LIES

OF MINE

A murder leads detectives to doubt past convictions

CHERYL REES-PRICE

THE
BOOK
FOLKS

Published by The Book Folks

London, 2021

ISBN 978-1-913516-60-4

www.thebookfolks.com

Lies of Mine is the fifth title in a bestselling series of murder mysteries set in the heart of Wales.

Chapter One

One year ago

Jay Parks stood at the door with a feeling of trepidation. He was about to step into a world that was alien to him. A world that had moved on and made him feel as though he had been frozen in time. Outside was a vast space he had not seen for fifteen years.

'Are you ready, Jay?'

Jay nodded at the prison officer who unlocked the door.

'Good luck, stay out of trouble, and stick to the rules. You'll be OK. This is your opportunity to prove you can be trusted. We don't want to see you back.' The prison officer opened the door.

'Thank you.' Jay stepped outside and inhaled as the door closed behind him. In his hand he clutched a bag of possessions. It wasn't much, just what he had on him when he was arrested and taken to the police station. He'd long outgrown the clothes he had been wearing at the time, and he would bin them as soon as he had the chance. There was a mobile phone which he doubted would work even if he could get a replacement charger. His wallet had his school bus pass, a cinema ticket, and a five-pound note. The money was out of date having been replaced with the smaller plastic version.

Jay took a step forward; he could feel his heart fluttering in his chest. Everything seemed brighter, the air smelled clean, and the noise of the traffic too loud. He'd only been outside the prison walls on a few occasions on resettlement release, and he had been escorted then. He'd never been out alone. He hadn't been alone since the day they had come for him. He moved along now heading for the bus stop. He was grateful to the charities that had helped him organise a place to live and set up a job. It wasn't the type of work he wanted but very few places would take on an ex-con, even one with his qualifications.

A bus pulled up and he hurried to jump aboard. He'd been given a travel grant, just enough to get him to the probation office, and a resettlement grant that would give him the basics. After that he was on his own. The bus pulled away as he headed for the back and took a seat. He didn't want to be seated where he could feel people's eyes on him. He looked like any other passenger, but he felt different, like there was a sign on his back that said, "Dangerous criminal. Keep away." He was sure someone would recognise him. The case had gained national coverage with the shocking details. It not only shattered the local community but spread darkness across the country and united people in their hatred for him. Every one of those people who spoke his name thought they knew him, but they didn't have a clue as to what really happened. He wished he'd been given a new identity, but very few prisoners were granted anonymity. There would be no escape nor a fresh start for him. He was stuck with who he was.

Jay was glad to reach his stop and get off the bus and away from people. He kept his eyes down as he walked towards the probation office. Just before he entered the building he heard someone call out his name. He turned and saw his brother, Mason, hurrying towards him. Relief washed over him at the sight of a familiar face and someone who was on his side.

'Sorry I'm a bit late,' Mason said. 'I had trouble finding a parking space.'

Jay smiled. 'You're just in time.'

'I would have liked to have been there when you got out, but I couldn't make it any earlier,' Mason said.

'It's no problem, you've done more than enough.' Jay put his arms around his brother. It had been so long since he'd felt human contact and it felt good to have his brother return the affection and not back away. 'Thank you for coming.'

'You don't have to thank me.' Mason patted his back. 'Come on, we better get inside.'

They were shown into an office where a man sat behind a desk. He stood as they entered. He was tall and broad. His sandy hair creeping past his ears and meeting with a ginger-flecked beard.

'Hello, Jay. I'm Oliver Wilson, your probation officer.' He held out his hand.

Jay shook Oliver's hand and introduced his brother before taking a seat.

'Today we are just going to go over the conditions of your license,' Oliver said. 'I understand it can be a little overwhelming when you're first released so it's good to see you have some support from your brother.'

'He's been great,' Jay said. 'He's picked up the keys for my flat, so it's all set for me to move in.'

'I've been in to set up the basics,' Mason said.

'Good,' Oliver said. He turned to his computer and hit a couple of keys. 'I see from your prison records that you have taken several courses over the years. You have some impressive qualifications.'

'I took my GCSEs and A levels when I was still at Glan-y-Wern, then I took a degree,' Jay said.

'More than one,' Oliver said.

'Yes, accountancy, business, and history. I've also got A levels in maths, English, law, and biology.'

Oliver smiled. 'Sounds like you worked hard to improve yourself. I see you've got a job lined up with Bright Start.'

'Yes, it's a community gardening project. I'm hoping when I've worked there long enough to get a good track record I will be able to move on.'

'I'm here to help in any way I can, but as you know it can be difficult to get work placements. For now, let's get you settled. Here's a copy of the terms of your license.' Oliver handed Jay a document. 'Take your time reading through then you can ask me any questions you may have.'

Jay sat back in the chair and started to read. Everything he did had to have preapproval. From the place that he lived to the work he undertook. He wouldn't be allowed to stay away for a night or even take a holiday. He was not permitted to leave the UK. He continued to read and saw a requirement that made his stomach flip.

'Everything clear, Jay?' Oliver asked.

'Erm… there's an exclusion zone.'

'Yes, you do understand that you are to have no contact with the victim's family?'

'Yes.'

'Well, the exclusion zone is for their benefit and yours. You wouldn't want to accidentally meet up with one of them, would you?'

The look on the family's faces in court had been enough. They had radiated pure hatred towards him. Jay shook his head. 'No, but do they know where I am?'

'No, but we can't guarantee that they won't find out. If you have any problems you are to contact me straight away.'

'How long is this for?' Mason asked as he took the document from Jay.

Oliver's eyes widened. 'Your brother is on life license. This will not change. Any breach of the conditions and he will be arrested.' He turned his attention back to Jay. 'You will also be asked to provide a urine sample on each visit for drugs testing. You must make any device such as a mobile phone or computer available for inspection. From time to time an inspection will be made of your place of residence.'

'I understand,' Jay said.

'OK, I think we have covered everything for today. I will see you next week and we'll see how you are getting on. Any questions?'

'No, thank you,' Jay said.

Oliver stood. 'If you go back to reception there are a couple of boxes for you to collect. It's a starter pack of bedding, towels, and kitchen equipment.'

'That's very kind,' Jay said. 'I appreciate it.'

'We get donations from charities,' Oliver said.

They collected the boxes and Mason drove to Jay's flat. Mason did most of the talking and kept the conversation light and upbeat. Jay just wanted to get into his flat, close the door and feel safe again.

'Here we are.' Mason pulled up in front of a semi-detached house that had been converted to flats. Jay's accommodation was on the ground floor. He turned to Jay. 'I would have like to have taken you home with me for a few days, but–'

'Your wife doesn't want a convicted murderer around the children,' Jay said.

'She'll come around,' Mason said. 'Let's get you inside.'

They took the boxes from the car and carried them inside. The front door led straight into a small sitting room. There was one armchair, a coffee table with two books placed on top, and an old CD player on the windowsill.

'We can get some more stuff,' Mason said. 'I picked you up a couple of books as I know you like to read. There's not much room here but we can get another chair.

The CD player has a radio, I thought it would give you some background noise, so you won't feel so lonely.'

Jay was touched by his brother's thoughtfulness. He felt his throat constrict but didn't want to show his emotions. He'd learnt to always keep them in check. He turned away and headed to the kitchen where he put down the box.

'I'll put this one in the bedroom,' Mason called.

Jay left the kitchen and joined his brother.

'Not much room in here,' Mason commented. 'We might be able to fit in a small wardrobe.'

'It's bigger than my cell,' Jay said with a smile. 'It's more room than I'm used to. I could get lost in here.'

Mason laughed. 'Well you're a free man now. You'll soon be wanting a bigger place.'

'I'll never be free.'

Mason shuffled awkwardly, his eyes scanning the room as though desperately thinking of something to say. 'Erm… right, I'll let you settle in then.' He left the bedroom and stood at the front door. 'Before I go I've got something for you.' He put his hand in his back pocket and pulled out a folded sheet of paper and handed it to Jay.

Jay unfolded the paper and looked at the five names listed with contact details.

'I've managed to track down all of them, I can tell you where they work, their routines–'

'Don't.' Jay held up a hand. 'I don't know about this. If I get caught…'

'You won't. It's what we planned. Do you want to end this?'

'Yes, but I don't think it will be that easy. We need to wait a while.'

'OK, but not too long,' Mason said.

'You better keep this.' Jay handed back the paper. 'If they search this place I don't want to get caught with that information.'

'I'll keep it safe. But this one you'll want to keep.' Mason pulled out a second piece of paper and handed it to Jay.

Jay looked at the information and felt a tightness in his chest. 'This is not far from where I'll be working.'

'No, so there is nothing to stop you going there. Oh, I nearly forgot. Here…' Mason took a phone and charger out of his jacket pocket. 'It's a pay as you go, I've put some credit on it and put in my number so you can call me if you need anything.'

'Thank you, I don't know how I would have managed without you.'

'I owe you. If I hadn't had—'

'It's in the past,' Jay said. 'None of this is your fault. I'm just glad you're here now.'

Mason lent in and gave his brother a quick hug. 'See you soon.'

With Mason gone, the flat felt unnaturally quiet. Jay moved to the kitchen and started to unpack. He needed to keep moving. The list that Mason had shown him was in the forefront of his mind. Each name brought back a memory. He could picture their faces. Had they felt any guilt at all? he wondered. He didn't know if he had the courage to go through with the plan, but they had all played their part and it was time they paid for what they did.

Chapter Two

Present day

As the small market town of Bryn Mawr came to life, DI Winter Meadows sat at his desk in the police station with a feeling of contentment. His paperwork was up to date, and there had been no violent crime recently. At present the team were dealing with local cannabis growers and a couple of cases of fraud. He'd started early this morning and was hoping to leave the office on time this evening and spend some time with his new girlfriend, Daisy. He was just thinking what he would cook for dinner when DCI Lester stuck his head out of the office door and called him.

Meadows saved the document on his computer and walked across the office passing DS Blackwell who raised his eyebrows. He stepped into Lester's office and closed the door before taking a seat.

DCI Lester headed up Bryn Mawr CID as well as two other stations and moved between them leaving Meadows in charge most of the time.

Lester sat forward and placed his folded hands on the desk. 'I've just had a call about a body found at Dinas Rock by a couple of hikers.'

'Doesn't Brecon cover that area?' Meadows asked.

'Yes, ordinarily but most of the CID are down with some virus, including the DCI. Sounds like half the station has got it so they are struggling. They've asked if we can help. What have you got on at the moment?'

'Not a lot, mainly low priority.'

'Good, take Edris and have a look. Could just be some poor soul had an accident. SOCO are already there as a precaution. By the way, how is Blackwell getting on?'

Meadows swivelled round in the chair and looked out at the office floor through the glass panel. He could see DC Valentine perched on the edge of DC Edris' desk. She had a cup in her hand and was laughing. DS Paskin was walking toward Blackwell with a mug in her hand. He saw Blackwell reach out a hand to take the mug. He turned back to Lester. 'He passed his fitness test; it was just a matter of having a stent inserted. I think he's up to the job.'

'He just has to keep his temper in check,' Lester said with a smile.

'If he weren't snarling and barking at everyone then I would be worried,' Meadows said.

Lester laughed. 'Yes, very little makes Blackwell happy.'

'I would imagine the heart attack has left him feeling low,' Meadows said. 'It must have been quite a shock for him. Blackwell isn't the type to make a fuss. I think the best thing is to treat him as if it never happened.'

Lester nodded and sat back in his chair. 'While you're here there is something else I wanted to discuss with you. The last couple of years has seen an increase in violent crime in our region. Given that we cover over 3,000 square miles and many remote rural communities, the task of policing the area comes with some difficulties. In response to this a specialised unit will be set up in Ystrad Amman. I would like you to consider heading up the MIT. It will mean a promotion for you.'

Meadows wasn't sure he wanted a promotion. 'I see. What about the team here?'

'That would be up to you. You could have a fresh start, or you could take the team with you. You appear to work well together and Edris is taking his sergeant exams.'

Meadows knew which he would prefer. He didn't want to start again with a new team. 'I guess that would be up to them.'

'Yes.'

'Will I still be reporting to you?'

'For now, but I'm hoping to be offered early retirement. It will be a good move for me. More time to spend with my family. Have a think about it and talk to the team.' Lester stood, indicating the meeting was over. 'Let me know how you get on at Dinas Rock.'

Meadows nodded and left the office. He briefed the team, picked up his coat and left with Edris.

DC Edris, a good-looking young officer with mischievous eyes and a quirky sense of humour, chattered away as Meadows drove.

'Say hello to the sleeping giant.' Edris pointed to the mountain ahead where a natural formation on top resembled a scene from *Gulliver's Travels*.

'Nice to have a change of scenery,' Meadows said.

'A change?' Edris laughed. 'Same view, different mountain.'

'What do you want? Skyscrapers?'

'Nah, I don't like the city with the crowds. I was thinking more of a tropical beach, few beers, and the sun warming my skin.'

'Take a holiday then,' Meadows said.

'It would be nice but between work and study, I don't really want to take the time off.'

'It will be worth it,' Meadows said. 'You'll be Detective Sergeant soon.'

'If I pass my exams.'

'Don't be pessimistic.'

'I can't help it,' Edris said. 'It's OK for you. You were born positive. Growing up with all that nature stuff and inner Zen, nothing seems to worry you.'

Meadows laughed. 'Inner Zen? I don't know what type of commune you think I grew up in.'

'Maybe I should go and stay. Would I be allowed?'

Meadows couldn't imagine the perfectly groomed Edris sleeping on the ground in the guest lodge, stinking of bonfire, and using a hole in the ground for a toilet. 'Not sure it's your cup of tea. If you want to get back to nature maybe glamping would be more your style.'

Edris grinned. 'Yeah you're probably right. So are we going to see the lovely Daisy today?'

'I don't know,' Meadows said. 'She's not the only pathologist in the area.'

'Yeah, but as you two are together I thought you'd know if she was attending this one.'

'We keep our work and social lives separate, well, as much as we can.'

'Thought you'd be shacked up in lovers' bliss by now,' Edris said. 'Your age you better get a move on.'

'Hey, I'm not even near my prime yet.'

'You wish.' Edris laughed.

Meadows would have liked to settle down but there were things about him that he had yet to reveal to Daisy. He knew she would find out at some stage and he would rather tell her himself. Telling her could mean that she would walk away from him, it could also cost him his career. No point in worrying about it now, he thought.

'Enough about my love life, let's examine yours,' Meadows said.

They arrived at Dinas Rock car park where two police cars, an ambulance, and a mountain rescue van were parked next to each other. There were three other cars and a minibus whose occupants stared out of the windows.

Meadows got out of the car and looked towards Dinas Rock, a limestone cliff popular with climbers. He expected to see some activity but no one was near the rock or could be seen above it. A uniformed officer approached them.

'What have you got for us?' Meadows asked.

'Body of a male found in the tunnel just after nine this morning by two hikers, Keira and Shaun Rogers. I've taken their statement and they've gone off for a walk to Sgwd Yr Eira,' the officer said. 'Mrs Rogers was shaken up. I thought it best they get some fresh air.'

'What tunnel?' Edris asked.

'There's a disused tunnel that runs from the old silica mine down to the lower mine. It's blocked off now so you can only access it from the top.'

'You've got to be kidding me,' Edris said as his eyes travelled to the top of the cliff.

The officer smiled. 'There's a path that runs up the side. It's steep but there's a handrail about halfway up. PC Ryan is at the top to direct you.'

'What about the people in the minibus, are they witnesses?' Meadows asked.

'No, a group of young offenders. They were about to start climbing as we arrived. They're waiting to see if they can continue.'

'How far away is the tunnel?'

'It's quite a distance. Not visible from the top of the rock.'

'Have they travelled far?'

'From Bristol.'

'OK, let them go ahead as long as they stay near the rock and don't wander off. They'll have to leave when we move the body. Have you identified the other vehicles?' Meadows asked.

'One belongs to the Rogers. The occupants of the others I guess are somewhere hiking.'

'Run a check on the other cars. One might belong to the deceased.'

'Right, of course.'

'Get the details of anyone that returns then they can go,' Meadows said. He turned to Edris. 'OK, best put on your walking shoes.' He opened the boot of the car and sat on the edge. 'Bet you're glad I persuaded you to get some decent footwear.'

'I'd rather they stayed in the boot,' Edris said as he slipped off his shoes.

The path that ran parallel to the rock led to a steep incline. To their left the River Mellte could be heard thundering over rocks and stones below. They kept their eyes down as they carefully picked their way up using the handrail to navigate the rocks. Meadows could feel the pull on his thigh muscles as he reached the top. A strong easterly wind whipped his hair and Edris could be heard breathing heavily behind him. He stopped and turned around admiring the view that stretched over the valleys.

'You OK?' Meadows asked.

'Yeah.' Edris drew in a lungful of air. 'I think I need to go to the gym.'

The ground was sodden from recent heavy rainfall and mud squelched around their boots as they followed the path. They found PC Ryan standing next to a wooden signpost looking cold and fed up.

'You look frozen,' Edris said.

'I am.' PC Ryan rubbed his hands together. 'I'm hoping someone will come and relieve me soon so I can go and get a coffee. The tunnel is down that way.' He pointed to the right. 'Careful going down. The path's not particularly good. You'll find a fork halfway down, take the path to the right.'

'Thanks,' Meadows said.

They continued on the path through trees that were starting to bud. All around them were signs of early spring and a damp earthy smell permeated the air. It proved just as difficult to make their way down as it had to climb up. They had to climb over a fallen tree and navigate slippery rocks with no handrail to help them. Then down steps made of wooden sleepers. To one side was a steep drop through trees, the other side was a limestone cliff face.

'Whatever this turns out to be, I think we can say with certainty the body wasn't dumped here,' Edris said. 'There is no way you could move someone over this terrain.'

'No,' Meadows agreed. 'It would be tricky.'

'Tricky?' Edris laughed. 'Impossible more like.'

At the bottom, the mountain rescue team could be seen standing in a group near a waterfall. The water gushed into a pool before cascading down to a second pool. The place had a mystic feel and Meadows could imagine taking off his boots and wading in the water despite the cold. He stopped briefly to introduce himself and Edris to the mountain rescue team, then walked over the bridge to the mouth of the tunnel which formed a perfect arch in the hillside.

SOCO were already busy scouring the area around the entrance. Meadows and Edris covered their shoes and took the path that had been laid out. Inside the tunnel the air was cool and damp. Floodlights lit the way powered by a generator whose humming followed them in.

'This place must be pitch black without the lights,' Edris said. 'I wouldn't like to walk down here on my own.'

'You'd certainly need a good torch.' Meadows looked around as they walked. There was no sign that anyone had frequented the tunnel. It would be a good place for teenagers to hang out, drink and smoke, he thought, but the area was clean, no litter, or even a dog-end. The ground was wet but as they walked further in, there were large dry patches.

The tunnel turned so that any light from the entrance disappeared. On each side the ground sloped upward and large, cavernous spaces appeared at intervals. After walking about a hundred and fifty meters, the floor gently sloped and they found Mike Fielding, the forensic officer, and

Daisy Moore, the pathologist. Daisy was crouched next to the body of a man.

'Hello.' Daisy smiled. 'I didn't expect you to turn up.'

'We're covering for Brecon station,' Meadows said. 'What have you got for us?'

'Male, thirty-one years old.'

'That's very precise,' Edris said.

'She's messing with you,' Mike said. 'We found his wallet inside his coat. Here.' Mike bent down to retrieve an evidence bag and handed it to Meadows.

'David Harris, address in Cwmtwrch,' Meadows said as he looked at the details. 'Not a robbery then. Anything else found on him?'

'Mobile phone. It's locked so I'll send it straight to tech.'

'And he was found like this?'

'Yes,' Mike said.

Meadows looked down at David Harris. His cleanly shaved face was waxen and set against cropped dark brown hair. He wore a grey suit, white shirt, and purple spotted tie with a dark grey woollen coat over the top. On his feet were a pair of lace-up muddy brogues. He lay on his back with his legs extended and his arms draped across his chest, left hand resting on his right. Everything about him looked ordered. It reminded Meadows of when he'd seen a relative laid out in a coffin in a chapel of rest.

'He looks like he has just laid down and died, poor soul,' Meadows said.

'Yes, but his position is too perfect. My guess is he's been laid out this way,' Daisy said.

'So, suspicious then?'

'Yes,' Daisy said.

'Any idea how he died?' Meadows asked.

'No, there are no obvious signs of trauma. You'll have to wait for the post-mortem.'

'Time of death?'

'I'd estimate he's been dead for a couple of days, given the temperature in here and secondary flaccidity, thirty-six hours or more.'

'So we're looking at around sometime Tuesday.' Meadows turned back to Mike. 'Did you find a torch or car keys?'

'No, just the wallet and phone,' Mike said.

'So, did he die here or was he dragged inside?' Edris asked.

'No scuff marks on his shoes,' Daisy said. 'So he wasn't dragged.' She lifted his trouser leg and examined the skin. 'Pooling would indicate that he wasn't moved after death. If he was it would have been very soon after.'

Meadows crouched down next to David and looked at his hands then took a closer look at his face. 'Looks like he came down here voluntarily and didn't put up a fight. No signs of a struggle. He's not a small man so one person couldn't have carried him alone, not dragged, and too clean to have been rolled. Looks like this is where he died.'

'How do you kill someone without leaving a mark?' Edris asked.

Daisy smiled. 'That's your puzzle to solve.'

'He wasn't dressed for a hike,' Meadows said. 'I'm guessing it wasn't his intention to come here. Either he came before work or after. The question is who or what would bring him here?'

'You wouldn't get me to come in this place,' Edris said.

Meadows stood up. 'I think you can photograph and move him. Perhaps we can get a better idea of what happened to him when we get him in the light. We'll leave you to it.' He took one last look at David Harris before turning away.

Outside seemed unnaturally bright after the darkness of the tunnel. Meadows stopped on the bridge and looked at the water cascading into the pool below. 'Why here?'

'It's quiet, no witnesses,' Edris said. 'That's if someone killed him. He could have swallowed a bottle of pills before walking up and laying himself down.'

'Yes, but most people would become delirious, or vomit. Depending on what they took. I can't see that he would stay in that position if he were alone.'

'Yeah,' Edris agreed. 'I suppose no one stays in the same position they fall asleep in, let alone die laid out like that.'

'I'm thinking this place had some meaning to him. Why else would he walk here when he is dressed for work? Come on.'

Meadows crossed the bridge and joined the mountain rescue team.

'It shouldn't be too much longer before you can move him. I don't envy you the task of getting up this hillside and down the rocky slope,' Meadows said.

'We've handled worse,' the group leader, a man named Tim, said.

'You must know the area well.'

'Yes, it can be dangerous if you don't stick to the marked paths. A few have got themselves into trouble. This area was silica mining until it closed in the sixties. As well as the mines you have a lot of natural caves that become flooded. Even experienced cavers have lost their lives,' Tim said.

'Any recent incidents, particularly in this spot?' Meadows asked.

'Nothing in the tunnel if that's what you mean. Some kid jumped off the rock a few months ago, suicide. There was a kayaking accident on the river last year. A young girl lost her life.'

'What about the mine murder,' one of Tim's colleagues said.

'Oh yeah, weren't you part of the search team, John?' Tim asked.

'Yeah, poor kid.'

'When was this?' Meadows asked.

'About fifteen years ago, we found her body in the mine, there.' John turned and pointed.

Meadows looked to where John indicated. A square entrance was cut into the rock. Brickwork ran up the sides and a rusted steel girder held up the top. A stony bank led from the mine entrance down to a fence and a warning sign.

'I have a vague memory of that murder,' Edris said. 'I was still in school. It was in all the papers. Bunch of teenagers hanging out up here and one of the boys killed a girl and hid her body in the mine.'

'Something like that,' John said.

'From what I recall there were drugs involved,' Tim said.

'Anything else?' Meadows asked.

Tim shook his head. 'Only broken legs or ankles from idiots that go hiking without the proper footwear.'

'Thanks for your time and patience,' Meadows said. 'I hope you won't have to wait much longer.'

'Do you think David Harris had a connection to one of the incidents?' Edris asked as they made their way back up.

'It's possible, he came up here for a reason. A suicide, an accident, and a murder. I don't believe in coincidences.'

Chapter Three

Meadows looked around the team as they gathered for the briefing. It was a small unit but one that worked well. He really didn't want to leave them and hoped they would all agree to make the move with him, but now wasn't the time to talk about it. Valentine sat next to Edris, she was the youngest member of the team, a bubbly woman with glossy black hair and chocolate eyes. She was the only one who could raise a smile from DS Blackwell. Blackwell sat with his legs stretched out and, leaning back in his chair, he had a couldn't-care-less look upon his face, but Meadows knew below the gruffness was a good detective. The last member was DS Paskin, a petite brunette that had a flare for finding information.

'David Harris, aged thirty-one, found in a disused tunnel at Dinas Rock this morning,' Meadows said. 'Early estimate is that he died sometime Tuesday.' He filled them in on all they had learnt so far. 'Until we know differently we are treating this as a suspicious death. David was found by a Mr and Mrs Rogers who were hiking in the area. According to their statement they took a detour off the main path to look at a smaller waterfall. They then used the torches from their mobile phones to explore the tunnel. The tunnel is easily visible from the waterfall and there are no warning signs upon entry. I think at this stage there is no reason to doubt the Rogers' story. This time of year very few visit the area, so it is likely that David wasn't meant to be found now or found at all given how far into the tunnel his body was discovered. All vehicles at the site have been identified so David either travelled with someone else or his car has been moved. Paskin, what have you found out about David Harris?'

Paskin tucked her hair behind her ear and read from her notepad. 'David Harris was a social worker. He mainly worked with young offenders. He has a wife, Tia, and two children Joshua and Alisha. He has a profile on Facebook but very rarely posts anything. I expect given his work he wanted to keep his personal life private.'

'If he's been dead since Tuesday why hasn't his wife reported him missing?' Valentine asked.

'Good question,' Blackwell said. 'Could be that she was the one that killed him. It would make sense as there were no signs of a struggle. Also, it would have to be someone he trusted. I doubt he'd go into the tunnel with a stranger or someone he'd had an argument with.'

'We'll be speaking to his wife soon and checking out her whereabouts on Tuesday,' Meadows said. 'In the meantime, we need to find out all we can about David's life. Once we have informed his wife and have a formal identification, we can start interviewing his work colleagues and friends. His phone is with tech, once it's back, we can see who he was in contact with before he died. The other thing to consider is the location. Why here?' He pointed to a photo on the board. 'There have been three fatalities in the locality. It's possible that David was connected to one of them. Paskin?'

'Ethan Pugh, aged twenty-two, jumped from Dinas Rock four months ago. Death was ruled a suicide at the inquest. Ethan had a history of drug and alcohol abuse. He also spent some time in Glan-y-Wern, the young offenders institute. He was in for theft and dealing.'

'David Harris probably knew him from work, you said his main role was working with young offenders,' Edris said.

'There was nothing suspicious about Ethan's death,' Paskin said.

'Yeah, but Ethan's family could have thought David was in some way to blame,' Blackwell said.

'It could be connected,' Meadows agreed. 'What about the accidental death?'

'Katie Taylor, kayaking accident on the River Mellte which is close to Dinas Rock. Coroner's report was drowning. Inquest verdict, accidental death. Then we have the murder. The victim was Ruth Williams. Thirteen years old. Jay Parks, aged fifteen at the time, was convicted of her murder in 2006. I don't have the full details yet. The case was in closed court as Jay Parks was a minor.'

'I can't see how a murder in 2006 would be connected,' Valentine said. 'It happened over fifteen years ago, and David Harris is too young to have been working with young offenders back then.'

Meadows rubbed his hand over his chin. 'You're probably right. We'll look at the more recent cases first although they may have no bearing at all on the case. It's just worth keeping in mind when we speak to his family and friends. There was a group of young offenders at Dinas Rock this morning on some climbing exercise. It's worth finding out if Glan-y-Wern takes groups to climb and if David Harris was involved in those sorts of activities but wait until we inform his wife. OK, Blackwell and Valentine, I'll leave you to look into the death of Ethan Pugh. Paskin, can you get the full details on the accidental death as well as finding out what groups use that area and if any of them were there on Tuesday. Edris and I will go and see Tia Harris.'

* * *

David Harris' house was a detached property set back off the road. Large planters sat either side of the door with green shoots just breaking through the earth.

Meadows knocked on the door and felt a flutter of anxiety. It always came when he was about to deliver bad news. It was the one part of the job that he hated. That moment when you changed someone's life. You could see it in their eyes. It's as though the world stands still for a moment then cracks in two. It becomes the world before death and the world after. He was about to throw David's wife and family into that unfamiliar territory. After this moment they could never go back to life as it was before he knocked on the door.

David Harris' wife, Tia, was a petite blonde woman with brown eyes set in a heart-shaped face. She was sitting on the sofa; the shock having robbed her face of colour. Upstairs the children could be heard playing. Edris walked into the room and placed a cup of tea in her hands. She looked at Meadows with a stunned expression.

If she had anything to do with David's death, she's an outstanding actress, Meadows thought.

'Are you sure?' Tia asked.

'Yes, we are fairly certain,' Meadows said. 'There will need to be a formal identification, but his wallet and mobile phone were found in his jacket pocket.'

'Oh.' Tia looked down and stared at the contents of the cup. 'But it still might not be him?'

'When was the last time you saw David?' Edris opened his notebook.

Tia looked up. 'Erm… Sunday.'

'Is it usual for him to stay away?'

'No, we've been separated for the last three months. He's staying in a B&B in Neath.'

'I'm sorry, we didn't know,' Meadows said.

'He hadn't changed his address on any documents and his post still comes here. He came to spend time with the kids on the weekend. I guess we thought we would sort things out.' Tia's voice cracked.

'Have you got the address for the B&B?' Edris asked.

'Yes.' Tia reeled off the address.

'Does David own a car?'

Tia nodded.

Meadows waited until Edris had written down the registration number. 'Do you mind telling us why you separated?'

'He's been drinking a lot the past six months and it was getting out of control.'

'Was he violent?' Meadows asked.

'No, nothing like that.' Tia wiped away a tear. 'It's difficult to explain. He wasn't himself when he drank. I couldn't talk to him. He would be brooding. He'd come home from work and the first thing he would do was open a can, or a bottle of wine. Then he would sit in the spare room, we use it as an office. I don't know what he was doing in there. When I'd call him for dinner, he'd say he wasn't hungry. By the time he'd come out of the room he was so drunk he could barely speak or talk. Next morning he'd be hungover and moody. Sometimes he was late going into work. I thought if I gave him an ultimatum he would stop, but instead he left. He said he needed time to sort a few things out then things would be all right.'

'Did he always like a drink?' Meadows asked.

'No, well not like that. He'd have the odd glass of wine if we went out, but he rarely drank at home.'

'And this started six months ago?'

'Yeah, I couldn't tell you exactly when.'

'Was there something that happened around that time?'

'No, not that he told me.'

'Any problems in work?'

'No, he loved his job. He worked with young offenders which was a little stressful at times. He always said they deserved a second chance, that they just needed someone to believe in them and guide them.' Tia wiped her cheek with the back of her hand. 'There was an accident about a year ago. David had taken a group out to kayak. Something went wrong and a girl died.'

There's the connection, Meadows thought.

'Would that be Katie Taylor?' Edris asked.

'Yes, there was an inquest and an inquiry at work. David was cleared of any responsibility.'

'Did David blame himself for the accident?' Meadows asked.

'At first, he kept going over that day but after the inquest things got better.'

'Do you think the accident was the cause of his drinking?'

'No, he didn't drink during that time. Yes, he was upset, anyone who was in charge of that group would have been.'

'Did David often take groups out?' Meadows asked.

'Yes, that was the main part of his job. Team and confidence building.'

'What about rock climbing?' Meadows asked.

'Yes, he was involved in all those activities.'

'So he would have the right equipment, boots, waterproofs, that sort of thing?'

'Yes, why?'

'When we found David he was wearing a suit and black lace-up shoes,' Meadows said.

'David only wore a suit if he had a hearing with one of the kids.'

'Can you think of any reason why David would go to Dinas Rock, before or after work, and walk near the old silica mines?'

'No.'

'Did he ever mention that area?'

'No, he may have taken the kids hiking there. Seren would know, Seren Hardy, she works with David.' Hope sparked in Tia's eyes. 'David was very particular about health and safety. He would never have gone up there without his boots. I'm sure there has been some mistake. It must be someone else that went up there and had an accident.'

'I'm sorry,' Meadows said. 'It may be that he wasn't expecting to go there. We are looking at the possibility that someone met him there.'

'Who? Are you saying someone killed him?'

'We don't know at this stage, but we are treating his death as suspicious. Can you think of anyone who may have wished to harm your husband?'

'No, David got along with everybody.'

'Any financial worries?'

'No, we're not well off but we do OK.'

'Did David ever mention Ethan Pugh?' Edris asked.

'The boy who killed himself at Dinas Rock? David knew him, he was one of his cases about six years ago, but he hadn't had any recent contact with him. He told me about the suicide. He was already drinking heavily by then. He said it was another one he had failed. He said something about paying the price.'

Another connection, Meadows thought. 'What do you think he meant by that?'

'I don't know, he was drunk at the time. He was just rambling on about his purpose in life, how he was supposed to make things better.'

'Is there anything else you can think of that was troubling him? Any unusual phone calls or visitors to the house?' Meadows asked.

'No.' Tia rubbed her hands over her face. 'It doesn't make sense. What am I supposed to tell the children?'

Meadows sensed that Tia was close to breaking down. The longer they questioned her the more reality seemed to be sinking in and he didn't want to cause her any more distress.

'Is there someone we can call for you?'

'My mum,' Tia said. 'I'll have to speak to David's mother. I don't think I can.' A sob escaped Tia's mouth and her body shuddered.

'Edris will call your mother and I'm going to arrange for a family liaison officer to come and help you. She'll be able to give you advice and will keep you informed. I'm going to do everything in my power to find out what happened to your husband. I'm so sorry this has happened to you and your family,' Meadows said.

They waited until Tia's mother arrived then left, the sound of Tia's sobs following them out the front door.

'Looks like you were right about David having a connection to the incidents at Dinas Rock. He knew Ethan Pugh and was involved in Katie Taylor's accident,' Edris said.

'Yes, but what happened in between?' Meadows said as he opened the car door. 'Tia said he had got over the accident and was drinking before Ethan Pugh killed himself.'

'What if Ethan Pugh didn't jump? He could have had something on David and was threatening to tell.' Edris clipped on his seatbelt.

'It's possible,' Meadows said. 'But there was an inquest and doubtless there would have been a thorough investigation. Blackwell is looking into it so I'm sure if David had anything to do with Ethan's death, he'll find a link.'

'Or it could be Katie Taylor's family.' Edris swivelled around in his seat. 'They could have blamed David and decided they wanted revenge for her death. They could have been threatening him and that's what was stressing him out.'

'Well, something was upsetting him and that's what we need to find out,' Meadows said as he started the engine.

Chapter Four

Jay got off the bus four stops early. It had been a year since his release and this was the only variation he made to his daily routine. He had an hour before he needed to be at work. Enough time to do what he planned and walk the rest of the way to the gardens. He had got off at this stop several times over the past month and just watched the house. The routine was always the same. The man left to walk the dog, a golden Labrador, at 7.30 a.m. Half an hour later he returned and ten minutes after he left for work. He walked the same route each morning. Jay had followed him on a few occasions but this morning he was just waiting. It wasn't the man he was interested in but the woman who sometimes appeared to wave her husband off to work. She was always in a dressing gown, and he wondered if she left the house at all. During the day he hadn't had the opportunity to watch her. Work kept him away.

He waited a few moments to make sure it was past the time for the man to leave with the dog then hurried to the door. He could feel the heat prickling his skin under his coat. It wasn't that it was a warm day, there was a strong wind lowering the temperature. It was anxiety that quickened his breath and made him light-headed and hot.

He'd prepared himself and got as far as the door twice before. Each time he had backed away. This time he would do it. He took a deep breath, knocked on the door, and hopped from foot to foot. Panic fizzled through his body, and it took all his effort not to turn and run.

The door opened and the man peered out at him. This wasn't supposed to happen, he was supposed to be walking the dog. Jay opened his mouth but not a sound came out.

'Yes?' The man frowned.

'Dad,' Jay blurted out.

Recognition flitted across the man's face and his eyes narrowed. 'What are you doing here?'

'Please, I just want to see Mum,' Jay said.

'Who is it, Wayne?' A woman appeared behind Jay's father.

'Go back inside, Ashya,' his father said.

'Mum,' Jay said. 'It's me, I just want to talk to you for a moment.'

His mother put her hand to her mouth and backed away.

'She doesn't want to see you,' his father said.

'Please, Dad, just talk to me for a minute. I want to explain.'

'Explain!' his father thundered. 'Do you have any idea what you did to us. The shame. We had to move, start again. I heard you'd been let out. They should have kept you locked up.'

'You don't understand,' Jay said. 'You never came to see me, you didn't even come to court to hear my side. I was fifteen years old.'

'There is no "your side". What possible excuse could you have for doing what you did?'

'But I–'

'Don't you dare. I don't want to hear it. Nothing you say could justify the humiliation you brought upon us. You disgust me. Now go. I don't want to see you anywhere near us or I'll call the police. You're dead to us.' His father stepped back and slammed the door.

Jay was shaking as he walked away. He hadn't expected a warm welcome but the look of hatred on his father's face had been a shock. His mother hadn't said a word. He wondered if it would have been different if he had caught her alone. I doubt it, he thought.

He arrived in work on time. He was always careful never to be late. Most of the other workers on the garden project were ex-cons or had been sentenced to community service, so you were generally treated as a lower-class citizen. The boss was OK most of the time, but he wasn't friendly. Sometimes people would pass by and cast a knowing look or give them a wide berth. Jay hadn't made any friends since his release. He kept to himself and got on with his work. There was a woman on the bus each morning that caught his eye. She had smiled at him a few times. Part of him wanted to talk to her but what was the point? She would find out one way or another who he was and would soon run. He resigned himself to the fact that he would be alone for the rest of his life. Mason called round now and again, but he had his own life and family. There was no one to talk to, and no one to understand how he felt.

Jay hit the shovel into the earth and pushed his foot down on the edge until it disappeared into the soil. He pulled the handle back, scooped up the earth and dumped it in the wheelbarrow. He didn't mind the physically demanding work. It made his body tired, although it did nothing for his mind which seemed to whirl constantly day and well into the night. The radio was playing in the background and as Jay stopped to take a drink of water the news came on. The first article was the report of a suspicious death at Dinas Rock. A coldness crept over him as he stood there unable to move. His mind was transported back sixteen years. He could see David Harris laughing as he handed him a drink, smell the arid ground scorched under the summer sun and feel the cool mountain water tricking down his arm. It was the last time he had been at Dinas Rock.

Jay had been the last to arrive that day. It had been another hot day, a rare heatwave that made everyone short-tempered. The sun had burnt his arms and sweat had soaked through his T-shirt as he struggled to peddle the bike up hill. Then had come the relief of the breeze on his face as he raced down the other side of the mountain road. He left his bike by the rock and walked the rest of the way. By the time he reached the waterfall his mouth was dry, and his head was pounding. He didn't bother to get undressed. He emptied his pockets, took off his trainers and jumped into the pool. The cold mountain water was a shock to his skin but at the same time a relief. He swam over to the waterfall, put his head under and opened his mouth to gulp down the water.

Goosebumps covered his arms and legs as he climbed up the bank and plonked down next to the others. The girls were giggling at something Aiden said and David was stretched out on his back.

'What took you so long?' David asked.

'Mason had gone out, so I had to find him first.'

'Did you get some?'

'Yeah, you got any food? I'm starving,' Jay said as he pushed his wet hair back.

'Didn't you bring any?' David sat up.

'No, I'm skint.'

David opened his rucksack and pulled out a drink and a packet of biscuits. 'Here, help yourself.'

'Jay!'

Jay was pulled out of his memories by his boss calling. 'What are you doing?'

'Nothing, I…'

'Just get on with it,' his boss said.

Jay pushed the shovel back in the earth, the memory left him feeling shaken. He tried to concentrate on the job but images kept invading his mind. The cold water, the darkness of the mine, and Ruth's blood seeping into his shorts.

Chapter Five

Edris yawned loudly as they walked down the corridor towards the morgue.

'Busy weekend, was it?' Meadows asked.

Edris grinned. 'Yeah, you could say that.'

'I hope you were studying.'

'Not exactly.'

Meadows pushed open the door. 'I don't think I want to know.'

'Morning, you two,' Daisy said.

'Morning,' Meadows said with a smile. He felt a warmth spread through him at the sight of her. She was sitting at her desk with her fingers poised over the keyboard. Her long black hair had been swept up into a messy knot at the top of her head. Although she spent the occasional night with him, work kept them too busy to spend any length of time together.

'I'll take you through to see David Harris,' Daisy said. She stood and put on her lab coat before pushing open the door to the examination room.

A metal table sat in the centre of the room with grooves running around the edges that sloped into a drain. David Harris was laid out, his neck supported by a block and a sheet covering him up to his shoulders. The smell of death hung in the air and mixed with chemicals. This and the over-bright lights made Meadows feel uncomfortable. He approached the table and looked down at David. He thought of the children that wouldn't see their father again, and Tia Harris who would never have the chance to work things out with her husband.

'See here.' Daisy pointed to a small bruise just above David's collar bone. 'I didn't see it when he was in the tunnel. It was covered by his shirt collar.'

'What is it?' Edris asked.

'Puncture wound from a needle. He was injected with gamma-hydroxybutyrate.'

'Do you want to say that in English?' Edris said.

'GHB,' Meadows said. 'Liquid ecstasy, G, get her into bed, among other things.'

Edris raised his eyebrows looking impressed at Meadows' knowledge.

'It's one of the club drugs.'

'Could he have injected himself?' Edris asked.

'I doubt it given the angle the needle entered and the force used. But not impossible,' Daisy said.

'There was no syringe found with him,' Meadows said.

'He could have thrown it in the river,' Edris suggested.

'But what would be the point?' Meadows asked. 'How far would he have been able to walk after being injected?'

'Not far,' Daisy said. 'Used in small doses it has a sedative effect, causes euphoria, and is also an aphrodisiac. The quantity found in his system would have rendered him unconscious fairly quickly. Also I doubt he would have had the coordination to do up his top button and straighten his tie after. He certainly wouldn't have laid himself out in the position we found him in and stayed that way.'

'I imagine he loosened his tie or took it off on the walk up past the rock, it's quite strenuous. It's an odd thing for

33

the killer to do, tidy him up and lay him out. I think it may be someone who cared for him,' Meadows said.

'Maybe he met someone for a bit of fun, and it went wrong,' Edris suggested.

'Then he would have taken it orally, put it in a drink,' Meadows said.

'Yes,' Daisy agreed. 'As far as I know it is rarely injected by users. It's extremely dangerous to take it that way.'

'Why GHB if not for fun? Surely there are other drugs which would be easier to get hold of and would have had the same effect,' Edris commented. 'Heroin?'

'The reason it's used as a date rape drug is because it leaves the body quickly and is not easy to detect. Maybe the killer thought there would be no trace. They didn't account for the fact that metabolism would stop minutes after death,' Daisy said.

'It's possible,' Meadows said. 'Anything else?'

'Time of death: Last Tuesday morning, between seven and nine. He hadn't eaten breakfast. There was alcohol in his system, looks like he had a heavy session the night before. He was fit, no underlying health conditions and no signs of previous substance abuse. There were fibres found at the puncture wound. I've sent them off for analysis together with his clothes. There was some blood on his shirt collar but that would be expected given the puncture wound.' Daisy turned away from David. 'I met his wife when she came into formally identified him. She came with her mother. Poor woman, there is always that bit of hope left before the viewing.'

'All we can do now is try and find her some answers,' Meadows said, as they followed Daisy out of the room.

'I'll send a copy of the report to you,' Daisy said as she sat at her desk.

Meadows was tempted to give her a kiss before leaving. It would be the natural thing to do but not very professional, he thought. Instead he gave her a smile. 'See you later.'

'To the office?' Edris asked as they walked out of the hospital.

'Yes, but we'll stop at the B&B first. I don't expect to get much from there but it's worth a look.'

* * *

Ann Sims owned Fairfield Guesthouse. It was a large, detached property set back off the road and behind enclosed walls. The garden was well kept with large shrubs and a decking area. Meadows wondered if David had sat outside in the evening talking to other guests as he drank. Maybe he met with someone here, another woman? He turned away from the garden and followed Ann inside. She led them into the lounge. The room was spacious with an open fireplace. Two armchairs were positioned near the fire and one by the bay window. A large sofa with scatter cushions faced the TV and as Meadows took a seat, his eyes travelled to the shelves which were crammed full of books.

'How many bedrooms do you have?' Edris asked.

'Four guest rooms and my own room.'

'How many guests do you have staying at the moment?' Edris opened his notebook.

'There was only David. Things don't usually pick up until Easter. I still can't believe it. David was such a nice man. No trouble at all.'

'And who else lives here besides yourself?'

'No one, it's just me now. The place was too much for me when my husband died so I started taking in guests to help with the bills. I have a local lad come in to help with the garden.'

Meadows thought it odd that David would live here rather than with his wife and children. He guessed Ann to be in her sixties so doubted there was anything between them. He found it hard to believe that David would choose drink over his family. There had to be another reason. Was he concerned for their safety? he wondered.

'Did David have any visitors?' Meadows asked.

'No, he was on the phone a lot. Mostly to his wife.'

'Did you see him on Tuesday morning?'

'Only briefly. He didn't have breakfast which was unusual. He said he had to attend a hearing, something to do with work, but had to meet someone first so he just had a coffee then left.'

'How did he seem?' Meadows asked.

'Erm… he was always quiet in the morning. I guess he seemed hurried, maybe a little stressed.'

'Did he give you any indication of who he was meeting? Did he say it was someone from work?'

'No, he didn't say.'

'What about last Monday night? Did you speak to him?'

'He said hello when he came in. I was watching TV.'

'What time was that?'

'About half seven. He went up to his room and I didn't see him after that.'

'Did he often stay in his room all evening?'

'Yes, mostly. There were a couple of nights he was home late.'

'OK, could we see his room?' Meadows asked.

'Yes of course.' Ann stood up. 'I'm afraid I cleaned the room and changed the bed. I didn't know.'

'It's fine,' Meadows reassured her.

Ann led them upstairs and pointed out a door on the right. 'I'll leave you to it,' she said.

'Thank you,' Meadows said and stepped into the room.

At the bottom of the bed a pair of lounge pants and T-shirt were neatly folded. A desk sat by the window with an open laptop. Edris stepped forward, hit the keys and the screen came to life.

'We need a password,' Edris said.

'Yeah, I would've been surprised if there wasn't one. Bag it up we'll take it to tech.' He opened the wardrobe and peered inside. Below the row of hanging clothes was a pair of hiking boots and two bottles of whisky. One empty, the other half-drunk. He closed the door.

'There isn't a lot to show for David's life here,' Meadows said, 'and his car is not parked in the grounds.'

'Looks like he did drive to Dinas Rock.'

'Yes, and whoever killed him took the car. They wanted to make sure no one went looking for him. I'm guessing they didn't want us to make the connection between Dinas Rock and David's disappearance.'

'And now we know that he had an arranged meeting,' Edris said. 'Someone he knew who made him nervous.'

'Yes but someone he trusted enough to go into that tunnel with. What was he doing every night hidden in this room and drinking? Ann said he was on the phone most nights. I don't think all those calls were to his wife. Give tech a call and ask them to get the information from his phone as top priority. I want to know who he was talking to and what secrets are on that laptop.'

Chapter Six

After dropping the laptop with the tech department Meadows and Edris headed into the office.

'You just missed Chris from tech,' Paskin said. 'He unlocked David's phone and I have a list of phone calls.'

'I wondered why he wasn't at his desk,' Meadows said. 'Anything interesting?'

'A few, I've concentrated on the last three months. He never cleared his call log history. I've also requested his phone records. Obviously his wife is top of the list, he called her often but not every day and he also called his mother frequently. Seren Hardy's number comes up a lot. She left a message the morning he died. Sounds work-related.'

'Yes,' Meadows said. 'She's one of David's work colleagues, we're seeing her today.'

'The other names that stand out are Naomi Collins – three calls, one the evening before he died; Oliver Wilson – he made quite a few calls to him over the last few months; Callum Vaughan – another regular contact; and Aiden Edwards. The rest of the calls are to Glan-y-Wern and a few other odd numbers pop up which I still need to check.'

'OK, good work. See what you can find out about the people on the list and what relationship they had to David.'

Edris brought in a tray of tea and biscuits and Meadows gathered the team around and updated them on what they had learnt from the post-mortem.

'So far we haven't got a lot to go on. I had hoped after David's name was released to the press on Saturday we would have more information. There were a few calls but nothing of interest. Blackwell, how did you get on with your inquiries into Ethan Pugh's death?' Meadows asked.

'There was nothing to suggest it wasn't a suicide, in fact there was a witness. A guy walking his dog saw Ethan jump. He was the one to call the emergency services. Ethan had been a user for some time and heroin was found in his system. I'll look to see if David had any recent contact with him and talk to Ethan's parents, but to be honest I don't think that Ethan's death has anything to do with David's murder.'

'I think you may be right,' Meadows said. 'That leaves Katie Taylor's accident. I'll see what more we can find out from David's colleagues. I don't think it is wise to talk to Katie's parents at the moment. I don't want to stir things up with an already grieving family unless it's necessary. I still feel that there is a reason David was killed at that particular location.'

'Could it be drugs-related?' Blackwell asked. 'Maybe he owed a dealer some money or he could have been supplying the kids he worked with and someone found out.'

'It's possible. There were no drugs other than GHB found in his system. It doesn't look like he was a user, still it's worth looking into the dealing. Find out if Glan-y-Wern has a drug problem. Also find out about the local circulation of GHB. It's mostly cannabis and cocaine in this area. I'm guessing it's come from one of the clubs. Have a word with vice.'

'Isn't GHB used as a date rape drug?' Valentine asked.

'Yes,' Meadows said. 'It's one of them.'

'What if he used it on someone? He knew the area around Dinas Rock. So, he takes someone for a hike, offers them a spiked drink, then drags them into the tunnel. Most of these cases are difficult to prosecute as the victim's memory is hazy, and a high number each year go unreported. It could be a revenge attack.'

'I don't see it,' Blackwell said. 'Why there of all places? A cold, damp, dark tunnel.'

'Maybe he liked the outdoors,' Edris said.

'Quiet, no witnesses,' Paskin said.

'I think that's a good theory,' Meadows said. 'It would've had to be someone known to him, someone who trusted him enough to go for a walk alone.'

'Some of the young offenders would know him well. Would have been on outdoor activities with him, or maybe a work colleague,' Valentine said.

'OK, Valentine, why don't you follow up on that. Go to Glan-y-Wern and speak to some of the young people that David has dealt with. See what impression they give of him. My feeling is if he was a sexual predator then it's unlikely he would have been able to keep it completely hidden. I would imagine someone would have picked up a vibe, even if it was just flirting. Tread carefully, these kids are troubled.' He looked at the board again. 'David's car is still missing, we need to find it. There are no cameras on the road leading into Dinas Rock. David could have picked up his killer who then disposed of his car. It could be anywhere if that's the case. Although I don't think the killer would risk driving it where they could be picked up on camera.'

'Unless they're not that clever,' Blackwell said.

'The best we can do for the moment is ask traffic and uniform to keep an eye out for it. Paskin, maybe it would be a good idea to put out an appeal for information on social media. Maybe someone in the area saw David arrive or saw his car parked somewhere nearby.'

'I'll get on to it,' Paskin said.

'Did you get anything on the groups climbing Dinas Rock on Tuesday?'

'No, I checked, there was no one booked in there on Tuesday. Uniform are canvassing the area. There are no houses overlooking the car park. The closest residents didn't see or hear anything out of the ordinary.'

'OK, thanks,' Meadows said. 'Valentine, I'd like you to talk to David's mother after you have visited Glan-y-Wern. It may be that he talked to her about what was troubling him, and check out Tia Harris' alibi with the school. She said she dropped the children off at breakfast club before going to work on Tuesday morning. Someone lured David to Dinas Rock, someone he felt safe with and I'm certain something happened there in the past. We need to find out what, when, who, and why. I'll see you all back here later.'

* * *

Seren Hardy met them in the reception area of social services and led them through to her office.

'Thank you for seeing us,' Meadows said as he took a seat.

'I'll try to help you anyway I can,' Seren said. 'I worked with David for the last six years. It's been an awful shock to all of us here.'

While Edris grabbed a chair and took out his notebook Meadows studied Seren's face. She was young, early thirties at the most, with straight blonde shoulder-length hair. He wondered if she could have been more than a colleague to David.

'Was David expected in work last Tuesday morning?' Meadows asked.

'Yes, well not in the office. He was supposed to attend a hearing. One of our clients was up for release. David didn't show. I received a call and tried to call David but it went straight to voicemail. I left a message. When I didn't hear back from him I attended myself.'

'Was it usual for David to be late or not turn up?'

'If you'd asked me a few months ago I would have said no. He was always first in and if there were any problems he would be the one to stay. Lately his timekeeping has been bad and on a few occasions he didn't come in.'

'Had there been any recent problems in work?'

'No, nothing out of the ordinary. We deal with young offenders and often these youngsters are troubled so the job can be stressful at times. There hasn't been anything that David hasn't dealt with before.'

'We understand that David was leading a group on an activity where a girl was involved in a fatal accident,' Edris said.

'Katie Taylor, yes, but that was nearly a year ago and David was cleared of all responsibility.'

'What about Katie's parents, did they make any complaints about David?' Edris asked.

'Katie's father was very verbal at the inquest.'

'In what way?' Meadows asked.

'He said we should be held responsible for the accident. He later sent a letter apologising for his outburst. He said he accepted that it was Katie's fault. I can show you a copy of that letter.'

'What happened that day?' Meadows asked.

'David and I took a group of eight kayaking. We'd been through the safety briefing with them, all had been taught to roll. We'd even walked that stretch of river showing them the take-off and landing points. They had the correct clothing and helmets. David led and I followed behind the group. All was good until we got to the landing. David landed the kayak, then got out to supervise the group as they came in. The first three stopped, Katie and one other were behind. Those two took off paddling fast. David shouted after them then jumped back in his kayak and took off. I got the other three to the landing and stayed with the group. I called the incident in straight away.

'There had been heavy rain for a few days before so the river was fast flowing. Katie went over the weir and capsized catching her chin on a rock. She was dragged down the river. By the time David got to her it was too late. He tried to revive her, but she'd been under too long. The inquest ruled accidental death by drowning.'

'Did David blame himself for the accident?' Meadows asked.

'He was upset, we both were, but there was nothing we could have done. It's the reason he moved departments. He no longer wanted to be part of the outdoor activities.'

That's not what his wife told us, Meadows thought, or maybe he didn't tell her.

'What department did David move to?'

'He mainly worked at Glan-y-Wern. Assisting with basic skills training, hearings, and support for when they left.'

'Can you think of any reason why David would be at Dinas Rock on Tuesday?'

'None at all, like I said it's been nearly a year since he was involved in activities in that area.'

'Would you say that he has been troubled since the accident?'

'Not really. He seemed fine. I think David's troubles had more to do with his home life than work.'

'What do you mean?'

'I know David and Tia had separated. It was about six months ago that he started to be preoccupied, missing meetings, late for work, not always responding to emails. I guess they must have been going through a rough patch before he moved out.'

'Did he talk to you about it?'

'No, he just said he had some problems at home and needed to sort through them.'

'I have to ask, do you have any reason to suspect that David was either taking drugs or supplying them?'

Seren's eyes widened. 'Absolutely not, David was anti-drugs. A lot of the young offenders we see have drug-related problems and David worked hard to get them help.'

'Offenders like Ethan Pugh?' Edris asked.

Seren looked at Edris. 'Yes, David worked with Ethan, and he was clean when he left Glan-y-Wern. Not all are success cases. I have a file full that are. David received many letters thanking him for the help he gave. He put them in a drawer. He was very modest.'

'Did he talk to you about what happened to Ethan?' Edris asked.

'He mentioned it, only to say how sad it was and that he felt he'd failed him.'

'Did David have any recent contact with Ethan?' Edris asked.

'Not that I am aware of. It's been five years since Ethan was released.'

'What was David like to work with?' Meadows asked.

'Great, he was very dedicated. He really believed that people deserve a second chance. I doubt you will find anyone who has a bad word to say about him. Everyone liked him.'

Someone didn't, Meadows thought. 'Did you get the impression that David was seeing someone else?'

'You mean an affair? No. He loved Tia and the kids.'

'Did you ever witness him be over-friendly with anyone at work?'

'No.' Seren shook her head. 'If you're asking if David was a womaniser, then no. In all the time we worked together he never once flirted or made an inappropriate comment, to me, or about anyone else.'

Meadows nodded at Edris.

'Could you have a look at this list of names and tell us if you recognise any of them?' Edris handed over the list that had been taken from David's phone call log.

Seren scanned the names. 'Only Oliver Wilson. He's a probation officer.'

'So David would have spoken to him regularly for work?' Edris said.

'No, Oliver works with adults released from prison. I only know Oliver because I was considering a change of career. I wasn't aware David and Oliver knew each other.'

'Anyone else on the list?'

'No, sorry.'

'Thank you for your time,' Meadows said as he stood up. 'You've been very helpful. We'll let you get back to work.'

'A lot of people are going to miss him,' Seren said as she walked them out of the building. 'He was genuinely a nice man. I just wish he had talked to me if he was in some sort of trouble.'

Meadows caught a glimpse of tears in her eyes before she turned away.

'Do you reckon she was in love with him?' Edris asked.

'I didn't get that impression,' Meadows said. 'It doesn't sound like David's troubles were work-related. The letter from Katie Taylor's parents exonerating David, and Seren's description of the accident make it just that, a tragic accident.'

'So now what?' Edris asked.

'We go and see Oliver Wilson and find out why David was in regular contact with a probation officer which had nothing to do with work.'

Chapter Seven

Naomi Collins lounged on the sofa flicking the screen on her tablet. It was her day off and she didn't feel like doing housework. She had just finished six days on shift and all she wanted to do was put her feet up while the kids were in school. She liked this feeling of tiredness and purposely kept busy until she came to her limit. Anxiety was never far from the surface. Only constant distraction stopped it overwhelming her and years of practice kept it hidden from those around her.

It was as she was trawling through Facebook that she came across a post that made her stomach flip. She sat upright and brought her face closer to the screen as she read the post again. Someone had shared an RIP David Harris page. It had a picture below the heading but no information. She scrolled through the comments, over a hundred, but they were all remarkably similar. She tried to find who had put up the post but couldn't find the administrator. She gave up and googled. The first article was from a local newspaper reporting that the body of a man found at Dinas Rock on Thursday morning had now been named as David Harris. An appeal had been made for witnesses. She felt sick, just the name of the place did that to her. She hadn't picked up her tablet in nearly a week or watched the news. An outbreak of norovirus on the ward had kept the staff so busy there wasn't time for gossip.

She switched back to the Facebook post and looked closely at his picture. He was kayaking, the paddle hitting the water sending droplets into the air, frozen in time. His head was turned towards the camera, he was smiling, his bright eyes full of life. It was a smile she had once loved. She stared at the photo until she was no longer looking at the man but the boy he had once been, a boy who had made her dizzy with happiness each time she saw him.

Naomi had thought he was a dick, just like the other boys in school. He was always messing around and laughing with Callum and Aiden. Sometimes Jay was part of the group, but he was always on the edge of their friendship. Then one day David had whistled at her when she was playing netball, the teachers had told him off and sent him on his way to the rugby pitch. She had thought it a joke. She wasn't used to the attention. She only had one friend, Amber, together they were the school's misfits. Those feelings of being different came back to her now as she looked at the picture. She had hated going to school each morning and watching the popular girls with their highlighted perfect straight hair. Not one of them had a blemish; if they did it was disguised beneath foundation. You weren't meant to wear make-up to school but somehow they got away with it.

Naomi wasn't allowed make-up or the latest fashion clothes. She had been brought up as a Jehovah's Witness by strict parents. Never allowed a friend home or to go out to the cinema. She hated her life, then everything changed. David started paying her attention, much to the shock of the other girls, then Callum started dating Amber, so they all hung out together at school breaks. Weekends were hard. Sometimes she could find an excuse and meet David in secret but there was always the fear that her parents would find out.

'We could have been so happy together,' she said as she touched his picture. It was easy to conjure up the feelings of happiness those days had brought her. She hadn't felt that way since. She loved her husband, but it wasn't the same as that first love she had felt for David. She lay the tablet down on the sofa, she didn't want to go down that path. Memory lane was a dangerous place for her, one she had worked hard to avoid. If she let her mind wander there, it would take her to that fatal day. There were nice memories from that day, but they couldn't be salvaged. Everything she had done then and every day since had been tainted.

Naomi got up from the sofa and made herself a cup of tea. She felt her anxiety building and spread through her body. She felt like a swing that had been twisted around until it was so tight that if you let go it would unravel and spin out of control. She was tempted to run from the house, keep running until she fell down exhausted. She wished now she was back in work where there wasn't room for a wandering mind. It was a trick she had used all her life. Keep busy, keep moving and don't think. She didn't want to think about death. She went back into the sitting room carrying her tea. It was no good; she had to know more, she had to find them all.

It didn't take long. Nearly everyone now had a social media presence and posted glimpses of their lives, just the good bits so that it appeared that they were doing so much better than the rest of the population. She only took a quick glance at Aiden and Callum. It was Amber she was interested in. She wished she could see her now and talk to her. Amber's profile showed she was married with three children, still living in the same area. She hadn't changed much since school, same ginger hair, but now it was styled. Naomi hadn't seen Amber since that day she had to say goodbye. The time before had been the day at Dinas Rock.

It was supposed to be a good day, a day of celebration. She leaned back on the sofa and let her mind wander back through the years.

It had been four days before her sixteenth birthday. It was the first time she would celebrate. Birthdays weren't celebrated in her family. She hadn't missed it at first as she wasn't allowed to attend parties, but she always saw the excitement on the faces of others as the special day approached. Celebrations were planned and gifts received. This time it would be different. She was the oldest in the group and together with Amber she had come up with a plan. Her aunt had given her a digital camera and Naomi told her parents that she was working on a school project, one for which she would have to visit and photograph waterfalls. They agreed to let her go.

David had been on the Four Waterfalls Walk with his parents so knew the area and had picked a place off the main track near the old silica mine. There was a smaller waterfall and a pool to swim. It would be quiet and apart from the odd walker the group would be on their own. David and Callum were going to meet them there.

Amber had baked a cake and managed to get a bottle of wine. When they arrived they sat on the wooden bridge and dangled their legs as they drank the wine from plastic beakers. A pleasant sensation spread through Naomi, the sound of the water, the heat on her back, and a day full of promise made her tingle with excitement.

'As soon as I'm eighteen I'm leaving home,' Naomi said. 'I can't wait to get my own place and do what I want.'

'Don't you want to go to uni?' Amber asked.

'Yeah, I suppose but that will mean another three years with my parents,' Naomi said and took another sip of wine.

'Only in the holidays.'

'No, if I go I am only allowed to apply to Swansea uni so I can travel home each day.'

'That's shit,' Amber said.

'You've no idea what it's like. I'd be as much a freak in uni as I am in school. No parties.'

'Well, apply to other universities. If you get in you can stay the whole time and not bother to go home. I'm sure my parents won't mind you spending the Christmas holidays with me.'

'I'm not bothered about Christmas holidays. I've never had a Christmas.'

'Must be really weird.'

'Not really. I'm given money for chores each week to save up for what I want, and Aunt Jenny takes me out shopping. She always buys me stuff I'm not supposed to have. I just have to hide it. Maybe I'll see where David is planning to go. We could go together. No more sneaking around.'

'Have you and David done it yet?'

Naomi blushed. 'No, have you and Callum?'

'Not yet, but he asked me.'

'What did you say?'

Amber laughed. 'I said I'd think about it.'

'Aren't you afraid you won't know what to do?'

'I don't think there is much to it. You just lie there.'

'I want it to be special with David. Maybe I'll ask him to wait. Come on let's go for a swim, it's boiling.' Naomi stood up. The wine and heat were making her feel light-headed.

Naomi brought herself back to the present. She smiled to herself. I had been so happy, she thought. Without warning the rest of the day flashed through her mind. The cold water, the heat drying her skin. The darkness of the tunnel, David's hands sliding over her body and then–

'No, no, you can't go there,' Naomi said as she put her hands on each side of her head and squeezed, but it was too late. The memory snaked around her stealing her breath until she felt like she was drowning. She pressed her hands down on to the sofa to try and ground herself.

'You're at home, you're safe.' She kept repeating this until she felt her breathing return to normal.

She looked down at her tablet and Amber's photo. Funny how I wanted to leave home so badly then, I got my wish sooner than I expected, she thought. No time to say goodbye to David. She started to type a message to Amber but what do you say after sixteen years? What do you say after what happened?

Chapter Eight

Meadows and Edris followed Oliver Wilson into his office and took a seat.

'What can I do for you, gentlemen?' Oliver asked.

'We're investigating the murder of David Harris,' Meadows said. 'We understand that you've had some contact with him the last few months.'

'Yes, I've spoken to David on a number of occasions. Awful business. I was sorry to hear the news. David was a nice guy.'

'Was he a friend?'

'No, he came to see me just over a year ago about a prisoner that was due for release.'

'Are you able to tell us the name of the prisoner?' Meadows asked.

'Yes, I don't suppose it would do any harm now. It was Jay Parks, one of the lifers.'

Meadows thought back on the conversation he had with mountain rescue at Dinas Rock and the murder in the silica mine. 'We've heard of the case,' he said. 'What was David's interest in Jay Parks?'

'David came to see me about Jay's release. He wanted to help.'

'Did he say why?' Meadows asked.

'No, he was evasive on that point.'

'Is Jay Parks out now?' Edris asked.

'Yes, he was released a year ago on life license.'

'In what way did David want to help him?' Meadows asked.

'David put in a word with the community garden project to get Jay a job. They usually don't take on lifers, it's mainly community sentence. David somehow managed to persuade them. He also spoke to the council to get Jay a flat.'

'So, David would have had a lot of contact with Jay,' Meadows said.

'No, as far as I am aware David had no contact with Jay. He wanted to remain anonymous. He even provided the basics for Jay's flat. Bedding, kitchen equipment, that sort of thing. He delivered it here. I told Jay they were from a charity. It's what David wanted.'

'Didn't you find it a little odd?' Edris asked.

'Not really. David had worked for several years with young offenders. Jay spent time in Glan y-Wern when he was first convicted. I know David worked there and helped a lot of the offenders. He seemed the type of guy that would go above and beyond his job to help people. Jay's family disowned him, apart from his brother, so I guess David would have known that Jay had little support.'

'Were there any other prisoners that he helped?' Edris asked.

'Not as far as I know, but I'm not the only probation officer, you would have to talk to the others in the area. I kept David's involvement confidential. So if he had helped others I doubt I would have heard about it.'

'And David kept in contact with you after Jay's release?' Meadows asked.

'Yes, he called me weekly to keep up to date on Jay's progress.'

'How has Jay been getting on?'

'Really well. Good reports from work and he never misses his appointments with me. He's passed all his random drug tests, and he hasn't been in any trouble. I hope that's not about to change.'

'No, we have no reason to believe that Jay has anything to do with David's murder. It sounds like Jay would have been thankful for the help if he found out. What can you tell me about Jay?'

'Jay was sentenced to fifteen years in 2006 for the murder of Ruth Williams. He was fifteen at the time. His records show that he was a model prisoner. He took his GCSEs and A levels while he was in Glan-y-Wern, even learnt to play the guitar. He went on to do an Open University degree. He was moved to an adult prison at twenty-one, again he settled down stayed out of trouble and took every course available to him.'

'He served the whole sentence,' Edris said. 'Wasn't he eligible for early release?'

'Yes, he would have been if it wasn't for the nature of the crime, that and his reluctance to accept responsibility. Each time he went before the board he refused to acknowledge his guilt. In fact he maintained his innocence the whole time.'

'Were there any appeals?' Meadows asked.

'No, there was never any justification for an appeal. No new witnesses or evidence came to light. My guess is he was off his face at the time he committed the crime and doesn't remember. Sad, really.'

'Did David ever talk about Jay's conviction?' Meadows asked.

'No, just asked how Jay was getting along with work. David was looking at other job opportunities for Jay. He thought Jay's education was wasted but he was finding it difficult to find a placement.'

'Does Jay ever talk about what happened in 2006? Mention anyone involved in the case?'

'No, he's polite, answers questions but he doesn't volunteer any information.'

'OK, well thanks for your time. We'll leave you to get on,' Meadows said.

'Please let me know if you need to speak to Jay or if you have any reason to believe that he has some involvement in what happened to David.'

'Of course,' Meadows said.

They left the probation offices and drove back towards Bryn Mawr station.

Meadows turned over the conversation they had with Oliver in his mind. He couldn't see why Jay would be involved in David's murder or why David chose to help Jay. Of all the prisoners that need help on release why him? He thought. Did David have a personal reason?

'It's quite a coincidence that Jay committed the crime at Dinas Rock and David was found there?' Meadows said.

Edris smiled. 'I thought you didn't believe in coincidence.'

'I don't, so what's the connection?'

'There has to be one,' Edris said. 'I don't buy that David helped him just because he was a good guy.'

'Maybe David had a guilty conscience, or he could have known Jay. They are the same age. Could be a distant relative, cousin maybe, and didn't want his connection known. It's worth checking out.'

'Maybe we should just talk to Jay Parks and ask him,' Edris said.

'Not yet. We have no reason to question him and why cause unnecessary trouble for him. Questioning him in connection to a murder could reflect badly on him and the terms of his license will be strict. Any sign of trouble and he could end up back inside.'

'You're too soft,' Edris said.

'No I'm not, I just like to be fair.'

Back in the office they found Blackwell at his desk with his fingers tapping away at the computer keyboard, Paskin was on the phone, and Valentine was still out.

'How did you get on?' Meadows asked Blackwell.

Blackwell stopped typing and looked up. 'Yeah, nothing of interest to report. Saw Ethan's parents. They said he was doing all right when he came out of Glan-y-Wern then he got back into drugs. They remember David well and said he went out of his way to help Ethan. They were singing his praises. As far as they knew, David hadn't had any contact with Ethan before he died. He sent a sympathy card to them but other than that they had no dealings with David. I spoke to vice in Swansea and Cardiff. They said GHB is circulating in the clubs but didn't have any intel on known dealers. There has been a steady increase in the number of GHB-related deaths reported in the UK since 2008. I've just been looking at the figures. Bloody waste of life. It doesn't look like it would be difficult to get hold of it. No reports that Glan-y-Wern has a drugs problem, but that doesn't mean there isn't one.'

'David's car has been found,' Paskin said. 'I just got off the phone with Ystrad. It was parked near Glynneath Football Club about a forty-minute walk away.'

'Did they find anything interesting?'

'A laptop, and the keys were in the ignition. They are waiting for the car to be picked up and taken to forensics. Maybe we'll be lucky and get some prints. The laptop has been sent to tech.'

'He could have parked the car there himself and walked to Dinas Rock. Maybe he didn't want to be seen,' Blackwell said.

'Yeah, but he wouldn't leave the keys in the ignition,' Edris said.

'Given the time he left the B&B he wouldn't have had enough time to walk that distance and make the climb. The latest time of death was 9 a.m.,' Meadows said. 'I think our killer moved the car so when David was reported missing Dinas Rock wouldn't be searched, and he would remain undiscovered. Given his drinking and recent separation it would be assumed that he went off on his own accord.'

'We're lucky no one nicked the car or laptop,' Blackwell said.

'Yes,' Meadows agreed. 'I would think that the laptop is for work and imagine there is some sensitive information on it.'

'Yeah, a list of his clients and drug suppliers,' Blackwell said.

'I'm not getting the impression that he was into drugs or dealing,' Meadows said. 'So far all I've heard is he was a good guy, a family man, who liked to help people who have got themselves into trouble.'

'Yeah, well I don't trust do-gooders,' Blackwell said.

'You don't trust anyone,' Edris said.

'Anything else?' Meadows asked before Blackwell got a chance to retort.

'I've got some more information on the contacts we took from David's phone,' Paskin said. 'Aiden Edwards is a solicitor working out of a Swansea office. I've set up an appointment for us to see him.'

'That's interesting,' Meadows said. 'Why would David be speaking to a solicitor in the weeks leading up to his death?'

'Maybe he was in trouble and needed advice,' Edris said.

'Could be or maybe he was planning on making his separation from his wife more permanent,' Meadows said.

'Yeah, and if he had a fat insurance policy I'm betting his wife will benefit. She wouldn't want him changing his will,' Blackwell said.

'Valentine is checking out Tia Harris' alibi but it's worth bearing in mind,' Meadows said. 'Anything else, Paskin?'

'Callum Vaughn is an old friend. I spoke to him briefly. He sounded upset by David's death. That leaves Naomi Collins. I haven't been able to get hold of her, but I've left a message for her to contact us.'

'OK, good work. As David called Naomi the evening before he died see if you can track down her address.'

'I'll get on it,' Paskin said.

Valentine walked into the office, put her bag down and plonked into a chair.

'How did it go?' Meadows asked.

'Checked out Tia Harris' alibi. She spoke to one of the teachers when she dropped the kids off at breakfast club at eight and she was in work just after eight-thirty. Nothing much from David's mother. She didn't think there were any extra-marital affairs on either side and although she noticed that David was distracted over the past few months, he didn't confide in her. I called in at Glan-y-Wern, that was an eye-opener. The language with some of them made my toes curl and I'm no prude, I'm used to Blackwell.'

'Oy,' Blackwell said. 'I don't swear that much.'

'Really?' Edris raised his eyebrows.

'Did you manage to get any of them to talk to you?' Meadows asked.

'Yeah, most of them were OK. Only good stuff to say about David from both residents and staff. If he was a sexual predator he did a good job of hiding it. You'd certainly need some patience to work there. I witnessed a kick-off and it wasn't pleasant.'

Meadows filled them in on what they had learnt from David's work colleague and Oliver Wilson.

'So, a nice guy, not into drugs. No financial worries, no affairs. Liked a drink and something upset him the past few months. Not held responsible for the suicide or death that occurred in the area. Basically, we have fuck all,' Blackwell said.

'I think there was a reason he was helping Jay Parks,' Meadows said, 'and I also think he knew he was in danger and that's why he left the family home.'

'Yeah but in danger from who?' Paskin asked.

Chris Harley from tech walked in the office at that moment carrying a laptop. Chris was softly spoken with a mop of wild hair. He was one of the few people in the station that was taller than Meadows.

'I'm glad I caught you before you left for the night. I've found something interesting for you,' Chris said before taking a seat and opening the laptop. 'Thought I'd come and show you.'

'Great,' Meadows said. 'We need all the help we can get.'

'These are some of the files we retrieved from David Harris' personal laptop,' Chris said as the team gathered around. 'He tried to delete them.' He called up the first file.

The screen filled with a picture that Meadows recognised as the entrance to the silica mine at Dinas Rock. Below were the words "August 2005". The next file was a darker picture. It showed a rusting tram cart resting on its side. It was only partially visible. It looked like a flash had picked out the main subject of the photo and the rest was darkness. Below was typed, "You know what happened here."

'August 2005 was when Ruth Williams was murdered,' Paskin said.

'Looks like we've found the reason David was helping Jay,' Edris said. 'He was somehow involved.'

'But in what way?' Meadows said.

'There is more,' Chris said.

The third picture was of the waterfall and pool, with the words, "You witnessed what happened here." The last photo was of the tunnel entrance with the caption, "you all lied."

'That's pretty much it. There is more of the same. Sent by email every week starting about six months ago,' Chris said.

'I don't suppose you have the details of the sender,' Meadows said.

Chris smiled. 'You suppose correctly. All from the same address. He had tried to reply but the emails got bounced back. It will take a while longer but I should be able to track down the sender.'

'Great, thanks,' Meadows said.

'I'll mail you copies of all the files,' Chris said as he headed out of the office.

'Those photos look like they were taken in the summer,' Meadows said. 'Whoever sent them wanted the area to look the same as it did when Ruth Williams was murdered. This has been planned to cause maximum impact.'

'Well, it's obvious that Jay Parks sent them,' Blackwell said. 'Let's bring him in.'

'On what grounds?' Meadows said. 'Part of his license agreement is that he doesn't go near Dinas Rock. I can't see that he would risk it. Until we get confirmation that he sent the emails I don't see how we can justify the risk of him getting his license revoked.'

Blackwell huffed. 'It's a murder investigation, he's killed before. We've got a link between Jay Parks and David Harris.'

'Have we?' Meadows said. 'All we know is that David was helping Jay anonymously. We don't know what David's involvement was in the Ruth Williams case. Jay has always claimed he was innocent. What if David went digging up the past and stumbled on some information or talked to someone who was involved? Jay has served his time, what possible motive could he have for killing David?'

'Maybe David was a witness, he was the same age as Jay,' Valentine said.

'Good point,' Meadows said. 'I want to look at all the information on the Ruth Williams murder. Paskin, can you request the files?'

'Yep,' Paskin nodded.

'Blackwell, I'd like you to speak to Aiden Edwards in the morning – see what David talked to him about. Valentine, can you look at the family backgrounds of Jay and David – see if there is a connection between the two. Edris and I will speak to his friend Callum Vaughn and pay a visit to Naomi Collins, see why she isn't returning our calls. At the moment Jay Parks is being monitored by probation so if he steps out of line he'll be arrested. Our priority is to trace the sender of the emails and find out why they drove David to drink and leave his family home.'

Chapter Nine

Jay picked up the local newspaper on the way to work as he had done each morning since hearing of the discovery of David's body. He scanned the pages as he walked flicking his eyes up now and again to make sure he didn't bump into anyone. There were no updates, just an appeal for witnesses walking in the area the morning David was murdered. Jay could have read the paper on his tea break at work, but he worried someone would notice his interest in the story. There was internet on the phone Mason had given him and he had been tempted to look for information, but the probation officer regularly checked his phone and search history. My life seems full of buts, he thought as he walked along.

Oliver Wilson had called and asked a few leading questions. He seemed particularly interested in whether Jay had visited any of the restricted areas. The boss had also mentioned that probation had been checking his timekeeping at work. All this made Jay feel anxious and he expected the police to turn up at any moment and arrest him. He didn't trust the police. There was no way they could trace the emails with the photos back to him, still he figured they would pin it on him all the same.

It had been Mason's idea to send out the emails. They had waited almost six months after he was released to make a move. Jay hadn't been able to go to Dinas Rock to take the photos, it was too risky. He wasn't willing to take that risk at the time, so Mason had gone instead following Jay's instructions. Jay had wanted to shake them up, it certainly did that, he thought, although he never intended for David to die. He just hoped that Mason hadn't taken things too far. He shook the thought away. He knew what it was like to have people think you were a monster. He wouldn't allow himself to think that of his brother. He'd seen in the paper that David had a family, young kids. He felt sorry for them, in fact he felt sorry for David. No matter what part he had played in the past, it wasn't worth his life. There had been enough suffering and Jay just wanted it over, to have some peace, but he doubted that would be the outcome. He had a feeling that things would be getting a lot worse.

He arrived at work, put the newspaper inside his coat and picked up a shovel. What now? he thought as he hit the earth. David was dead and he hoped the truth didn't die with him. The others would be scared now. It was time they knew what it felt like. He had been scared back then. The police had come to the house and taken his trainers and clothes. At first he had lied, kept to the story they had agreed. The others had changed their story, he guessed they had all met up without him. He'd been left alone to take the blame and it was too late to tell the truth. No one believed him.

He tried to think now whose idea it had been to go into the silica mine. It couldn't have been planned but it had sealed his fate later. His mind drifted back as he continued to dig the earth.

'I don't think we should go in there,' Ruth said hovering by the fence. 'It's dangerous. Can't any of you read? Look at the sign.'

Naomi glanced at the sign and shook her head. 'Don't be such a baby.'

'The sign is just to scare people and keep them out. It's safe enough,' Callum said. He climbed the fence and swung his legs over, landing easily on the other side.

Amber climbed over next. 'Come on, it will be fun,' she said.

David followed then held out his hand for Naomi. Naomi climbed to the top of the fence then jumped into David's arms.

'You next,' Aiden said giving Ruth a smile. 'I'll help you.'

Ruth seemed flattered by Aiden's attention and took his hand. Jay was last over the fence. He was beginning to feel like a spare wheel. It was the same in school, they didn't always want him around. He followed them up the bank watching as Ruth stayed close to Aiden. He couldn't see how Aiden would be interested in her. He guessed she was kind of pretty, but she was two years younger and seemed to complain about everything.

They stepped through the entrance of the silica mine into the darkness. It took Jay's eyes a moment to adjust after being in the bright sunlight. A draft of cool damp air raised goosebumps on his arms and the sound of dripping water echoed through the tunnels. Both Callum and David had brought torches and as they shone them around, the beam picked up cigarette butts, empty cans, and bottles on the rough floor.

'See, others have been in here,' Aiden said.

'Yeah, I heard that divers use this place,' David added.

'Why would divers come in here?' Ruth asked.

'It's flooded further down so you need equipment to explore. I bet that would be cool.'

'Don't think I'd like that,' Amber said. 'Imagine being underwater in the dark.'

'Come on, I'll show you the water,' David said.

'I don't think we should go in any further. We could get lost, or trapped,' Ruth said.

'If you're afraid, you can hold my hand,' Aiden said.

'Come on,' Naomi said. 'We won't go too far. You'll be able to see the light from the entrance so we won't get lost.'

'All right,' Ruth said.

Jay watched Aiden take Ruth's hand and lead her forward. David and Callum led the way with the torches, and he was left at the back. He didn't like being last, but he felt a sense of excitement and adventure as they walked deeper in. The torch beams picked out the thick stone pillars. They curved upwards like tree trunks and were spaced close enough to form archways. They moved slowly as a group, keeping to the right.

'That one's flooded.' David shone his torch at the furthest tunnel. 'We'll go down this one.' He moved his torch over.

The light from the entrance was getting further away and when Jay peeked behind, all he could see was inky blackness. He moved closer to the group. As they moved further in the tunnel, the torches picked up a large entrance to the right. David stopped and shone his torch through. The ground sloped down to reveal a body of water.

'I don't like it,' Ruth said. 'Let's go back.'

'Yeah,' Naomi said. 'I think we've gone far enough.'

David laughed. 'Might have known you lot would chicken out.' He turned around and led the way back to the entrance of the tunnel and handed Naomi his torch. 'You go back, we'll meet you at the entrance.'

Jay was tempted to go back with the girls. He didn't trust the boys. They'll probably play some joke on me, leave me in the dark, he thought. He followed David into the furthest tunnel which sloped down until they reached the water. David shone his torch on the still surface. The floor of the mine gradually faded away in the depths.

'Anyone fancy a swim?' Callum asked.

'No way,' David said. 'That looks pretty deep, you probably wouldn't get out that easily. I bet it's slippery and your feet would sink and get stuck.'

Jay took a step back. He didn't trust them not to push him in.

'Let's go back,' David said. He led the way back to where the girls were sitting on a slab just inside the entrance.

'Skin up then,' Callum said before taking a seat next to Amber.

Jay took a pouch from his pocket, rolled a joint, lit it, and inhaled. 'Ooh, that one's a bit strong.' He handed it to David.

They all took turns except Ruth who had her hands folded across her chest and her eyes full of judgement.

'Let's play truth or dare,' Amber said with a giggle.

Jay didn't want to play the stupid game, but the others agreed. When it got to his turn, he chose dare. It was Aiden's idea that the dare be to go deeper into the mine and take the furthest tunnel until he reached the water then dip his foot in.

'I want to see the water on your trainers,' Aiden said. 'If you come back with dry feet we'll know you chickened out.'

'Gimme the torch then,' Jay said holding out his hand.

Callum gave Jay his torch which was the smaller of the two and didn't give out as much light. Jay set off further into the mine. He could hear the others laughing. The torchlight picked out debris left behind when the mine was abandoned. He passed an old rusty tram cart left on its side. As he got further in he could feel the darkness pressing against his back. He could no longer hear the others and thought they had probably left him in there alone. He was determined to get to the water to prove he wasn't afraid. Large rock pillars held up the ceiling taking on an orange hue in the torchlight. Ahead he could see three tunnels, there could have been more but he couldn't see beyond. He chose the tunnel to the right and as he walked along he shone his torch upwards and saw a large rusting hook. His first thought was that it looked like it belonged in a horror movie. In his haste to move away he tripped over and felt something smash into his shin as he landed face down. The torch flew out of his hand.

'Ow, fuck.' He rubbed his leg to try and soothe the pain and could feel a warm trickle of blood. He scrambled forward and picked up the torch, shining the beam around to see what had caused his fall. He saw a piece of railway track with a thick bolt protruding from the top and was glad it wasn't anything more sinister. The darkness was starting to play with his imagination. He got up and hurried on. His shoulders were hunched up to his neck and his body tensed with fear. The sooner he got to the water the quicker he could get out. The ground beneath him changed until he could feel water seeping into his trainers. He shone the torch in front of him and the beam picked up the water, dark deep, and eerie, as the ground sloped downwards and became fully submerged. Jay imagined these waters would be freezing and if he moved any further he would plunge deep in and be unlikely to get back out. The thought made him shudder. He balanced carefully and dipped his feet in the water one at a time then turned and hurried back. It was silent as he made his way towards the light of the entrance. He couldn't see the others. So they did leave me, he thought. A hand squeezed his shoulder and he let out an involuntary scream. The mine filled with laughter.

'Bastards,' Jay said.

'Shit yourself, did you?' Aiden said.

'It's not funny.' Jay stormed out of the mine. Outside, the sunlight stung his eyes.

Aiden and Callum came out behind him laughing.

'Come on, I have a little something that will make you feel good,' Callum said.

Jay walked down the bank and jumped over the fence. David was sitting with the girls. He sat down and pulled off his trainers. Callum sat down next to him and picked up his rucksack. From inside he took out paper cups and lined them up before filling them from a large bottle of cherryade.

'There you go.' Callum handed him a cup. 'Enjoy.'

Jay was thirsty so he downed the drink. Food had been pooled together so he helped himself. He watched the waterfall filling the pool and the bubbles popping on the surface. He began to feel relaxed.

I can't remember what happened next, Jay thought. He rubbed his hand over his face as he chased away the past. He stopped digging and picked up a bottle of water. I know I went back into the mine later, he thought, but I was alone. Everything from that point seemed jumbled as if the memories from that day had been put in a pot and stirred. He couldn't fix a timeline. He was sure he remembered most of the day but there was a grey area. He could picture Ruth now, dressed in cropped pink trousers and a cotton, sleeveless blouse, her hair pulled back in a ponytail. Her face had been pink from the sun. So young, he thought. I couldn't have hurt her, I saw her after that. Of that he was certain. The evidence against him had been damming but he had an explanation, if only someone would have listened.

Chapter Ten

Meadows turned the car into a haulage yard in Hirwaun industrial estate and parked next to an articulated lorry with the words "Vaughn Haulage" printed on the side. Forklift trucks were whizzing about loading and unloading pallets.

'Busy place,' Edris said as he kept step with Meadows who was weaving his way through the workers.

'Yes, father and son business but from what I can gather Callum Vaughn mainly runs the place.'

Stairs led to an open-plan office and as they entered they heard raised voices. Two men were stood facing each other. One, a thickset man, with cropped dark hair and designer stubble, who looked to be in his early thirties. The other man was slim and in his sixties. Meadows guessed the former to be Callum Vaughn. As the two men continued to argue the rest of the office workers had their heads down appearing to be working.

'You're fired,' Callum said.

'It wasn't my fault, mate,' the older one said.

'Don't mate me, Jeff.' Callum puffed out his chest. He turned to a woman sitting closest. 'Izzy, sort out his P45.'

'But—'

'Just do it!' Callum said.

'I've been here from the start,' Jeff said. 'I worked with your father when it was just two drivers.'

'Yeah, well maybe it's about time you left then. Things have moved on and if you can't keep up…'

'This is unfair dismissal,' Jeff said.

'Tell someone who cares,' Callum said.

'I'll take this up with your father. As far as I am aware he still owns this company.' Jeff turned away and hurried past Meadows and Edris.

Callum turned his attention to Meadows. 'Who are you?'

Meadows introduced Edris and himself.

'Oh right, you better come into my office.'

They followed Callum through a door which led into a spacious office. It was furnished in black and chrome with modern art hung on the wall.

'Take a seat,' Callum said as he shut the door. 'Sorry about that. When you're at the top you have to make some tough decisions. Now I don't have a lot of time, so I'd appreciate it if you keep it brief.'

Meadows wasn't fazed by Callum's arrogance and had no intention of being hurried. He had a feeling that Callum was used to getting his own way. He sat back in the chair. 'We understand that David Harris was a friend of yours.'

'Yes, he…' Callum's voice broke and he cleared his throat. 'Sorry, I just can't believe he's gone. I've tried distracting myself with work and staying here as late as I can but all I've ended up doing is making a mess of things.'

'Had you known David long?' Meadows asked.

'All my life. We started nursery school together.'

'Did you see a lot of him?'

'We got together every couple of weeks when work didn't get in the way. We usually went out for a couple of pints and a catch-up.'

'When was the last time you saw him?' Edris asked.

'Erm… it must be about three weeks ago maybe a little more.'

Edris flicked through the pages of his notebook. 'According to David's phone records, he called you three times in the week leading up to his death. Was it usual for him to call that often?'

'We hadn't had a chance to meet up, so he phoned.'

'What did you talk about?' Edris asked.

'Work, family, just general stuff. He just wanted a chat. He sounded like he had drunk a fair bit.'

'How did David seem to you in the past few months?' Meadows asked.

'Fine.' Callum shifted in his chair. 'Well, he had split with Tia, so I guess he was a bit down about that, perhaps drinking a little too much. I told him he needed to go out and have some fun, if you know what I mean.'

'Did he talk to you about the break-up? Give you a reason why he had left the family home?' Meadows asked.

'No, not really. He just said that they were having a few problems.'

Meadows thought it odd that David didn't talk to his best friend about his marital problems. He wondered if this was true, or was Callum holding back to protect his friend?

'Do you think David was involved with someone else?' Meadows asked.

'No, David wasn't like that. He loved Tia and the kids and I'm sure he would have told me if he thought Tia was having an affair.'

'They must have had some serious problems for David to move out of the family home. Didn't you find that odd?'

'No, why would I? I expect he needed some space, and I didn't ask him why, it was none of my business.'

Again Meadows found this statement odd. Was it the case that David was a private man? It made him wonder what else was in David's past that he didn't share with those closest to him.

'Did David ever mention a Jay Parks?'

'Jay… no.' Colour rose in Callum's cheeks.

That got a reaction, Meadows thought.

'But you know Jay Parks?' Meadows said.

'We went to school together.'

'So you would remember the murder of Ruth Williams?'

'Yeah, everyone in school at the time knew about it?'

'Were you and David friends with Jay?'

'We were in the same year. I wouldn't say we were friends. But we knew each other.' Callum rubbed at the palm of his hand with his thumb. 'It was a long time ago.'

Meadows thought that Callum looked uncomfortable and took a chance. 'What was David's involvement in the case?'

'Involvement? David didn't have anything to do with what happened to Ruth.'

'Did David know Ruth?'

'She was in the same school as us, but she was two years younger.'

Meadows looked at Edris who flipped back through his notebook. Letting someone think you had information was a trick that Meadows found worked well and Edris was quick to pick up on the cue.

'Were you aware that Jay Parks was released from prison a year ago?' Edris asked.

'I think I might have heard it somewhere,' Callum said.

'Did David tell you?' Edris asked.

'He might have mentioned it.'

'Can you think of why David would have had a particular interest in Jay Parks now?' Edris asked.

'No. Look, I don't see what this has to do with what happened to David.'

Edris glanced down at his notebook. 'There are certain aspects of the case that we can't disclose now. It would be really helpful if you would tell us everything you know about Ruth Williams' murder.'

'All I know is that Jay Parks murdered her. We saw Jay at Dinas Rock that day.'

That's interesting, Meadows thought. 'You and David were there that day with Jay?'

'Yes, no, David and me went up there. Jay turned up and we saw him with the girls.'

'What girls?' Edris asked.

'Ruth, Amber, and Naomi. We helped look for Ruth later that day when she went missing.'

'Were you questioned at the time?' Meadows asked.

'Yeah, we all gave statements.'

'Did you give evidence at the trial?'

'Yes, but like I said it was a long time ago and I put it out of my mind. I can't really remember that day. I was just a kid.'

Meadows was sure that Callum would clearly remember a day a girl from his school got murdered, even more so the trial.

'Have you had any contact with Jay?' Meadows asked.

'No, why would I?'

Meadows glanced at Edris.

'We found some photos on David's laptop of the silica mine and the surrounding area. There was a reference to the Ruth Williams case. Did David mention this?'

'No.'

'Have you received any similar emails?' Edris asked.

'No.' Callum shook his head.

'Do you think David could have had any involvement in Ruth's murder?' Meadows asked.

'No.' Callum's eyes narrowed. 'David had nothing to do with what happened. He was with me the whole time.'

'Why were you and David up at Dinas Rock that day?' Meadows asked.

'We just went for a hike. David liked to do that sort of thing, even as a kid.' Callum sighed and rubbed his hands over his face. 'I'm sorry, I'm finding this really difficult. David was a good guy, my best friend. There is nothing more I can tell you about what happened to Ruth Williams. If David had any contact with Jay it would have been because he wanted to try and help him. It's what David did.'

'OK, we'll leave it there for now,' Meadows said and stood. 'We may need to speak with you again. Oh, one more thing. Could you tell us where you were last Tuesday morning between seven and nine?'

'What, you don't think—'

'It's just a matter of eliminating you from our enquiries,' Edris said.

'I would have been here,' Callum said.

'Can anyone confirm that?'

'I was in here all morning. I got in early, before the other staff. There would have been drivers around and the loaders. I'd have to check to see who was around when I arrived.'

'OK, if you could do that and let us have the details of each person that saw you that morning,' Edris said.

'Thank you for your time,' Meadows added.

Meadows waited until they were back in the car before voicing his opinion. 'Now we know David's connection to Jay Parks and Dinas Rock. I also get the feeling that Callum wasn't telling us everything.'

'Yeah, I got that impression. He was edgy about something. Maybe he's worried that Jay is out for revenge. If both he and David saw Jay at Dinas Rock that day and gave evidence, then he would be the next target.'

Meadows started the engine. 'That thought did cross my mind but surely it would make sense for Callum to tell us what he saw that day, and that he is worried for his safety. Besides, Jay has served his time. What would be the point of going after those who testified against him?'

'Unless David and Callum lied back then.'

'That's a possibility. I find it hard to believe that Callum has such a poor memory of that day. We'll have to wait until we get the files and see exactly what they witnessed. Meanwhile let's see Naomi Collins, according to Callum she was there that day.'

The road took them close to Dinas Rock then up higher until they were looking at the views across the Brecon Beacons with the Vale of Neath behind.

'It wouldn't take Callum long to get to Dinas Rock, kill David, and get back to work in time for a bacon butty,' Edris said.

'No, and David would trust Callum, but what would be the motive? Unless David knew something about Callum's involvement that day and kept quiet about it. Then after Jay is released he decides to come clean. Make sure you follow up on Callum's alibi,' Meadows said.

Twenty minutes later they arrived at Pontardawe where Naomi Collins lived. The house was a semi-detached positioned halfway up a steep hill. Meadows parked the car, got out and stretched.

'Let's hope she's in,' Edris said.

'If she isn't we'll try at her workplace. It's a little concerning that she hasn't returned our calls. That's a good sign,' – Meadows pointed at the car in the driveway – 'we may be in luck.'

They walked up the path and Meadows knocked on the door. A few moments later it was opened by a woman wearing a denim pinafore dress over a green jumper. She had brown wavy hair and blue eyes set against pale skin. Beneath her eyes were dark shadows.

Meadows introduced himself and Edris. 'One of our officers left you a message regarding a contact of yours, David Harris.'

'Oh, yes, sorry I meant to call back, but I've been busy. I work shifts.'

'Is this a convenient time to talk?' Meadows asked.

'I have to pick the kids up from school soon,' Naomi said.

'It won't take long,' Meadows said and smiled.

Naomi hesitated. She seemed reluctant to let them in. 'OK then, but like I said I haven't got much time.'

Naomi led them into the sitting room and sat down in an armchair with her arms folded across her chest.

Meadows and Edris took the sofa. Meadows glanced around. The room was set up for a family with a large TV, games console, and DVDs stacked at the side. He turned his attention to Naomi.

'As you are probably aware from the phone call and the recent coverage in the news, David Harris was found dead last Thursday morning at Dinas Rock. We are treating his death as suspicious. Do you mind telling us how you knew David?'

'I wouldn't say I knew him as such. We went to school together. I haven't seen him in years.'

'According to his phone records he called you on Monday the 7th of March, the evening before he died,' Edris said. 'He also called you twice the week before and on a few occasions before that.'

'Yes, it was a bit of a surprise. He was trying to set up a school reunion. He rang a few times as he was having difficulty tracing a couple of people and he wanted to see if I knew anything about them. If they had married or moved away, that sort of thing.' Naomi's hand travelled to her hair as she spoke, and she twisted a lock around her finger.

Meadows thought that Naomi was probably unaware of the tell-tale sign that she was uncomfortable and at this point he didn't believe one word she had said to them.

'What did you and David talk about last Monday evening?' Meadows asked.

'Nothing really, he just wanted a chat. I think he had drunk a few.'

It's what Callum said, Meadows thought. 'Do you know Callum Vaughn?'

'He was David's friend at school. I haven't seen him or spoken to him since we were kids. I'm sure David mentioned that he had kept in contact with him.'

'What about Jay Parks?'

Naomi visibly recoiled at the mention of his name. 'That's one person I definitely wouldn't have contact with.'

'But you knew him?'

'Of course I bloody knew him. He killed my sister.'

Meadows felt like an idiot. Naomi was married so had a different surname from Ruth. Without the files he couldn't have made the connection. Callum had mentioned the girls being at Dinas Rock but he made it sound like a group of friends.

'I'm sorry,' Meadows said. 'We didn't know Ruth was your sister.'

'Maybe you should have done your research before coming here and dragging up the past,' Naomi snapped.

'It wasn't our intention to upset you. Jay Parks' name came up in our enquiries.'

'Why? It happened years ago,' Naomi said.

'Did David mention your sister or Jay Parks?' Meadows asked.

'No, why would he bring up something like that?'

Meadows chose his next words carefully. 'We believe that someone contacted David about the case.'

Naomi didn't comment. Meadows let the silence hang in the air for a moment. 'Have you ever had any contact from Jay Parks or anyone asking about the events of that day?'

'No, Jay Parks isn't allowed to contact me or my family. He's not allowed to come near this area.'

'We spoke to Callum Vaughn earlier today. He told us that both he and David were witnesses. He also mentioned that you were at Dinas Rock that day with another girl, Amber?'

'I don't want to talk about it,' Naomi stood. 'I was sorry to hear about David, but I don't see how I can help you. I only spoke to David a few times, there is nothing more I can tell you.'

'OK.' Meadows stood. 'If you remember anything that David mentioned, even if it doesn't seem important, please give us a call.' He handed Naomi a card.

Naomi glanced at the details then put the card down on the coffee table. 'I'll see you out.'

Meadows and Edris stepped outside and the door was closed promptly behind them.

'Bit odd, don't you think?' Edris said. 'David contacts her after all these years for a reunion, she claims, then he gets murdered.'

'I don't think she was telling us the truth. David was troubled over the past few months and I'm guessing he wanted some sort of information from Naomi.'

'Well, whatever was troubling David is to do with Jay Parks and the murder, that much is clear,' Edris said.

'Yes, and I'd like to know what Naomi and Callum are afraid to tell us.'

Chapter Eleven

Naomi's heart was beating an unnatural rhythm in her chest, and it felt like the floor was moving. She moved quickly to the sofa and sat with her head between her legs waiting for the dizziness to pass. She hated herself for being so weak and wished that any mention of the past didn't bring on a panic attack. She had considered counselling but that would mean talking about it and she never wanted to do that. She had tried so hard not to dwell on what had happened, but it kept creeping up on her. She had found herself in a trance the last few days as she went about the housework. It was as though she was outside her body looking in. She took a few breaths and attempted to sit up and rest her head against the back of the sofa. I need to pull myself together before I pick up the kids and go back to work, she thought.

Naomi felt guilty now that she had been rude to the detectives, but it had been a shock hearing them mention Jay Parks. She hadn't wanted to hear what they would say next, the questions. She'd had enough of questions in her life. They had been endless back then and her parents relentless in their demand for details. Ruth hadn't meant to be with her that day. Her parents could never see that, ultimately it had been their decision, one that had ended Ruth's life and ruined hers. She closed her eyes now and allowed herself a memory. Her childhood bedroom, with Ruth sitting on the bed.

'Who is going with you tomorrow?' Ruth asked.

'I told you, just Amber,' Naomi said as she put her sunglasses into her rucksack.

Ruth grinned. 'Emily Lane saw you kissing David Harris in school. Are you sure you're not sneaking out to meet him?'

'No, and don't go telling that to Mum and Dad or I'll never be allowed out again.'

'I won't say anything,' Ruth said. 'Just let me go tomorrow.'

'You'll be bored. All we're doing is walking and taking some photos. We'll spend most of the time on the bus. It will take us nearly two hours to get there.'

'No it won't,' Ruth said. 'It's not that far.'

'Yeah it will. If you don't believe me, check it out yourself. Because we live in this stupid place you can't just catch a bus straight there. You have to catch a bus to Swansea then change. It's ridiculous, it only takes twenty minutes by car.'

'You could ask Dad to take you,' Ruth said.

'Oh yeah, I can see how that would go. I'm lucky to be able to go at all. Anyway he's got work. He won't go out of his way to drop me off.'

'I'm going to end up stuck here on my own with Mum all day,' Ruth complained.

'Don't you have any friends of your own?' Naomi asked. She wished Ruth would stop moaning and leave as she wanted to finish packing her rucksack. She didn't want her sister to see what she was putting in.

Ruth scowled. 'You know I'm not allowed to hang around with anyone outside of school. Everyone is a bad influence according to Mum and Dad.'

'I'm allowed to see Amber.'

'Only because you say you are working on a school project.'

'Then make something up.'

Ruth's eyes widened. 'What? Lie?'

'Just a little one. I won't tell.'

'It's not fair.' Ruth folded her arms.

'It's not my fault. Why don't you go and do something instead of sulking in here? I'll go somewhere with you Friday.'

'Where?'

'I don't know. You think of somewhere.'

Ruth seemed satisfied. She jumped off the bed and left the room.

Naomi opened her wardrobe and retrieved the clothes and a pair of sandals hidden in the back. She put them in the rucksack and put a folded towel on top before adding her camera. She had clothes hidden in different places. They were the type that her mother forbid her to wear. Her aunt wasn't part of the faith and whenever Naomi would visit she would give her something. Make-up, bits of jewellery, and clothes. All of which had to be kept secret. Naomi knew her aunt would do the same for Ruth when she was older.

Naomi sat down at the computer and logged on to MSN to chat to Amber. Her parents never checked the computer like they did her phone. It was the only safe form of communication. Excitement fizzled in her stomach as she went over the plan with Amber. Amber's older brother was going to drive them to Dinas Rock. The boys were cycling and would meet them there. Another hot day was forecast so they would be able to swim in the river.

'Naomi.' Her mother's voice drifted up the stairs.

Naomi shut down the screen. 'Yes?'

'Come down here.'

The tone of her mother's voice put Naomi on edge. She left the room and walked slowly downstairs. In the sitting room her father was reading a book and her mother was perched on the edge of the sofa with a needle and thread in her hand and one of her father's shirts draped across her lap. Ruth was sitting next to her mother, her eyes downcast as she fiddled with her nails.

'I think you should take Ruthie with you tomorrow,' her mother said.

'What, no. I said I would go out with her Friday.'

'So she said but I want you to help me clean the house on Friday. Besides, I don't want you going out on your own.'

'I won't be on my own. Amber is going with me.'

Her mother pursed her lips as she pushed the needle through the cotton. 'I'm not sure I'm comfortable with you going with that girl.'

'You've met Amber,' Naomi said.

'Yes, she seems like a nice enough girl but she's not like us. Doesn't hold the same values. It's easy to get led astray. If Ruthie goes with you then you are less likely to get into trouble.'

'What trouble? I'm going out to take photos of a waterfall and have a picnic.' Naomi's voice rose.

Her father put down his book. 'Don't raise your voice to your mother,' he said.

Naomi could feel her anger bubbling under her skin. 'Sorry,' she said. 'I promise I'm only going to Dinas Rock and nowhere else. I'll be back at six.'

'That's a bit late,' her father said. 'It's not going to take you all day to take a few pictures.'

'It's because the bus takes so long.'

'OK, you can come home at six, but you are to take Ruthie with you.'

'But–'

'That's my final word.' Her father picked up his book.

Naomi knew there was no point in arguing. She went back to her room seething. Ruth followed her up.

'I didn't say I wanted to go,' Ruth said. 'Only that we were going to go out on Friday.'

'Just leave me alone,' Naomi said.

Naomi felt like there was no point in going now but if she didn't it would look suspicious. She logged back onto MSN and vented to Amber. Amber was quick to find a solution. She would arrange for her brother to meet them at the bus stop and make it look as if he were just driving by. He would offer them a lift. She would contact the boys and ask them to come an hour later than planned so they could accidently meet up. It wasn't ideal but it was Naomi's only option.

The plan worked and the next day Naomi's anger was forgotten. She even managed to drink the wine Amber had brought by pouring it into a plastic cup when Ruth wasn't looking. Ruth thought they were drinking lemonade and was happily snapping pictures with Naomi's camera. Naomi changed into the clothes she had hidden in her rucksack, high-cut shorts and a cropped top. Ruth commented that they were inappropriate so Naomi promised she would give them to her to wear when she was older.

'It's too hot,' Ruth complained. 'How long are we going to stay here?'

'You knew we were coming out for the day,' Naomi said.

'Yeah to walk. We haven't gone that far. Can't we go to the big waterfall? There are trees there and it'll be cooler.'

'That's why I packed a change of clothes. It's too hot to wear trousers,' Naomi said. 'I told you to pack your swimsuit. You could have gone in the pool. I'm going in later. I packed a bikini. When I change you can wear these.' She pointed to her outfit.

'I can't wear those, what if someone sees?' Ruth said.

'There's no one here,' Amber said. 'Come on, let's paddle in the water, it will cool you down.'

While they were dipping their feet in the water, David, Aiden, and Callum turned up, but they didn't join them straight away. Instead they said a quick hello and walked across the bridge and up the bank on the other side.

'What are they doing here?' Ruth said.

'The same as us,' Amber said. 'They have to take photos for the school project.'

'I hope they are not going to come back here.' Ruth picked up a stone and threw it in the water.

Ten minutes later the boys came back and settled on the bank. Ruth was uncomfortable in their company but once Aiden started to flirt with her she relaxed. Naomi thought that the day wouldn't be so bad after all. She had David by her side, holding her hand and maybe they would find time to sneak off alone.

Jay was the last to turn up and jumped in the pool. To Naomi's surprise, Ruth laughed and seemed to like Jay, but it was Aiden she paid the most attention to. It hadn't been easy to persuade Ruth to go into the silica mine. Naomi thought it would be exciting, and it would be a chance to kiss David without Ruth seeing.

'I don't want to go exploring in there,' Ruth said grabbing Naomi's hand and holding her back.

'Why not, it will be fun,' Naomi said.

'It will be dark and what if it collapses and we get trapped?'

Naomi huffed. 'Fine, let's go to the fence and we can watch the others go in.'

It was Aiden that managed to persuade Ruth to enter the mine. As they got further in, Naomi felt David's arm snake around her waist then he moved his hand up over her breast. Her body came alive under his touch and she forgot all her worries and even took a drag of the joint when it was passed around. That had been a mistake. It was a step too far for Ruth and as soon as Jay had set off on his dare to go further into the mine she had stomped off.

'Ruthie,' Naomi called following her out of the mine. 'Wait.'

'I want to go home,' Ruth said.

'Oh, come on, we're having fun.'

'I'm not, you took drugs. If you don't take me home now I'm going to tell Mum and Dad.'

'Tell them if you want, they've probably smoked weed themselves.' The thought made Naomi giggle.

'You're stoned,' Ruth said.

'No, I'm not, I only had a bit.'

'I'm going.' Ruth turned away.

'OK, fine. Let me have something to eat first. I'm starving. Then I'll go with you.'

Naomi wished that she had taken Ruth home then, because it was after they all sat down to eat that everything changed.

Chapter Twelve

Aiden Edwards sat behind his desk in his office clicking the top of a pen. The click-clack filled the silence of the office and his knees jiggled to the rhythm. It was times like this that he wished he hadn't given up smoking. He was waiting for the detective to arrive. He had called to say he was on his way but hadn't given any details on what he wanted to discuss and this made Aiden nervous. He wanted to be prepared, know the questions before they were asked, but he knew it didn't work that way.

He suspected, from the moment he heard of the discovery of David's body, that they would want to talk to him. More so as David had called him and visited the office. Now the time had come he felt like a fifteen-year-old boy again. He had been questioned back then about Ruth Williams' murder and he could still remember the feeling of being intimidated by the detectives. They hadn't said or done anything to make him feel that way. It was the mere presence of them in his house and the fear that they would find out he was lying.

His mind wandered back to that day as he stood up and looked out of the window. It was supposed to be a boys-only day out, that's what Callum had said. Aiden had been looking forward to getting away from the village. It was the summer holidays, and his family never went anywhere. Both his parents worked and there wasn't enough money for a holiday away. He'd filled his rucksack with food and drink, packed a towel and had ridden his bike to the next village and met with Callum and David. It was as they were pushing their bikes up the hill that David mentioned that Amber, Naomi, and her little sister Ruth were going to be there. Aiden had stopped his bike. He could recall the disappointment. It seemed so childish now but back then, filled with teenage hormones, it had been a big deal. It was bad enough that he didn't have a girlfriend and already felt left out most of the time, but to spend the day watching them stick their tongues down each other's throats was too much.

'No,' Aiden said. 'Callum said just us boys. There is no point in me going.'

'Oh come on,' David said. 'It will be a laugh. The girls are OK.'

'You could have invited someone for me. I'm going to feel like a right dick,' Aiden said.

'You can have Naomi's sister,' Callum said and laughed.

'Piss off.' Aiden turned his bike around.

'It was only a joke,' Callum said.

'Yeah, well it's not funny.'

'Jay is going to be there,' David said. 'So you won't be on your own. Actually, I need you to do me a favour. I need an hour alone with Naomi. Just keep Ruth occupied, you know, distract her, flirt a little.'

Aiden turned round to face them. 'Hell no, you can get Jay to do it.'

'Please,' David said. 'I'd do the same for you.'

'I'll give you my phone.' Callum pulled the phone out of his back pocket and wiggled it in front of Aiden.

'Hey, you promised to give that to me,' David said.

'Do you want to get laid or not?' Callum said.

'Fine,' David said.

'Look, it's got three games. It's a good phone,' Callum said.

Aiden didn't have to look. Callum always had the latest gadgets, and anything was better than the crappy mobile he had. 'You've only just had that phone.'

'Months ago,' Callum said. 'Dad's getting me a new one for my birthday. One with a camera.'

'Can we go now?' David said. 'We're never gonna get there.'

'OK.' Aiden turned his bike round. 'Just one hour though. I don't want to be stuck with Ruth any longer.'

By the time they got to Dinas Rock, Aiden was so hot and sweaty that all he wanted to do was get to the river and jump in. They left their bikes near the rock and took the steep climb up. When they descended the other side, the girls were paddling but they couldn't stop. They had to make it look like their meeting was accidental. They waved as they crossed the bridge and Aiden saw Ruth scowl at them. The task of keeping her occupied is not going to be easy, he thought. They walked for a while. It seemed like hours in the heat and Aiden was pissed off by the time they joined the girls and in no mood to be polite, but he really wanted Callum's phone.

Naomi and Amber laid towels out and were lying on their backs with David and Callum lying next to them. Ruth sat on the concrete slab that overlooked the river. Aiden sat down next to her and made some crack about being a spare wheel. Ruth smiled at him. She's pretty, he thought. It was a shame she was two years younger. He kept up the conversation and she seemed to be warming to him until Jay turned up and jumped in the river. Ruth laughed and watched Jay swimming. Aiden didn't know why he felt jealous, maybe because a lot of girls looked at Jay and not at him. He was the one that was supposed to keep Ruth company and he wasn't about to be upstaged by Jay's good looks.

'You know he's a druggy,' Aiden said.

'I heard the police arrested him last year for drugs. It was all over the school,' Ruth said.

'Yeah but he only got a caution. Best stay away from him,' Aiden said.

Jay got out of the water and sat down next to David. Aiden took a packet of crisps from his bag and offered one to Ruth. She dipped her hand in the packet, her attention now back on him. When they all decided to explore the silica mine he was pleased with himself that he managed to persuade Ruth to go in. He hoped that David and Callum would remember the part he played in making the day go smoothly. It was while they were inside the mine that Ruth became upset because they had all shared a joint. He heard her snap at Naomi and storm out of the mine. The weed made him feel chilled so he didn't care now if the girls left. He stayed inside with Callum and hid while Jay took a dare to go further in. They jumped out at him when he returned. Jay shrieking like a girl made his day and he doubled up laughing until his stomach hurt.

Back out in the sun the girls were sitting together, Naomi looked upset, and Ruth was pouting. He took out his sandwiches and sat next to David to eat. It wasn't long after that that things became hazy. He could remember the feeling of euphoria, the water sparkling with the foam bubbles popping on the surface. Then Ruth stood up and pulled off her top and trousers. They were all laughing as she slid down the bank and jumped into the water. Aiden felt a tightening in his groin. In that moment of madness she looked like the most beautiful woman he had seen.

The shame of that memory came down on him wrapping around his body and making his skin prickle. Don't think of it now, he thought. The images of what happened after flashed through his mind making him feel sick. A knock at his office door made him start. The door opened and his secretary appeared.

'Detective Sergeant Blackwell is here to see you,' she said.

The detective entered the office. He was thickset with a triangular neck and sharp eyes.

'Take a seat.' Aiden sat behind his desk and tried to force a smile. 'How can I help you?'

'As you will be aware, we are investigating the suspicious death of David Harris and his phone records show that he called your office on three occasions. Your secretary also confirmed that he visited you here without an appointment.'

This one gets straight to the point, Aiden thought. 'That is correct.'

'Was David Harris a client?'

'More of an acquaintance. I've known David a number of years.'

'So was it a social call David made on' – Blackwell flipped open his notebook – 'the 5th of March?'

Aiden wondered how much the detective knew. He hadn't once smiled and his manner was brisk. He would have to keep it simple. The less he said the better. 'David was estranged from his wife and wanted some advice.'

'What advice did he want?'

'Just what would happen if the split became more permanent. The house, child custody, things like that.'

'And what about his visit to the office?'

'Again, it was just an informal chat.'

'I see,' Blackwell said. 'But he turned up without an appointment.'

'Yes, just on the off chance I was free. As it was I didn't have any clients in at the time.'

'Did he discuss with you why he had left his wife?'

'No, he didn't go into details.'

'Was there anything else he talked about?'

Aiden could feel the sweat soaking through his shirt and was glad he was wearing a jacket so the detective couldn't see. 'No, nothing of consequence, just general talk.'

'He phoned you again after he had been to see you. What was that call about?'

'Just a chat. To be honest, I think he was a bit lonely and was drinking.'

'Did you get the impression he was troubled? I mean something other than his marital problems.'

'No.' The lie slipped from Aiden's lips easily.

'OK, that's about all, I think,' Blackwell said and shut his notebook.

Aiden felt his body relax. Every muscle in his body had been taut during the conversation.

'Oh, one other thing. Did David mention Ruth Williams or Jay Parks?'

The words came like a blow. 'Erm, no.'

'Are you familiar with the case?'

Aiden chose his words carefully. 'Yes, I remember it well. I think most people that lived in the area at the time would find it difficult to forget.'

'Can you think of any reason why David would have an interest in the release of Jay Parks?'

'No, only that David worked with young offenders. He helped people that had been in trouble so maybe his interests included adult offenders.'

Blackwell stood. 'Thank you for your time. If you remember anything from your conversations with David please let us know.'

'Of course.'

As soon as Blackwell left the office Aiden started going over everything he had said to the detective. They will look at the case and he'll know I lied, he thought. But I didn't lie. He asked about David's interest in Jay Parks not mine. Aiden could visualise David in the office. He had been upset and wanted to know everything that Aiden had seen that day. He knew what had sent David off on his quest for the truth, but Aiden couldn't tell the detective that, it would mean exposing his own lies.

He moved to the window and watched Blackwell get in his car and drive off. After waiting a few minutes he grabbed his phone off the desk and left the office.

'I have to go out for a couple of hours,' he told his secretary.

'You have a client coming in in half an hour,' she said.

'Call them and reschedule. I'll be back as soon as I can.'

He hurried out of his office. With a bit of luck Callum would be at work. He couldn't call ahead as the police would have a record. He needed to speak to the others to make sure they would stick to the story.

Chapter Thirteen

The Ruth Williams case files were piled up on his desk when Meadows got into work the next morning. He started with the witness statements. There were eyewitness accounts of the girls arriving and later David, Callum, and Aiden followed by Jay. It had been a hot summer's day with a full car park. Some hikers had arrived at the same time. Others had walked the path up to the turning at either the same time as the girls or the boys. There had also been a group climbing the rock. All the boys had arrived by bicycle and asked the group leader to keep an eye on their bikes. The statements Meadows was most interested in were the ones from David and Naomi. He picked out David's and started to read.

> *I went to Dinas Rock with my friends Callum and Aiden. We hiked up from home. We were going for a walk and to swim in the river. We turned off to take the path that goes to Penderyn. We wanted to go into the old silica mine and tunnel to explore. When we got there we saw Amber Thomas, Naomi Williams, and her sister Ruth. They were paddling in the river. We stopped to talk to them then looked in the mine before going in the tunnel then walking further up river.*

We came back to the mine later. I don't know what time but we had been walking for a while. Naomi and Amber said that Ruth was missing so we said we would help them look. We searched around the area and down the river. We met up with Jay Parks and asked if he had seen Ruth. He said he had seen Naomi and Amber and he was helping them look for Ruth. He looked in the mine but didn't find her. We all kept searching but we couldn't find her, so Aiden, Callum, Jay, and me left as we had to bike home.

'Anything interesting?' Blackwell asked.

Meadows looked up, he had been concentrating on the statement and didn't notice Blackwell coming in. 'Just going through the statements. There's a lot of them.'

'I'll grab a coffee and give you a hand.'

'Great.' Meadows picked up the account from Naomi and read.

I went up to Dinas Rock with my friend Amber and my sister Ruth. We took some photos and went paddling in the water. We saw David Harris, Aiden Edwards, and Callum Vaughn. They were going for a walk. They spoke to us then went into the mine before going off for a walk. We had a look in the mine and tunnel then Amber and me went off to take some photos. We left Ruth sunbathing by the waterfall. I don't know how long we were gone. Maybe an hour. When we got back she wasn't there. I thought she might have gone for a walk so we waited. When she didn't come back we went to look for her. We saw Jay Parks, he said he would look in the mine. We looked everywhere. We met up with the boys again and they hadn't seen her so I had to call my mum and dad. The boys left before they came.

Blackwell came back into the office and placed a cup of tea on Meadows' desk before grabbing a file and sitting down. Meadows was reading through Jay's statement when he heard Blackwell curse.

'Lying little bastard,' Blackwell said.

Meadows looked up. 'What have you got?'

'Statement from Aiden Edwards. He didn't say a thing about being a witness in the case.'

'Did you ask him?' Meadows asked.

Blackwell huffed. 'Yeah, I asked him about David's interest in the case. All he said was that he remembered the case.'

Meadows smiled. 'Technically he didn't lie. He just omitted to tell you the facts.'

'That in itself is fishy. Most people would spurt that out if asked.'

'I'd keep the conversation to a minimum if I were faced with you,' Valentine said as she took a seat at her desk.

'For your information, I was pleasant. I usually am,' Blackwell said.

Meadows saw Paskin's lips twitch as she switched on her computer.

Edris was last in. 'Are we going to read through all these files?' he asked eyeing the pile.

'Good of you to join us,' Blackwell said.

'I'm not late. Maybe a few minutes,' Edris said.

'Grab a file,' Meadows said before Blackwell and Edris got into their usual morning spat. He couldn't understand why the two of them couldn't get on. He guessed it was a personality clash and Edris had a way of ruffling Blackwell's feathers.

The office became silent with only the odd comment and Paskin tapping away at the keyboard. Once Meadows had finished reading through the post-mortem report, he called the team to join him around the incident board where Paskin had put up photos relating to the case.

'You've all had a chance to look through the files. As we know, Jay Parks was convicted for the murder of Ruth Williams in August 2005. Ruth was thirteen years old and Jay fifteen at the time. Ruth's body was discovered in floodwater in the old silica mine. She had suffered a trauma to the back of the head so was unconscious when she went in the water. There were also traces of GHB in her system. The timeline is sketchy. The girls arrived at 10.30 a.m. and the boys an hour later, with Jay arriving at 12 p.m. According to the statements, the girls stayed near the water until about 2 p.m. then went off for a walk, leaving Ruth. After talking with the girls the boys went off walking, not one of them could give a time they returned. It's estimated that the girls returned from their walk around 3 p.m. They then searched for Ruth. Naomi called her parents at 6 p.m. It was after 10 p.m. that Ruth's body was discovered by search and rescue.'

'David was found near enough the same place as Ruth,' Valentine said. 'And the same drug was used. It has to be Jay Parks.'

'I agree, David Harris' death is connected to Jay Parks and the murder of Ruth. I spoke to Oliver Wilson, Jay's probation officer, this morning and he confirmed that Jay was in work the morning David was killed, with plenty of witnesses,' Meadows said.

'Yeah, but that doesn't mean he hasn't got someone helping him,' Blackwell said.

'Jay has a brother, Mason. He's the only member of the family that has any contact with Jay,' Meadows said. 'It's worth checking to see if he made any close friends inside. Valentine, was there any family connection between David and Jay?'

'No, none at all. I traced back to grandparents. Both David's parents are Welsh, family originally from Merthyr. Jay's father is Welsh, his family is from Cardiff. Jay's mother's family are originally from India, they moved to Wales in the sixties. There are no distant relatives that connect the two families.'

'OK, so David was helping Jay either because he was an old friend and he did it out of the goodness of his heart, or he somehow felt guilty. Perhaps he suspected that Jay wasn't wholly responsible for Ruth's murder.'

'The evidence against him was solid,' Blackwell said.

'Yeah, but doesn't mean he acted alone,' Edris said.

'There were five others there that day. The initial statements taken at the time tell the same story. The girls went up to Dinas Rock for a picnic, they met David, Aiden, and Callum out for a walk. Later they see Jay. All say they saw Jay going into the mine after Ruth went missing. Jay's statement differs slightly. He said he had arranged to meet the boys at Dinas Rock. So what's wrong with this picture?' Meadows asked.

'Well, Aiden didn't say he was a witness when I spoke to him yesterday,' Blackwell said.

'Callum didn't say that Aiden was with them when we spoke to him,' Edris said.

'And Naomi didn't tell us anything,' Meadows added. 'The statements from Aiden, Naomi, Amber, Callum, and David are too alike. They lack detail. It's as though they all stuck to the same story and kept it simple. The other thing that struck me is why would Jay go to Dinas Rock alone that day? Think about it. A fifteen-year-old boy. He lived in Ystrad at the time, and it would have taken about an hour to cycle there. I think it unlikely that he would have cycled that distance to take a walk on his own. It's more plausible that he arranged to meet the group there.'

'What does it matter?' Blackwell asked.

'Why lie? They all distanced themselves from Jay. Did they witness something? At the time they gave their statements Jay wouldn't have been in the frame for murdering Ruth, but their statements certainly point the finger.'

'But there was evidence against him,' Valentine said.

'Yes,' Meadows agreed. 'But what else happened that day? Why did Jay attack Ruth?'

'Jay already had a record for dealing,' Blackwell said.

'Cannabis, not class A drugs,' Meadows said. 'The evidence against him was blood found on his shorts and trainers matching Ruth's blood. There was also Jay's blood and skin cells found on a piece of old railway track along with blood and tissue from Ruth. Prints from his trainers also matched prints leading down to the water. Like you say, the evidence was damming. The theory is that Jay drugged Ruth and took her into the mine and sexually assaulted her. Ruth's shirt was torn with buttons missing. It is thought that Ruth fought back and there was a struggle. She was knocked unconscious and dragged to the water's edge. She was alive when she was put in the water. Cause of death was drowning.'

'It sounds like he was off his face. He comes across Ruth sunbathing and alone and attacks her,' Blackwell said. 'And if anyone else was involved why would Jay cover for them?'

'He did change his statement later to say that the whole group had planned to meet up, not just the boys. We would need to look at the interview tapes to see what else Jay said about that day at a later point. Better still, I think we should talk to the SIO who worked the case at the time. DI Dylan Finch. Paskin, can you track him down? We also need contact details for the other witness, Amber Thomas.'

'Yeah, I'll get on to it,' Paskin said.

'Let's assume for the moment that everything the witnesses said was true and Jay was guilty despite protesting his innocence to date. Then who sent the photos to David?'

'Jay,' Valentine said.

'But why? And why those words? "You know what happened" and "Tell the Truth"? It implies that Jay thought David knew something about that day or was involved in Ruth's murder.'

'The photos worried David enough to cause him to hit the bottle and move out of his home,' Edris said.

'Yes, and he contacted the others, except for Amber Thomas,' Valentine said.

'It's possible that he could've visited her if he knew where she lived. We won't know until we talk to her,' Meadows said.

'Maybe David was afraid,' Paskin said. 'He testified against Jay. Jay is released and he sends photos.'

'It doesn't make sense though,' Meadows said. 'Why would Jay kill David now? If David had simply recounted what he saw that day, why would Jay want revenge? He's served his time and is out. Why risk going back to prison? And why would David help Jay if he was afraid he was going to harm him? Why didn't David report the photos to the police?'

'Because he didn't want Jay to get into trouble,' Edris said. 'Maybe the photos sparked something in David's memory, and he started to suspect one of the others was involved so he started digging and got himself killed.'

'That would make more sense,' Meadows said.

'We should just bring Jay in,' Blackwell said. 'He's obviously the one that sent the photos.'

'If we bring him in it's likely he'll end up back inside. We have no evidence that he sent the photos. We have to wait for tech to track down the sender. We'll talk to Jay, but at home after he's finished work. Keep it low key. Edris, you'd better give Oliver Wilson a call and tell him that we will be visiting Jay. Make it clear that he is not a suspect. Paskin, can you get a detailed map of Dinas Rock and draw up a timeline for the original case?'

'All this would have been done at the time,' Blackwell said.

'One would hope so,' Meadows said. 'Jay was arrested fairly soon after the murder. There were no other suspects. The evidence was there so there was no need to look any further. Callum, Aiden, and Naomi are all hiding something. If Jay did send the photos then he thought that David knew something. David would have told the others. I intend to find out if they all lied back then and what they lied about. Blackwell and Valentine, speak to Mason and see if he has an alibi for the morning David died. Also check out who Jay shared a cell with, if he made any friends and who has been released recently. While we wait for Jay to finish work we'll talk to David's mother, see what she remembers from that time. David may have told her something at the time of Ruth's murder that she didn't think mattered or maybe she wanted to protect her son and told him to keep quiet. It could be the thing that cost her son his life.'

Chapter Fourteen

Vanessa Harris led Meadows and Edris into her sitting room which was filled with flowers.

'Everyone has been so kind,' she said. 'Bringing flowers and food for Tia and the kids. They drop it here as they don't want to disturb her. Most of them knew David as a child and it helps to have visitors. David's father has gone back to work. He couldn't bear sitting around. Please take a seat.' She sat down in an armchair, but her body remained taut.

Vanessa's pain was almost tangible, and Meadows felt a keen sadness for her. It was against nature for a child to die before their parents and he imagined that the hole left behind could never be filled.

'I'm so sorry for your loss and to intrude on you at this time,' Meadows said as he took a seat. 'We just need to ask you a few questions if you're up to it.'

'Yes, I want to help in any way I can. Visitors are also a welcome distraction. I already spoke to another detective. Valentine? Lovely girl. I told her everything I know so I'm not sure how much help I can be. David was upset by the split with Tia but I'm sure they would have sorted things out eventually.'

'We wanted to ask you about David's earlier life, particularly his teenage years, when he was a witness in the Ruth Williams murder case,' Meadows said.

'Oh, right. All that happened a long time ago,' Vanessa said.

'Yes, but we have to explore every avenue and that means looking at David's past. Jay Parks was released from prison a year ago and David had been helping him. Although David asked that his involvement remain anonymous. Did he speak to you about it?'

'No, but it wouldn't surprise me. David was friends with Jay when they were young, and he liked to help people.'

'Can you tell us what you remember about that time?'

'Jay Parks would come to our house often. David always had the boys around. They would stay for food and could they eat.' Vanessa smiled. 'I knew all their parents. From what I recall Jay's father had lost his job and things were a little tense at home. He was always polite, a nice boy. It was a shock that he would do such a thing. That poor child. I didn't know Ruth. Her parents kept to themselves. David talked about Naomi, from what I gathered she was his girlfriend. He didn't say much about it. You know how secretive teenagers can be. I'd heard the other boys tease him and Callum was seeing Amber, Naomi's friend. Callum and David were good friends. Callum called around to see me yesterday. He was in a bit of a state. He's taken David's death badly.'

Meadows let her talk. He found it better not to interrupt, that way snippets of information slipped out easily. Naomi hadn't mentioned she was David's girlfriend at school. Now he knew that Amber and Callum were involved he was sure the boys had planned to meet with the girls that day. It was no coincidence that they met at that location.

'Did all the boys leave to go to Dinas Rock together that day?' Edris asked.

'Callum was here,' Vanessa said. 'They were going to meet Aiden as he lived in Coelbren at the time. They packed their rucksacks full of food and drink. I wasn't working then as I liked to be around when the kids got home from school. David's two sisters are younger. I expected the boys to be gone for the day but I started to get worried when David didn't come home for dinner. It must have been after seven when he got back.'

'Was he upset or acting out of character?' Meadows asked.

'Oh, I don't know. It was a long time ago and the girls were young. I guess I would have been distracted. I think I asked him why he was so late back. He said something like they had met up with Amber, Naomi, and Ruth and they stayed later because Ruth had gone missing, and they had helped to look for her.' Vanessa bit her lip in concentration as she appeared to be sifting through memories.

'He did seem concerned that Ruth was missing. I think he was more worried because it was Naomi's sister. He didn't want food and went straight to his room. I remember I didn't think much of it at the time. It's a safe area and there had never been any incidents in the past that would cause concern. Callum came over later I remember that he was out of breath and it was late for him to be calling. He told us that Ruth had been found dead in the old silica mine. Accident was my first thought. I asked David if he had been into the mine. He said they had all been exploring earlier in the day. I told him I didn't want him to go to that place again. At the time I was so grateful that no harm had come to him and thought how easily it could have been any one of them that died in that place. Of course later we heard that poor girl had been murdered.'

'How did David react to the news?'

'He was upset, both boys went to his room. I phoned Callum's parents to say that he was with us. I offered for him to stay the night, but he went home. David wanted to be alone. He stayed mostly in his room, didn't eat anything. I was worried about him. The police came to talk to him. I sat with him while he answered their questions.'

'Did you get the impression that David knew more than what he told the police?' Meadows asked.

'It was difficult to tell. He was withdrawn and I suppose uncomfortable talking to the detectives. They were very nice. David gave his statement although he wasn't very forthcoming. My guess would be that they were up to some sort of mischief, as boys that age usually are. Smoking or drinking maybe.'

'Looking back, do you think David saw something, maybe witnessed Ruth's murder?'

'No, I'm sure he would have said if he saw Jay kill Ruth. If that's what you mean. He wouldn't have lied about something that important. I just think the whole business shook him up. I offered to take him to see Ruth's parents to give our condolences. I thought he might like to see Naomi. He didn't want to go so I didn't push him.'

'Did David seem surprised at Jay's arrest?'

'It shocked everyone. David was called as a witness along with the others that were there that day. He didn't want to give evidence against Jay. I think he was frightened of going to court and Jay had been his friend. He had plenty of support and handled it well, but it still affected him badly. He didn't go out for a long time after that. It took time for him to get over it and to return to normal. I recall Naomi was sent to live with relatives after and her parents moved away from the area. That's about all I can tell you.'

'Do you think David was helping Jay because he felt guilty about something that happened that day or something he said in his statement?' Edris asked.

Vanessa turned her attention to Edris. 'No, I'm certain that David told the police everything he knew and the truth. If he was helping Jay Parks, then it would have been because they were once friends. It's what David did, help people. I really can't see that what happened back then has anything to do with David's death.'

'We have to look at all avenues. If we are to have a chance of catching the person responsible for taking your son from you then we must look closely at David's past,' Meadows said. 'Can you remember anything from that time, maybe something that didn't seem important or didn't feel quite right?'

Vanessa thought for a moment. 'No, David threw himself into his studies and went off to university. He stayed friends with Callum, I don't think he saw much of Aiden when they left school. I suppose if I thought anything odd it was that Naomi was sent away. You'd think after losing one child they would cherish the remaining one, keep her close. That's just my opinion. Perhaps they wanted Naomi to have a fresh start, or maybe her parents weren't coping.'

Meadows nodded. 'Thank you for talking to us.' He stood up.

'David wasn't an extraordinary man. He didn't do any great deeds. He was just a normal man, a family man. He probably made mistakes like anyone else, but he was my boy,' Vanessa said.

'We'll do everything in our power to find out what happened to your son,' Meadows said.

'Thank you.' Vanessa led them to the door and closed it quietly behind them.

'Sounds like David knew more than he was telling,' Edris said.

'Yes, it's possible he knew Ruth was dead before Callum came to tell him. But why keep quiet if he saw something?'

'Unless he thought Callum had something to do with it. They were best friends,' Edris said.

Meadows opened the car door, climbed inside, and started the engine. 'The other question is, why was Naomi sent away? Vanessa Harris is right, all the grieving families I have encountered tend to stick together.'

'Unless they blamed Naomi,' Edris said.

'My thoughts exactly,' Meadows said. 'Right, let's go and see Jay Parks. I want to hear his version of events from that day.'

Chapter Fifteen

The strumming of a guitar accompanied by singing could be heard outside Jay's flat.

'Nice voice,' Meadows said before knocking the door.

'I guess he's had a lot of time to practice,' Edris said.

The singing stopped and a few moments later the door was opened by a man wearing jeans and a T-shirt. His feet were bare. The first thing Meadows noticed was his striking eyes, soft brown and doleful framed by long dark lashes. He had thick, jet-black hair and an open face.

'Jay Parks?' Meadows asked.

Jay sighed. 'Can I put on some shoes and lock up before you take me in, please?'

'We're not here to take you in,' Meadows said. 'Unless you give us a reason to do so. Detective Inspector Meadows and this is Detective Constable Edris, but I think you already guessed.'

'Yeah.' Jay smiled. 'I don't get any visitors and you kinda look like cops.'

'We just want to ask you a few questions. Can we come in?'

'Sure.' Jay stood back to let them in then closed the door.

They entered a small sitting room where Meadows noticed there were only two chairs and a coffee table.

'Have a seat,' Jay said as he moved the guitar that was resting against the armchair. 'I'm happy to sit on the floor.'

Meadows figured that Jay would feel more comfortable if they were sitting. He took the armchair nearest the window and nodded to Edris to sit in the other chair. Jay sat cross-legged near the coffee table.

'Why did you think we were here to arrest you?' Meadows asked.

'I heard about David Harris' murder on the radio and read about it in the papers. As it was at Dinas Rock and David was one of the people to give evidence against me then I guessed you'd come knocking. Part of my license is to stay out of trouble so being questioned by the police in connection to a murder is bound to get me put back inside.'

'You understand why we have to question you?' Meadows asked.

'Yeah, I had nothing to do with David's murder, but I don't suppose that matters,' Jay said.

There was no anger in Jay's tone and Meadows thought he sounded resigned, as if he expected the worse to happen.

'We are just interested in the truth,' Meadows said.

'The truth?' Jay laughed. 'It didn't mean shit last time.'

'I promise you I will not be biased because of your past conviction. I'll treat you the same as anyone else that has had a connection to David in the past. I can assure you that you are not the only one that we've spoken to.'

'Fair enough,' Jay said. 'What do you want to know?'

'Have you had any recent contact with David?'

'No, the last I saw David was at my trial.'

'Did you try to contact him?'

'No, I'm not supposed to have any contact with the victim's family, and that also extends to witnesses. I'd be stupid to try.'

'Before David was murdered he was sent photos of the silica mine and surrounding area. Do you know anything about that?'

Jay shook his head, but Meadows saw him glance away for a split second before looking him in the eye and answering. 'No.'

'Were you aware that David was trying to help you?'

'Help me? In what way? I told you I haven't been in contact with him.'

'He put in a good word for you to get the job with the garden project. He arranged with the council for you to get this flat and even provided the basics.'

Jay looked genuinely surprised. 'I was told the stuff was from a charity. Why would he do that?'

'That's what we want to find out. Did David write to you when you were in prison?' Meadows asked.

'No, no one did.'

'What about the internet?' Edris asked. 'You can find out a lot of information on social media. Do you have an email account?'

'No, what would be the point?'

'Information, job searches. Almost everyone has a social media presence.'

'Well, not me,' Jay said. He picked up his mobile from the coffee table. 'There is internet on here, but I don't use it. Check it if you want.' He held out the phone to Edris.

Meadows nodded and Edris took the phone.

'If you didn't send those photos to David then who do you think did?' Meadows asked.

'I don't know,' Jay said.

Meadows had the feeling that Jay wouldn't freely offer information. He guessed that he had learnt from experience the less said the better. It was going to be difficult to break down his guard. He was sure that Jay knew who sent the photos and why. First he would have to gain his trust.

'The photos that were sent to David referred to Ruth Williams' murder. As well as the photo of the mine there was a photo of the tunnel opposite the mine and one of the waterfall and pool. Captions had been written underneath. "Tell the truth" for the mine photo and "you witnessed what happened here" for the pool and waterfall. What do you think the sender meant by that?'

Jay shrugged his shoulders. 'Obviously David needed to tell the truth.'

'About what?' Meadows asked.

Jay didn't comment.

'Do you think David lied about what happened that day in the mine?'

'They all lied.'

'You must have been angry,' Meadows said.

'I was at the time, but I had to let it go. I wouldn't have survived otherwise. I served time with some of society's worst and damaged individuals. There was one guy who killed the man who molested his child. Was it right? None of us knows what we would do if pushed to our limits. I didn't want to carry all that anger. The injustice weighed me down for so long and nearly drove me insane. I spent a lot of time talking to the prison chaplain. He talked a lot about forgiveness, not for the benefit of those who had lied, but for my own self-preservation. He was right. We were all kids at the time. All of us were scared of getting in trouble.'

'In trouble for what?'

'Doing things we shouldn't have been doing.'

'Like taking drugs?' Meadows said.

Another shrug. 'Just stuff kids do at that age, drinking and smoking.'

'So you don't blame the others at all for giving evidence against you?'

'I don't blame them for what they did at the time but now, well they should know better. They've had more than enough time to put things right, but they are probably as scared as they were back then. One of them killed Ruth and as long as I was in prison they were safe. No one was going to knock on their door.'

'Do you think that David killed Ruth?'

'I don't know, it could be any one of them. For all I know they were all in on it. Covering for each other.'

'Why don't you tell us what happened?' Meadows said.

'What's the point? No one listened back then and it's too late now.'

'Too late for what?'

'For me. I can never get my life back. I was convicted for Ruth's murder, and I will never be anything but an ex-con. Living under restrictions waiting for a knock on the door the next time something happens, and I fit the bill.'

'There was evidence against you,' Edris said as he handed back the phone. 'Ruth's blood was found on your clothes.'

'Which I explained at the time.'

'And blood on your trainers as well as other evidence.'

'So you come to the same conclusion as they did back then. Now you think I killed David because he helped convict me.'

'Did you?' Edris asked.

'No, but then I doubt you will take my word for it.'

'Where were you on the morning of the 8th of March between seven and nine?'

'Work. I catch the bus at seven-thirty as I like to get in early. I usually stop off at the shop to get a paper and a bar of chocolate then I have a cuppa before I start. You can check.'

Meadows didn't want to tell him that they had already checked.

'Do you catch the same bus every morning?' Edris asked.

'Yes, well on a few occasions I caught an earlier bus.'

'Why was that?'

'I wanted to see my parents. I shouldn't have bothered. They're like the rest of the world. They think I'm a murderer so don't want anything to do with me.'

Meadows wondered if Jay had managed to convince himself over the years that he was innocent. He was very convincing. The only alternative was that he was telling the truth.

'Jay, if you say you didn't kill Ruth despite the evidence then you must have some idea who did,' Meadows said.

'I don't know and I'm not going to point the finger. I know what that feels like.'

'You said they all lied, so tell us, what did they lie about?' Meadows asked.

'Does it matter now? It was five against one and no one believed me then so why should it make a difference now? Are you going to look at the case and find Ruth's real killer?'

'We are trying to find out who killed David. It looks like whatever happened back then is the reason David was murdered. If you didn't kill him then it's in your own interests to help us find out who did. Like I said before, I'm only interested in the truth and finding David's killer so I can give his family some answers. Tell me what happened that day. You've already served your time so what harm can it do?'

Jay looked down and rubbed his hands over his jeans. He seemed to be weighing up his options. It was clear that Jay didn't trust them, but Meadows was hoping that Jay would take this opportunity to tell his version of the events that day.

'I didn't go up to Dinas Rock alone that day. It had been arranged that we all meet there. I lied in my original statement. I said that I met up with the girls accidentally. Callum and David asked me to go as they wanted me to bring some weed. That was probably the only reason.'

'You expected the girls to be there?' Meadows asked.

'Yeah, that was always the plan. They wanted to celebrate Naomi's birthday. David said he wanted to make it special. Naomi's parents were religious and strict.'

'Did you know she was bringing Ruth with her?'

'No, it was only supposed to be Naomi and Amber.'

'Did you take cannabis with you?' Edris asked.

'Yeah, but nothing else. I swear I didn't take GHB. I wouldn't have had the money for a start.'

'OK, so you cycled up with the boys,' Meadows said.

'No, I arrived later than the others. I had to find my brother to... I had to see Mason first.'

'To get the weed?' Meadows asked. 'We're not bothered about where you got a bit of weed from sixteen years ago.'

'OK, yeah. I got it from Mason.'

'So you arrived later than the others. What were they doing when you got there?'

'They were all sitting around by the river. I jumped straight in as I was so hot. Then I joined them. David gave me something to eat and drink. I hadn't brought anything with me. We had a couple of shots. Callum had a bottle of vodka. We hung out there for a while then we went into the mine to explore. I can't remember whose idea it was. David and Callum had torches. We went inside and walked down one of the tunnels. The girls went back to the entrance. The rest of us walked to the water in the flooded tunnel, then went back to the girls and all shared a joint.'

'All of you?'

'Yeah, well except Ruth. She wasn't too happy about it. I think I put too much in, it was more of a blunt. We were all stoned. We messed around for a bit but it wasn't like we were out of control. I took a dare to go further into the mine alone. When I got back to the entrance only the boys were still in the mine, the girls had gone out. We joined them at the river. There was a large concrete slab that they were sitting on dangling their feet over the edge. We all had something to eat and drink, I had to share with the others. I think they pooled all the food. After that, things got a little crazy.'

'In what way?'

'I started to feel really good at first, that feeling when everything is wonderful and exciting. I thought a lot about it over the years. I think maybe my drink was spiked or it could have been in the food.'

'Who do you think spiked your drink?' Meadows asked.

'I honestly don't know.'

'What happened after?'

'It's a little hazy but at some point Ruth stood up and stripped down to her underwear. Maybe her drink was spiked as well. She was acting strange so whatever it was she had too much. Everyone was laughing and clapping. She slid down the bank and jumped into the water. She swam to the other side and tried to climb the rocks but kept slipping. She fell and went back into the water. She kept going under and no one was taking any notice, they just kept laughing. To be honest, I think they were all high. I don't know whether it was because I hadn't drunk as much alcohol as the others, or maybe just something in my head clicked. I knew she was in trouble. I went in after her. I tried to get her out, but she kept slipping back in. It was like she didn't have the energy or couldn't be bothered. She was sort of floppy. Eventually I got her out of the water and persuaded her to climb on my back. She had cut her leg and that's how the blood got onto my shorts.'

'Did you have your trainers on when you went to get Ruth out of the water?' Edris asked.

'No, I don't think so. I took them off. I remember the stones and rocks digging into my feet, why?'

'So how did the blood get on the bottom of your trainers?' Edris asked.

Jay's shoulders hunched and he twisted his hands together. Meadows could tell from Jay's face that it must feel like it had sixteen years ago. The questions, the implication that he was guilty. In that moment he appeared younger than his years and vulnerable.

'What happened after?' Meadows asked.

Jay sighed. 'I'm sure you can get all your answers from the court transcript. The testimony of the others. The so-called expert witnesses.'

'We'd rather hear it from you,' Meadows said.

'Why don't you ask the others that were there that day, starting with Aiden? I think it's time they answered some questions.'

'OK,' Meadows said. 'Thank you for talking to us. I appreciate how difficult it must be for you to go over past events.'

'It's fine. I've gone over it so many times in my head over the last sixteen years, looking for answers. I hope you find David's killer and maybe this time get it right.'

As soon as the door shut on Jay's flat they heard the strumming of the guitar.

'Do you think he is telling the truth about the blood on his shorts?' Edris asked.

'I think there is a lot that he isn't telling us, but past experience has taught him to be guarded. He has no reason to lie to us now. I also think they all could have taken GHB and that's why they gave a sketchy version of events and had no idea of the time.'

'That's if Jay is to be believed. In his own words he said he lied in his original statement about meeting the girls so he could be lying now. He could be making up the fact he felt like he was drugged. He needed an excuse for getting blood on his clothes. So he makes up the story that Ruth is also drugged and falls when she is in the water. Even if it was true, it doesn't mean he didn't kill her later or that he didn't kill David. He has motive.'

'But no opportunity,' Meadows said. 'I want to talk to DI Finch and see if he got the impression the others were lying about the events of that day. If they all smoked weed there will be some evidence and it will give credit to Jay's version of events. Let's go back to the office, check the evidence log and see how the others have got on. I want to know if there is someone helping Jay.'

'If it turns out that Jay is telling the truth about smoking weed with the others then what else did they all lie about? And why did he want us to talk to Aiden first?'

'That's what we need to find out, but we have a bigger problem,' Meadow said. 'If Jay is telling the truth and he didn't kill Ruth, then who did? That would mean there has been a miscarriage of justice and a killer has been free all this time.'

Chapter Sixteen

Aiden was sitting in his car looking in his rear-view mirror at the pavement behind. He was waiting for Amber to get back from picking up her children from school. He wanted to catch her by surprise and get a chance to talk to her before her husband got home. He could have phoned her, but he didn't want a record that the police could check.

It had been easy to find her as she hadn't moved far from her childhood home and Callum had given him all the details he needed. He glanced at the clock on the dashboard. She should be walking down the road at any moment, he thought, unless she'd stopped off for a coffee with one of the other mothers.

He thought back to the conversation he had had with Callum. He was reassured to find that Callum was as worried as he was, and wanted to stick to the original story. He hadn't asked Aiden any questions as to why he wanted to meet or about the concerns he had. Aiden figured that Callum had as much to lose as he did if the truth came out.

Amber appeared in his vision holding a child's hand in each of her own. She wasn't difficult to spot. Same flame hair and voluptuous figure. He stepped out of the car and stood on the pavement outside her house.

'Hello, Amber,' he said.

She stopped and he saw a look of confusion on her face.

He smiled. 'It's Aiden.'

'Oh hello, I didn't recognise you for a moment. I haven't seen you since we left school. You haven't changed much.'

Aiden thought he saw a look of worry flit across her face. It was only fleeting so he couldn't be sure.

'It's been a long time,' he said. 'I went to university then got a job in Bristol. I'm back living and working in Swansea for the past eight years.'

There was an awkward silence and the children fidgeted next to her.

'I should go,' Amber said. 'These two will be wanting their dinner.' She looked down at the two little girls. 'Was there something you wanted? I guess it's no coincidence that you are standing outside my house.'

'No, it isn't.' Now he was face to face with her he didn't know how to begin. 'The police came to see me about David.'

'Really. Did you two stay in contact?'

'No, but he came to see me before he died. I don't really want to talk about this here. Can I come in for a minute? It won't take long.'

Amber looked hesitant. 'I was sorry to hear about David and where it happened brought back memories. The thing is I haven't had anything to do with him or any of the others for years. If you're planning some sort of send-off I don't think it's appropriate for me to be involved.'

Aiden knew she was lying. David had been in contact with all the others. He would have spoken to Amber.

'I know David came to see you, he told me. We need to talk about what happened,' Aiden said.

'Mum.' One of the girls pulled on Amber's arm. 'Can we go in?'

'Yes, darling.' Amber moved past Aiden. 'There's nothing to talk about.' She took a set of keys out of her pocket.

'Please,' Aiden said as she opened the door. 'I'm really worried.'

'Fine.' Amber turned to face him as the girls ran inside. 'Five minutes. Right, you two…' she called after the girls, 'go and play upstairs. I'll call you when dinner is ready.'

Aiden followed Amber into the sitting room and took a seat. It wasn't going to be easy as he had no idea what she had seen that day. 'Nice home you have,' he said looking around. The room was messy with an ironing board left out next to a stack of washing. There were toys piled up in a corner and an empty mug on the coffee table.

'Cut the crap, Aiden.' Amber plonked down on the sofa. 'What did the police ask you?'

'They wanted to know what David said when he came to see me. I made up some stuff. I told them he wanted some advice about the split with his wife. What did David talk to you about?'

'The same thing as you want to talk about. That day.'

'And what did you tell him?'

'What is this? We were all there that day and we all lied.'

'That's because of you,' Aiden said.

Amber's eyes flashed with anger. 'Don't you dare blame me.'

'You're the one that went running to Callum to tell him the police had found Ruth's body. You're the one who suggested Jay only went into the mine to look for Ruth because he didn't want us to find her, and you're the one that insisted that we tell the police that it was a chance meeting.'

'That's because I wanted to protect Naomi. She had enough to deal with losing her sister, she didn't need to get

119

into any more trouble. It was down to you, Callum, and David. You're the ones who decided to tell the police that Jay just turned up. Why did you do that?'

'I don't know. It seemed like a good idea at the time. We didn't want the police to associate him with us after what he did.'

'Maybe he didn't do anything,' Amber said. 'David had it in his head that Jay was innocent. Why was that? Look, I don't see the point in dragging up the past. What's done is done. We can't change what happened. The police are not interested in all that. They will be looking for David's killer.'

'Have you even stopped to think that it may have been Jay that killed David, and if that's the case then none of us are safe.' Aiden saw the colour drain from Amber's face. 'The police asked me about Jay. They've already made the connection and it won't be long before they come to talk to you. We need to get our stories straight.'

'I think we need to tell them the truth,' Amber said.

'What truth is that? What do you think will happen to us?'

'Us? I've nothing to hide. We were all just kids at the time. What difference does telling the truth make now? Yes, it's going to be embarrassing and it's possible we will get into some sort of trouble for lying back then, but it's a better option than ending up like David.'

All right for her to say, Aiden thought. I'll lose my job, possibly my family and my freedom depending on what the others saw that day. 'If we admit to lying back then they will wonder what else we lied about. They're not going to believe a word we say. Look, it was sixteen years ago, we were off our faces, why change our story now? Just let the police do their job. If we confuse things now they will get distracted. They'll focus on the past instead of putting Jay back in prison where he belongs.'

'Are you sure that's where Jay belongs? Are you certain that he killed Ruth? David had his doubts. What did you see that day? Coming to think about it, where were you?'

Aiden felt his skin prickling. 'I could ask the same of you.'

'I was with Callum.'

'The whole time?'

Aiden saw the doubt in Amber's eyes. 'No,' she said, 'but he couldn't have.'

'Really? Any one of us could have. You were so sure that it was Jay back then.'

'There was evidence.'

'Yes, but we all saw him pull Ruth out of the pool and her leg was bleeding.'

'But it wasn't just that, was it?'

'No,' Aiden agreed. Amber was talking herself into believing in Jay's guilt. It's what Aiden wanted. He needed to confuse her so she doubted her own memory. All he had to do was plant the seed of doubt. 'What if Jay isn't guilty? You helped put him in prison. Have you thought about that? And what about Naomi?'

'What about her?' Amber asked.

'Have you spoken to her?'

'Not yet. She contacted me after David died.'

'What did she want?'

'Just to catch up.'

'Did she ask you about that day?'

'No, why would she and I'm not going to bring it up when we meet.'

'Good, no point in upsetting her.' Aiden stood. 'I would think carefully before you talk to the police if I were you.'

'You make that sound like a threat,' Amber said.

'Take it as you want, but David was going around asking questions and look what happened to him.'

'I think you should leave now.'

Aiden was satisfied he had made his point. All he had to do now was talk to Naomi. It was going to be difficult, but he was sure there were things she wouldn't want known about that day. The thing that troubled him most was not knowing how much David had told Naomi before he died. When David had visited him he had been persuaded to tell more than he wanted. Even then he had given an edited version of the truth. It had been enough to make David look concerned. Enough to make David ask more questions. Aiden looked back at Amber's house. What if David had relayed these concerns to Amber? What if this time they turned on him?

Chapter Seventeen

Meadows stood with the rest of the team looking at the incident board. Paskin had put up a map and pinned copies of the photos sent to David.

'We know what happened in the mine, then there's the incident in the pool where Ruth cut her leg, that leaves the tunnel. What happened here?' Meadows tapped the photo.

'It's only Jay's version of what happened at the pool,' Blackwell said.

'Then why send the photos to David? That's assuming that it was Jay. It's clear that he wanted David to admit to seeing him pull Ruth from the water with a cut leg. The thing that would explain the blood on his clothes.'

'I thought you wanted evidence that Jay sent the photos before we go down the road of tearing apart the original investigation,' Blackwell said.

'Yes, I do. I don't think he sent them himself, but I got the feeling that he knows who did. How did you get on in the prison?'

'Yeah, from what I can gather he was well liked by inmates and prison guards. He made friends easily. He shared a cell with a number of offenders over the years. Some of them are out now. Valentine?'

Valentine flipped open her notebook and reeled off a list of names.

'Better get them all checked out,' Meadows said. 'What about Mason Parks?'

'He didn't have a lot to say to us. He has an alibi for the morning David Harris was murdered. He was in work at seven. Clocked in. Rest of his answers were one syllable,' Blackwell said.

'Shouldn't we be warning the others that testified against Jay?' Valentine asked. 'If David was killed because he was a witness, it's possible that if Jay has a mate helping then one of them could be the next target.'

Meadows looked at the faces of the witnesses pinned to the board. 'No, if we do that it will look like Jay is a suspect in David Harris' murder. Questions will be asked as to why he hasn't been arrested. We have no solid evidence that links Jay to the murder of David. We do need to speak to all of them again. I want to know why they lied about meeting up that day.'

'If Jay is to be believed,' Edris said.

'I'm more inclined to believe him. It makes more sense than they all met by coincidence. Paskin, did you find an address for Amber Thomas?'

'Yes, she's Amber Richards now.'

'Good, she's the only one that David didn't contact, as far as we know. She may be able to tell us something about that day. I also want to know why Naomi was sent away after her sister's murder. Blackwell, Valentine, can you go and see Ruth Williams' parents. You'll need to tread carefully. Find out what Naomi's behaviour was like leading up to and after her sister's death.'

'Don't you think we should be concentrating on finding David Harris' killer instead of digging up all this?' Blackwell swept his hands towards the pile of files. 'If we start asking too many questions it's going to make people question the original investigation. Just because Jay Parks claims he is innocent doesn't justify looking at the case. There is no new evidence to contradict the conviction.'

Blackwell has a point, Meadows thought. He had no intention of throwing doubt on Dylan Finch's conduct during the Ruth Williams investigation. But there was a possibility that Finch's team didn't have all the information at the time. He rubbed his hand over his chin as the team looked at him.

'David Harris' murder does bring up questions. Why now and why the photos? How many convicted murderers do you know of who have been released from prison then go after the witnesses?'

'Mafia?' Edris said.

Blackwell sniggered.

'Yes, but we are not talking about a gang-related killing,' Meadows said. 'These were a group of teenagers that went out for the day. Not one of them witnessed the actual murder. I think David was killed because he knew something.'

'If that was the case then surely he would have been silenced long ago. Why now?' Valentine asked.

'Because of the photos,' Edris said.

'Then we are back to Jay Parks,' Blackwell said. 'Let's say for argument's sake that Jay is innocent. The killer has been free for sixteen years. Why would they send the photos now and stir things up?'

'That's a good point,' Meadows said. 'OK, what if Jay somehow organised the photos to be sent and it stirred up the past. David starts to ask questions and the killer gets jumpy.'

'Then why send them to David? It implies that David was the killer,' Blackwell said.

'Jay Parks may be guilty but just wanted to clear his name so he can be free of life license. So he sends the photos, and... no, it doesn't make sense,' Valentine said.

'Exactly,' Meadows said.

'Unless he is a clever little bastard and he sent the photos to throw us,' Blackwell said.

'Right, I want background checks on all the witnesses,' Meadows said. 'Get clearance to monitor their phones. Also check social media. I want to know if they are in contact with each other. Paskin, anything from forensics from the crime scene or the car?'

'Not yet, I'll chase it up and see what they've got so far.'

'It's late. You should all get off home and we'll look at this with fresh eyes in the morning.'

As the team were packing up for the night, Chris from tech ambled in.

'All right.' Chris looked at Meadows. 'I've tracked down that IP address for you. This one wasn't the brightest spark. Didn't make much of an effort to cover their tracks. Device is registered to an address in Ystrad. Mr and Mrs Mason Parks.'

'Lying little fuck,' Blackwell said.

Chris glanced across at Blackwell. 'I leave you to it.'

'There you go, his brother is in on it,' Blackwell said.

'OK,' Meadows said. 'I want Mason Parks brought in first thing in the morning. Pick him up at work and check to see if his alibi holds up.'

'Yeah, no problem,' Blackwell said and took his jacket off the back of his chair. 'See you in the morning.'

Meadows was the last to leave. He picked up a bunch of files from the Ruth Williams case and carried them out of the office. It was dark and rain started to pick as he drove his way up the valley. Most of the villages he drove through were quiet, the cold wet evening having driven the occupants indoors. By the time he reached his home village the rain was coming down heavily. He took the turning off the main road and plunged into darkness as he pulled the car into the farm track. His cottage was halfway down. It had been his family home after they had left the commune and he had taken it over when his mother moved to a flat.

He parked the car and hurried into the house. The heating was timed so it was warm inside and once he put the lights on it felt homely. After changing into lounge pants and a jumper he made himself a cup of camomile tea and settled in the armchair to read through the files. He was certain now that David's death was a result of something that happened that day. He just had to find out what David knew or had found out.

Callum and David had remained friends over the years but not Aiden. That's not unusual, he thought. School friends lose contact, but the fact that Jay had suggested that Aiden knew more made him think that there was another reason why David had distanced himself from Aiden.

Meadows tried to look at the points that were consistent with Jay's version of events. They all cycled together, and Jay arrived later. Amber stayed with Naomi during the search and the boys cycled home.

It was Callum that told David about the discovery of Ruth's body according to David's mother. That meant that Amber would have called Callum or Aiden to let them know. Other than Naomi, Amber would have been the only one to have that information at that time. Callum could have phoned David to let him know. Why cycle to David's house, then stay? Was it because they needed to concoct a story?

Meadows sighed, put the files down and stood to retrieve a small wooden box he kept on a shelf behind his books. He rolled a joint and peered out of the window. It was still raining, and he didn't feel like standing outside to smoke. No one was going to call around, so he grabbed an ashtray, sat back in the chair, and lit up. He inhaled deeply and closed his eyes as he tried to imagine the teenagers sitting by the river. It had been a hot day. They would have been in high spirits, no school, no one watching them.

They were caught in that time between childhood and adulthood. Wanting to feel free of any constraints but not yet mature enough to take responsibilities. They had all shared a joint, strong by the sound of it. That would have mellowed them out, he thought as he took another drag. Cannabis alone hadn't made one of them violent, but a mix of alcohol, GHB, and maybe even something else could have had an adverse effect. They certainly would have been high, their sense of reality blurred.

His phone pinged, pulling him from his thoughts and alerting him to a message. He picked it up and looked at the screen. It was a text from Daisy saying she had finished work earlier than expected and was on her way.

'Oh, hell.' Meadows stubbed out the joint and went around the cottage throwing open the windows. He found an incense stick in a drawer and lit it. He emptied the ashtray and dashed upstairs for a shower. He was just putting on fresh clothes when he heard the door open.

'Be down in a mo,' he called.

He checked his reflection in the mirror before heading down the stairs.

'It's bloody freezing in here,' Daisy said from the sitting room.

'Yeah, sorry, just wanted some fresh air,' he said as he joined her.

'Am I disturbing you?' She had a curious look on her face.

'No.' He pulled her against him. 'I'm glad of the distraction,' he said before kissing her. He saw the box he had left out on the table as he pulled away. He would need to move it, but he didn't want to draw Daisy's attention to his stash. 'Drink?'

'Please, I brought my own teabags.'

Meadows laughed. 'I guess herbal tea is an acquired taste.'

He filled the kettle then went round closing the windows. By the time the tea was made Daisy was sitting on the sofa with her legs tucked beneath her.

'Is that the David Harris case?' She said pointing at the files.

'Yes, well sort of.' He filled her in on the Ruth Williams case.

'It does sound like they are connected,' Daisy said. 'Do you think that Jay Parks could be innocent?'

'I don't know. All the evidence is there.'

'Want to talk me through it?'

'No, we agreed no work.'

'Yes, but I turned up unexpected. I don't mind, honestly. It might help you to sound off on someone other than the team. As I carried out the post-mortem on David Harris I'm involved. I don't think we'd be breaking any official rules by discussing the case.'

'No, I guess not. Here, look at this.' He handed her the file with Ruth Williams' post-mortem report. 'Tell me what you think.'

Daisy read through the report and looked at the pictures. 'Poor kid,' she said. 'She was alive when she was put in the water. What's troubling you about the report?'

'Jay Parks claimed that Ruth cut her leg on a rock earlier that day. There is a cut on her leg. Could it have been from a rock?'

'It's difficult to tell. She had a lot of marks on her body, particularly on her back. These would be consistent with a struggle on a rough surface. There are also these marks on her neck.' Daisy took a closer look. 'Looks like friction marks, something pulled, straps of a bag maybe.'

'I'll check the evidence log and statements to see if she had a shoulder bag. From what I remember they all had rucksacks apart from Jay. I'm sure the marks on her neck would have been looked at in detail. There was never a confession from Jay so what happened that day is pieced together from the evidence and the rest is unknown. I'm more interested in Jay's explanation for the blood on his clothes. Could he be telling the truth and that cut on her leg came from a rock?'

Daisy peered at the photograph and looked at the measurement. 'It's deeper than the other marks which are more like scratches. It's also ragged. I guess it could have been earlier that day and from a sharp-edged rock, but I couldn't say with certainty. The wound was clean which would tally with her being in the water when it happened. But her body was immersed in water for quite some time after she died. Any traces of dirt would have washed away if she had sustained that injury on the floor of the mine.'

'If it were only the blood found on Jay's shorts then it could be explained by him carrying Ruth earlier that day, but there was blood on his trainers as well as his shoeprints leading down to the water.' Meadows opened another file, took out photographs, and laid them across the coffee table. 'Skin and blood from Jay was also found here,' – he pointed to one of the photos – 'as well as Ruth's blood and other matter.'

Daisy leaned over the photo. 'That's nasty, what is it?'

'Piece of an old rail track. Rails used to run through the mine; the carts would travel in and out then get hooked up to a pully system. This bit still had a large bolt protruding. It's where Ruth sustained possibly a fatal injury.'

Daisy nodded. 'From the post-mortem report it appears that even if she hadn't drowned her chances of survival were slim. The bolt penetrated the back of her neck and damaged her cervical spine. It would have resulted in paralysis at best.'

'Would she have appeared dead to her attacker?'

'To the untrained eye, given the amount of blood, and added to the fact it was dark, I would say so. Why?'

'I wondered why she was moved to the water. Is it because the killer wanted to make sure she was dead? Or it wasn't their intention to kill her, and they wanted to conceal the body.'

'They could have been trying to wash away evidence. Anyway, that is for you, detective, to work out.' Daisy smiled. 'From what you've told me and from reading the files, it looks like they got it right when they convicted Jay Parks.'

'Which would work if David Harris hadn't been sent those photographs and murdered shortly after. Unless—'

'Enough for tonight.' Daisy closed the file and stood up. 'What you need is an early night.'

'I can't argue with that.' Meadows took her hand and led her upstairs.

Chapter Eighteen

Blackwell was waiting impatiently by the office door as Meadows took a quick gulp of tea and picked up a file from his desk.

'OK, let's see what Mason Parks has to say for himself,' Meadows said. 'I'll let you take the lead.'

Blackwell nodded and Meadows saw a hint of a smile on his lips as they walked downstairs and into the interview room. Mason was sitting behind the desk with his arms folded across his chest. Like his brother, he had jet-black hair and deep brown eyes, but he was heavier set. Meadows pulled back a chair and sat, placing the file on the desk.

'You understand why you have been brought in this morning?' Blackwell asked as he took a seat next to Meadows.

'Not really. I hope you are going to compensate me for loss of earnings. I'll get docked for the hours I've missed this morning.' Mason huffed. 'Am I under arrest or what?'

'For now you are helping us with our enquiries,' Blackwell said. 'Whether we arrest you or not will depend on how you cooperate and answer our questions.'

Meadows took the photographs of the mine, tunnel, and river from the file and placed them on the desk. 'What can you tell us about these photographs?' he asked sliding them towards Mason.

Mason shrugged his shoulders. 'If I were to take a guess I would say they are of the old silica mine at Dinas Rock. Went up there a few times as a kid. As you will be aware, I am also familiar with the place given what happened to my brother.'

'Happened to your brother? You mean the place where your brother murdered a thirteen-year-old girl?' Blackwell said.

Mason glared at Blackwell for a moment. 'Just because he was convicted it doesn't mean he was guilty. There are plenty of cases of innocent people being banged up.'

'Well, we're not here to talk about your brother,' Blackwell said. 'When was the last time you were at Dinas Rock?'

'Dunno, when I was a teenager, I think. Took a hike up that way with my parents to see the waterfall.'

'Are you sure you haven't been up more recently to take some photos?' Blackwell asked.

'Yes.'

'Take a look at the words under the photos. I think the meaning is clear, don't you? August 2005.'

'Yeah, it's when someone murdered Ruth Williams.'

'Why did you send the photos to David Harris?' Meadows asked.

'I didn't.'

'Stop wasting our time,' Blackwell snapped. 'They were sent from a device registered to your address. You have to do better than that to hide the origins of emails.'

'Fine, I sent the emails.' Mason sat back. 'It's not illegal to send photos.'

'Well, in this case they could be taken as threatening given that the recipient was murdered,' Blackwell said.

'I didn't kill him,' Mason said. 'I only wanted him to tell the truth.'

'You sent the photos for your brother,' Meadows said.

'Jay didn't ask me to send them. He doesn't know anything about it.'

'I find that hard to believe,' Blackwell said.

'Believe what you want,' Mason said. 'I took the photos and sent them.'

'Why David Harris?' Meadows asked. 'Did you think that he knew something about the murder?'

'I sent emails to them all.'

'All?' Meadows asked.

'Yeah, Amber, Callum, David, Naomi, and Aiden. Lying bastards have kept their mouths shut for long enough. Look, it was only meant to rattle them, get one of them to feel guilty and tell the truth. It certainly did that. Maybe you should be looking to them for answers.'

Interesting that not one of them mentioned receiving the photos. Why? Meadows thought.

'You sent this photo' – Meadows tapped the one of the silica mine – 'to the victim's sister. Why would you do that?'

'She was there that day like the others and lied.'

'OK, let's say you took these photos and sent them without your brother's knowledge. Why now? It's been sixteen years,' Blackwell said.

'Because I now believe my brother didn't kill Ruth Williams, which means one of the others did.'

'What made you change your mind about your brother's guilt?' Meadows asked.

'What do you mean?'

'We've looked at Jay's prison records. He had no visitors until two years ago. You waited thirteen years before you went to see him.'

'I was a mess back then,' Mason said. 'I was out of it most of the time, taking drugs and drinking. My life wasn't so easy. I was the brother of a convicted murderer, and I couldn't escape from that. At the time the police came to our house and pulled it apart looking for evidence. We were the talk of the village and beyond. My parents forbade me to see Jay, I was still living at home with them. They locked themselves away. We didn't even go to the trial. When Jay was convicted, we were staying with relatives in India. My mother cried constantly and my father, well, he was just angry. We came back and moved house. I just wanted to get away from them all. I was on the streets for a couple of years.

'When I finally got my act together I did some research. The papers said that Jay had drugged Ruth and that he had already had a caution for possession. They made him out to be a druggy. He wasn't. A few months before Ruth was murdered I took Jay out on a run with me. He didn't know what I was up to. I'd just started driving and it was a quick way to make cash. I was worried I was being watched so I parked the car a few streets away and I sent Jay to make the pick-up. I waited in the car. The police stopped Jay when he had the gear. They'd been watching the house. Jay took the rap for it. He didn't tell the police he was doing it for me. I let him take the blame as he was a minor and I thought he would get off lightly compared to me. He never said a word. Not even when my parents grounded him. That caution was used against him.'

'Why didn't you say anything at the time?' Blackwell asked.

'I wasn't going to admit to dealing and what good would it have done? Anyway, I felt guilty about that, and I started to think about the day Ruth Williams was murdered. Jay had come to find me that morning. I was hanging out at a mate's house. He wanted some weed. He said his mates wanted to try some and they were having a get-together, some sort of party for one of the girls. I gave him enough for a few joints. That's all he had, no other drugs. There is no way he had GHB, besides, he wouldn't have known where to get it. It wasn't like he went out clubbing. If he had wanted something stronger than weed he would have asked me. I owed him. Jay had been grounded with no pocket money because of the caution. He had only just been allowed out and he had to be in at seven each evening.'

'Did you see Jay later that day?' Meadows asked.

'Yeah, I went home for dinner. We were all sitting at the table. He was OK, said he had had a good day. He even mentioned that Ruth was missing. He said they were all a little pissed off as they had to look for her and she'd probably caught the bus home. There was nothing in his behaviour to suggest that something was wrong. If he had killed Ruth then I can't see that he would sit down for a family dinner talking and laughing just like any other day.'

'So you decided to go and see him,' Meadows said.

'Yeah, I requested a visiting order. I didn't think he would want to see me after I'd turned my back on him. He accepted the visit. He never once asked why I hadn't come to see him before. He was just so pleased to have a visit. I saw him as often as I could after that, and he told me everything about that day. I believe him. He's not a murderer.'

'Don't you think there would have been grounds for an appeal if your brother was innocent?' Blackwell asked. 'No one came forward with new evidence, no new witnesses.'

'That was the point of sending the photos. I thought one of them might have a conscience. Enough time has passed. They are all adults and things that they were ashamed of then wouldn't matter so much now. I thought one of them would help.'

'Did you try and contact any of them, other than send emails?' Blackwell asked.

'No, I didn't think they would speak to me.'

'What did you think would happen?' Blackwell asked.

Mason shrugged his shoulders. 'I just kept sending them.'

'I think you met up with David and took it a bit further,' Blackwell said.

'No, I told you already, I was in work the morning David was murdered.'

'Yes, and I checked, but just because you clocked in doesn't mean that you didn't sneak out. It's also possible you could have given your card to someone else to clock in for you.'

'I work on a production line. Any gap would be noticed. You can check.'

'I will be talking to all your work colleagues,' Blackwell said.

'I didn't kill David Harris and neither did Jay. What would be the point?'

Meadows had to admit that what Mason said made sense. If he or Jay had killed David out of revenge for his testimony then why bother to send the photos. Then again if Mason thought his brother was innocent and David was guilty of killing Ruth, that would give him motive. He might have got David to confess. David was troubled before he died. These thoughts went through Meadows' mind as Blackwell continued with the questioning.

'Can I go now?' Mason asked. 'I've answered all your questions, and it is not illegal to send emails.'

Meadows nodded at Blackwell.

'You're free to go for now,' Blackwell said. 'Don't leave the area as we may need to speak to you again. In the meantime, I would suggest that you refrain from contacting Ruth Williams' family and the witnesses involved in the case.'

Blackwell didn't look happy as they made their way back to the office.

'I don't think Mason is in the frame for killing David Harris,' Meadows said.

'I'm not sure,' Blackwell said. 'Just because he didn't stick the needle in doesn't mean he isn't involved.'

DCI Lester was waiting for Meadows when they walked through the door. He left Blackwell to fill the team in on the interview and followed Lester into his office and closed the door.

'I see you have all the files from the Ruth Williams case and understand that you have requested the physical evidence,' Lester said as he took a seat.

'Yes, we now believe David Harris' murder is connected to the case.'

'I see.' Lester sat back and folded his hands. 'You are going to need to tread carefully. Your actions imply that you think there has been a miscarriage of justice which would bring the original investigation under scrutiny.'

'I understand that. I will be speaking to retired DI Dylan Finch today. He led the investigation. As far as I can see all the evidence is there to back up the conviction against Jay Parks, but it may be the case that they didn't have all the facts at the time. I believe that the witnesses lied.'

'But if the evidence is there,' Lester said, 'I can't see how a lie told by one or more of the witnesses would have had any bearing on the outcome of the case. Unless you think that someone else was involved in Ruth Williams' murder and Jay Parks protected their part in it.'

'That's one possibility, although I don't believe that to be the case. Jay did explain the blood found on his clothes. Maybe there is an explanation for the other evidence against him. Given recent events I think it is worth revisiting the case. Mason Parks admits sending the photographs to all the witnesses. The fact that not one of them reported this implies that they have something to hide.'

'OK, but if you are to continue with this line of enquiry then it can't appear as if we are re-opening the case.'

'I'll be discreet. To be honest, it could go either way. I'm on the fence with Jay Parks but we have to make sure that he was responsible for killing Ruth Williams. If he didn't then a killer has been free for sixteen years and has killed again.'

Meadows could see that he had made his point by the look of concern on Lester's face.

'I'll let you get on,' Lester said. 'Keep me updated.'

As soon as Meadows stepped out of the office his phone rang on his desk. He picked it up, it was Oliver Wilson.

'I just wanted to let you know that we picked up Jay Parks this morning,' Oliver said.

'Why?'

'You questioned him in connection to a murder. I'm sorry, I had no choice.'

Meadows thought that Oliver really did sound sorry, but it didn't make the situation any better for Jay Parks. He also felt responsible for taking away Jay's freedom and possibly costing him his job.

'I had no option but to question him,' Meadows said. 'For what it's worth, I don't think he killed David Harris.'

'Unfortunately, given his past record we can't take a chance,' Oliver said. 'His license has been revoked and he will remain in custody until you charge someone with the David Harris murder.'

'Thanks for letting me know. I'll keep you updated.' Meadows put down the phone and joined the others at the incident board. 'OK, Paskin, what have you got for us?'

Paskin stood up and flipped open her notebook. 'Initial reports from forensics. They are still processing the crime scene, but this is what they have for us so far. David's car didn't yield anything of interest. The only prints found on the steering wheel were David's and his wife's, Tia. Lots of hair and fibre which you would expect from a family car. These are being tested against family members although Tia said that she used the car on several occasions. She gave friends lifts as well as being part of the school run, with various friends of the children. They are working on eliminating hair and fibres found on or near the driver's seat. The laptop found in his car was for work. There was no personal information.'

'Nothing useful there,' Blackwell said.

'Except that some fibres match those found on David. Well, those fibres found on his neck where he was injected.'

'Like I said, nothing useful. The killer wore gloves so until we find the killer we have nothing to match.'

'It will be useful evidence though,' Meadows said.

'We should get a warrant to search Mason's house and Jay's flat,' Blackwell suggested.

'On what grounds?' Meadows said. 'They both have alibis.'

Blackwell huffed. 'Yeah, until I'm certain that Mason didn't sneak out of work, my money is on the brothers.'

'We haven't yet established alibis for the witnesses,' Meadows said. 'Both Callum and Aiden claim they were in work, that needs to be verified. We'll talk to Amber and Naomi today and ask them to account for their whereabouts on the morning David was killed.'

Paskin cleared her throat to get the attention of the team. 'Do you want to hear the rest?' she said.

'Yes, sorry, go ahead,' Meadows said.

'Shoeprints taken from inside the tunnel. Given that the area is protected from the outside elements there were a large number of impressions. The majority of these could have been from any time before David was found. Prints from the Rogers, who found David's body, have been eliminated together with David's shoeprints. Impressions concentrated around the body are a boot size six.' Paskin pinned a photograph to the board. 'These prints lead both in and out of the tunnel as well as branching off in various directions within the tunnel. It's more likely that these came from a walker who explored the tunnel close to the time of David's death. These prints were also found underneath David's body. The second noticeable impression came from a size-ten boot. Again, this led both in and out of the tunnel and was concentrated near the body, but no prints were found underneath. The fibres on the body, notably near the wound are a wool mix, burgundy in colour. As mentioned earlier, matching fibres were found in the car. A thorough search of the area was conducted but there was no sign of the syringe.'

'So we're looking for a man with size-ten feet or a woman with a size-six or both. Wearing woollen gloves which wouldn't look odd at this time of year,' Blackwell said.

'Thank you, Paskin,' Meadows said. 'Blackwell and Valentine, I'd like you to continue looking into Mason and Jay's possible connection to David's murder. Look for any gaps in their alibis and look at everyone connected to the brothers. Edris and I will look closely at the four remaining witnesses in the Ruth Williams murder. I think we can all agree they lied to some degree at the time. Paskin, can you find any information you can on them? Also, put in a request for phone records. We'll start with Amber this morning and then talk to DCI Dylan Finch about the original investigation this afternoon.'

'Oh, yeah,' Paskin said. 'I almost forgot. Amber called the station and asked if she could meet with you after five. She had to go out this morning and she wants to take the kids to their grandmother before she talks to you.'

'It could be that whatever she is going to tell us she doesn't want her children to hear. That's fine. We'll call on Aiden instead. That leaves Callum. I'll leave him until after we've spoken to Amber. I want to move fast and find answers. If Jay is innocent I don't want him spending any more time in prison than he has to.'

Chapter Nineteen

Aiden was sitting behind his desk in his office staring at the wall opposite. He had just finished seeing his first client of the day and the meeting had been a disaster. Aiden's mind had been elsewhere. He just couldn't concentrate. The client had rattled on, and Aiden had just nodded as the words flowed over him.

He felt more troubled now than he had before he had seen Amber. He hadn't known that David had gone to see her and didn't know exactly what he had told her. He wished David had never come to his office that day. David knew there was more than Aiden was telling. Shame burnt at his skin. He'd told David the bit before and the bit after and glossed over the details of the in-between. It was easy to do as they were all stoned but could David have worked it out? He should have told the police that he had been a witness. It was stupid to have kept quiet. They would know by now and be wondering why he didn't say anything. It had just taken him by surprise. He hadn't expected them to make the connection that quickly.

Aiden's secretary knocked at the door and poked her head round.

'Detectives Meadows and Edris to see you,' she said.

The two men stepped into the room. Aiden felt a coldness creep over him. He hadn't expected them to come again so soon. Have they spoken to Amber? was his first thought.

'Oh.' Aiden stood. 'I wasn't expecting you and I have a client coming in shortly.'

'We won't take up much of your time,' Meadows said.

'You've got about ten minutes before your next appointment,' his secretary said and smiled. 'I can give them a cup of tea or coffee if you need longer.'

Aiden felt like slapping her. It wouldn't surprise him if she listened behind the door once it was closed. 'That would be great, thank you, Fiona.' He forced a smile. 'Please take a seat.' His legs felt weak, and he was grateful to sink back down into his chair.

Aiden looked at Meadows. He had thick dark wavy hair and bright green eyes. Although he had a friendly face his gaze made Aiden feel uncomfortable. He felt the slightest gesture would give him away. His eyes flicked to Edris who had taken out a notebook and pen.

'What can I do for you?' Aiden asked.

'When my sergeant came to talk to you, you didn't mention that you had been a witness in the Ruth Williams case. We just need to go over the statement you made back then,' Meadows said.

'Oh, right. Well, he didn't ask me. It did cross my mind after he had left but I didn't think it was important. He certainly didn't mention that it was connected to David's death.'

'We are looking at all aspects of David's life and during our enquiries the murder of Ruth Williams came up on more than one occasion. We now believe that the two cases are connected.'

'In what way?' Aiden asked.

Meadows ignored his question and nodded at Edris.

Edris flipped back the pages in his notebook, appeared to read, then looked up.

'A number of emails with photographs of the silica mine and reference to the date of Ruth Williams' murder were sent to witnesses. Did you receive any correspondence of this nature?'

If they have traced the ones sent to David, it's possible they know I've received some too, Aiden thought. Maybe this was their way of trying to catch him in a lie. 'Yes, there was something like that sent a while ago.'

'Why didn't you report it?' Meadows asked.

'I erm… I didn't think much of it, I thought it was some sort of prank. I knew of course that Jay was out of prison and perhaps he was upset that we had spoken against him.'

'Why didn't you mention it when you spoke to my sergeant?'

'I forgot.'

'Did David mention that he had received the same email when he came to see you?' Meadows asked.

'No.'

Edris flicked another couple of pages. 'You gave a statement to the police following Ruth Williams' murder, can you just take us through the events of that day?'

'It was quite some time ago so obviously I can't repeat word for word what I said back then.' Aiden could feel his mouth getting dry. 'I went up to Dinas Rock with David and another friend, Callum Edwards. We went for a walk and met up with Amber, Naomi, and Ruth by the river. We stopped to talk to them for a while then went on our way. When we came back later there was only Amber and Naomi. They said that Ruth was missing so we helped them look for her. It was getting late so we left the girls and cycled home.'

'With Callum and Aiden?' Edris said.

'Yes, and Jay Parks.'

'Pretty much what you said back then,' Edris said.

'When did you meet up with Jay?' Meadows asked.

'Erm, it was later.'

'Later, when? After you first met the girls? Or after you went off for a walk?'

'I think he turned up when we were talking to the girls, then we saw him again later and he joined in the search for Ruth.'

'Did you go into the old silica mine?' Meadows asked.

'Yes, we went in exploring. Callum and David had torches but that was before, I mean before Ruth went missing.'

'Did Jay go in with you?'

'I don't recall Jay being with us.'

'Did you and the boys smoke a joint when you were in the mine?'

Aiden could still remember pulling the smoke into his lungs and coughing. He didn't like it much, he only joined in because the others were smoking.

'No, well, I didn't, I think David and Callum had a smoke.'

'So which one of them brought the cannabis?' Meadows asked.

Fuck. 'Erm... I don't know.' Aiden picked up his cup and took a sip of the cold coffee. He couldn't say it was Jay that brought the weed, he'd just said Jay wasn't with them in the mine. 'It could have been either of them.'

'And you say it was just you, David, and Callum in the mine?'

'As far as I remember.'

'So the girls didn't go in with you?'

Aiden could feel the panic twisting his stomach. What if Amber told them we all went in? he thought. 'No, they were paddling in the river. They may have gone in on their own at some time during the day.'

'I see,' Meadows said. 'The thing is we have had a different account of that day.'

'From who?'

'According to a witness you all went into the mine together.'

'Maybe your witness was mistaken. It was a long time ago.'

Meadows looked at Edris who again flipped his notebook.

'You claim you saw Jay Parks go into the mine,' Edris said.

'Yes, that's correct.'

'Was that before or after Ruth went missing?'

'After, he offered to go in and look for her.'

'Why do you think he did that?' Edris asked.

'What do you mean?'

'If Jay Parks had murdered Ruth why would he draw attention to the mine?'

'I really couldn't tell you. You would have to ask him. My best guess would be that he didn't want any of us going in and finding her.'

'Did you offer to go into the mine to help him look?' Edris asked.

'No, I went to the car park to see if she was there, from what I recall.'

'There was an incident earlier that day where Ruth went swimming. She got into trouble and Jay helped her out. Do you remember that?' Meadows asked.

An image of Ruth stripped down to her underwear flashed through Aiden's mind. He had clapped with the others as she slid down the bank to the water. 'No, I don't remember that.'

'Right, I think that's about all for now,' Meadows said. 'If there is anything else you remember about that day, even if it doesn't seem important, please let us know.' He stood up.

Edris closed his notebook and put it in his jacket pocket before standing.

'I'm sorry I couldn't be of more help,' Aiden said as he rose from the chair.

'Oh, you've been very helpful,' Meadows said with a smile.

Aiden wondered what the detective meant by that. Had he given himself away with his answers? It didn't matter now. He was glad they were leaving.

'Oh, one more thing,' Meadows said.

Aiden felt his stomach clench.

'On the morning of the 8th of March, you said you were in work. Can you confirm what time you arrived at the office?'

'I was here just before eight that morning.'

'We spoke to your secretary, and she said she had a dental appointment that morning and didn't get in until after nine. Is there anyone else who can confirm the time you arrived at the office?'

'No, I don't think so.'

'You didn't speak to anyone on the way in? Maybe stop off to get a coffee?'

The heat was rising in Aiden's body. He could feel his skin prickling and his collar felt too tight. He thought of Jay and how easily the evidence had built up against him. 'No, I may have a parking ticket, but I generally throw them away.'

'OK, if you do find one let us know. It would be useful to eliminate you from our enquiries. We'll let you get on.'

Aiden followed the detectives out of the office and was relieved to see his next client hadn't arrived. He waited until it was just him and his secretary in the room.

'Could you give me a few minutes? I have to make a few phone calls.'

'No problem,' his secretary said. 'By the way, this came for you this morning.' She held up a bottle of wine. 'Looks like it's from a grateful client.'

Aiden was tempted to grab the bottle, open it, and drink the lot. It will be the first thing I do when I get home tonight, he thought. He went back into his office and closed the door. He could feel himself unravelling. What had the others said? Clearly they had spoken about being on the bank of the river when Ruth jumped in. They had all thought it so funny at the time. The memory made Aiden's skin crawl. Ruth was just a child but so was he at the time. He told himself this to try and justify his actions. He was a teenager with all the raging hormones and girls on his mind. He had to endure talk of sex from the other boys. The sight of Ruth stripping that day had aroused him and he was so out of his head he wasn't bothered if the others noticed. Then Jay had gone in after her, acting like some sort of hero. Aiden couldn't understand now why he had been so jealous at the time. He had watched Ruth cling to Jay and wished it was him. He was the one who was supposed to be keeping her occupied, she should have been giving him attention. That was how he had felt. Did any of them see what happened after? Jay could have seen and that's why he sent the emails. He felt sick. If it came out, he didn't think he could bear the shame.

Chapter Twenty

Retired DCI Dylan Finch answered the door wearing a dirty pair of jeans and an old woollen jumper. 'You're just in time. I've just come in from the garden and about to make a cuppa.'

Meadows and Edris followed Dylan into the kitchen and watched as he grabbed two mugs from a cupboard and placed them next to his.

'I was always grateful for a cup of tea when I was working.' Dylan smiled. 'Can I get you anything to eat?'

'Tea is fine, thanks,' Meadows said.

'I wouldn't say no to a biscuit,' Edris said.

Dylan opened the cupboard again, took out a packet of biscuits and handed them to Edris. 'Help yourself. Go take a seat in the sitting room and I'll bring in the tea.'

Meadows walked into the sitting room which had large display cabinets filled with ornaments and family photographs. He guessed Dylan's wife to be out at work and imagined that he was grateful for the company. Not easy, he thought, to go from working a full time often stressful job into retirement.

Meadows took a seat and Dylan appeared with a tray of tea and placed it on the coffee table.

'Help yourself to sugar,' Dylan said as he picked up his mug and took a seat.

Edris grabbed a mug, took a sip and opened the biscuits.

'How are you finding retirement?' Meadows asked.

'OK now spring is on the way. Plenty in the garden to keep me occupied. The winter is not so good. It will be different when the missus retires. We hope to do some travelling. So what can I do for you, gentlemen?'

'We wanted to talk to you about the Ruth Williams case. I'm sure you've heard that we are investigating the murder of David Harris,' Meadows said.

'Yeah, I've followed the story in the news. Of course as soon as I heard the name it brought back memories of the case. It's one I'll never forget, and I remember all the kids involved at the time. Do you think that David's murder is connected to what happened to Ruth Williams?'

'Yes, although that is not public knowledge,' Meadows said with a smile.

'I understand,' Dylan said. 'It's strange being on the other side. My mind is always asking questions, looking for information. Old habits I guess.'

'What was your impression of David Harris back then?'

Dylan took a sip of his tea. 'Like any other teenage boy at that age, I suppose. He was upset by Ruth's murder, a little withdrawn. He didn't offer a lot of information. I guess it must have been quite a shock, added to that he had cycled back with Jay Parks completely oblivious to what Jay had done. That must have played on his mind. He was the oldest of three children. Stable family life. There was nothing to indicate that he knew what Jay had done before we found Ruth. It wasn't as though he pointed us in Jay's direction. He was reluctant to give testimony at the trial, but it was a big thing for a youngster and quite nerve-wracking.'

'What about the others that were there that day?'

'Pretty much the same. I remember Callum being a cocky little bugger. Maybe a little defensive. His family was wealthy, and his father sat in on the interviews and kept interrupting, you know the type. Aiden, like David, was quiet. He was a nervous boy, again he didn't offer any information, we had to coax him. Neither Callum, David, nor Aiden had been in any previous trouble. Good grades at school. No trouble within the families. All three boys told a similar story.'

'What about the girls?'

'The girls were very tearful, particularly Naomi as you would expect. I felt really sorry for her. She was sobbing uncontrollably through the interviews. I think she took a lot of blame upon herself. It was her little sister and she kept saying she never should have left her alone.'

'Did you get called out at the onset or after the body was discovered?' Meadows asked.

'Before. Uniform attended initially and search and rescue were on the scene, given Ruth's age and the fact that she had gone off without telling her sister. Added to that, her phone was either switched off or out of range. It was later found in her pocket. Her rucksack had been left by the river. There were concerns for her safety. I was called out as a precaution. There were a lot of people around the area walking the Four Waterfalls trail, so we had to cover every possibility. We thought that she had most likely wandered off and had had some accident or got lost. She had been missing a number of hours by the time I got there. I never expected the outcome.'

'The timeline given by the other kids was pretty sketchy according to their statements,' Edris said as he pulled another biscuit from the packet.

'Yes, we had a rough idea of when they all arrived, and the time Naomi called her parents, but no fixed time for when the girls left Ruth by the river and what time they returned.'

'Didn't you find that odd?' Edris asked.

'Not really. They all had phones so could check the time, but I guessed they had been out enjoying themselves and not paying attention to how much time had passed.'

'Were Ruth's parents there during the search?' Meadows asked.

'Yes, Naomi had called her mother to tell her she couldn't find Ruth. The girls were supposed to be home at six. Mrs Williams called her husband and they drove up. They called the police not long after they arrived.'

'What did you make of the parents?' Meadows asked.

'They were polite. Anxious about their daughter but, well, through the whole investigation... it's difficult to explain. I suppose people deal with grief differently. They were very religious, and I guess they found strength in that. I never got close to them. They never let me in, I suppose you would describe them as guarded. When it went to trial Naomi had already been sent away to live with her aunt.'

'Didn't you find that a bit strange? You'd think they would want to keep her close,' Meadows said.

Dylan shrugged. 'Maybe the parents needed time alone to grieve.'

'Maybe they blamed Naomi for not looking after her sister and couldn't stand having her around,' Edris suggested.

'Like I said they weren't easy people to get to know.'

'Did you get the impression that all was not well at home between the parents and the girls?'

'Naomi was in a state when I first arrived, that was before we found Ruth's body. She was crying and her parents made no attempt to comfort her. Amber was still there at that point, and they stayed together. The parents didn't speak to Amber at all. If anything, they appeared angry with both girls.'

'Did they all stay the whole time?'

'Yes, apart from Amber. Her brother came to pick her up. After that Naomi stood alone when we waited for news. Search and rescue were scouring the area. Naomi and her parents were in the car park as it was getting dark. We didn't want the risk of them getting lost while searching. Naomi told us they had searched the mine and tunnel before she called her parents. It seemed unlikely that Ruth would have gone in alone without a torch. To be thorough, and as a last resort, search and rescue went inside the mine after they had exhausted the area. One of the team noticed the blood. If they hadn't we probably wouldn't have found her that night. They followed the trail to the water and then divers were sent in to retrieve the body.'

'Your worst nightmare,' Edris commented. 'Dead teenager and the parents on the scene.'

'Yes, I can't forget that feeling in the pit of your stomach when you have to deliver the news.'

Meadows knew that feeling too well. 'I imagine it must have been quite difficult to handle the parents and Naomi.'

'Yeah, they wanted to go and see her and pray. It took a lot of persuasion to get them to go home. Naomi fainted, poor girl. It was one of my officers that dealt with her. I guess the parents were in too much shock to look after her. We had already questioned Naomi when we arrived at the scene, so I thought it best to leave her until the next day. I got one of my officers to take the family home and stay with them. I later learnt that Naomi phoned Amber to tell her that we had found Ruth. By the time we interviewed the boys, they all knew.'

'What was your first impression of Jay Parks and his family?' Meadows asked.

'He certainly didn't act like someone who had just murdered a girl. He was polite and calm. He wasn't what I'd call comfortable in our presence, but nothing more than you would expect from a teenager being questioned by the police. There was some tension in the house. His father had been made redundant and the older brother, Mason, was a bit of a handful.'

'Jay gave the same story as the others at first,' Meadows said.

'Yes, that they had come across the girls when they were walking. The only difference being that he said that he had arranged to meet up with the boys, he just happened to arrive later than the others. He later changed his statement. He was terrified when we arrested him. His father initially sat in on the interviews as an appropriate adult, but we felt that Jay didn't want to say too much in front of him. We got in a social worker. He admitted to going into the mine alone, drinking, and smoking cannabis but not to taking GHB. It was too late to test him after we had arrested him as it would have been out of his system. He kept changing his story, adding bits. Well, you saw the evidence against him. He tried to explain some of it away but at that stage we couldn't believe a word he said, and his explanations weren't plausible.'

'Did you have any doubts at the time?'

'No, I think he was likely off his face when he killed Ruth. He was pretty convincing about his innocence but that's because I think he believed it himself, probably couldn't remember what he had done. He might have even blocked it from his mind.' Dylan took a swig of his tea. 'The case was watertight. The CPS were happy to prosecute on the evidence we had. Everything was done by the book.'

'I'm sure it was,' Meadows said. 'I've looked over the case notes and given the evidence and the witness statements at the time, I can't see how there would have been any other outcome. What changes things is David Harris' murder, and the possibility that there was some evidence withheld at the time. There are some aspects of the case that we can't discuss with you, but some information has come to light that firmly ties the motive for David's murder to the Ruth Williams case.'

Dylan looked relieved for a moment then his face creased with concern. 'Do you think I missed something?'

'No,' Meadows said. 'I think it's possible that you didn't have all the facts at the time.'

'But we had all the evidence against Jay Parks. I don't see how there could have been any other alternative.'

Meadows could see Dylan's unease, and if the roles were reversed he knew how he would feel. Having another detective pick holes in your investigation, throwing doubt in your own mind. He didn't want to cause that anxiety. 'It may be that we draw the same conclusions and it's not my intention to throw doubt on the original investigation. I can assure you that your conduct at the time will not be brought into question. You have nothing to worry about.'

'Thank you,' Dylan said. 'Although that won't stop me wondering.'

'I'm sure,' Meadows said. 'You believed that the motive for Ruth Williams' murder was sexual?'

'Yes, Ruth's shirt was torn and three of the buttons were missing. They were found at the bank of the river where her sister said she left her sunbathing. There were no signs that she was dragged into the mine. It's more likely that she ran in there to get away from Parks.'

'Did Jay Parks have a girlfriend at the time? Or was there any inappropriate behaviour with girls prior to the attack on Ruth?'

'No, not that we turned up. He had a good record at school. Good grades, he hadn't got into any fights. Other than the caution for drugs there was nothing in his past. Reports were that he got plenty attention from girls. He was a nice-looking boy. No one came forward with a complaint against him at the time.'

'What about the others?'

'Same thing. They were just a bunch of regular teenagers out for the day.'

'Did you get the impression that any of them were lying when you questioned them?' Meadows asked.

'I got the sense they weren't telling everything that happened that day. My guess was that they were up to something they shouldn't have been, and they didn't want to get into trouble. Drinking and smoking cannabis most likely. Parks' DNA was on the remnants of the joint we found but his wasn't the only one.'

'Which would confirm his story that they all shared a joint in the mine,' Edris said.

'Yes, my gut feeling was that one of them was responsible for Ruth's murder. They all gave the same story apart from Jay. None of them offered information freely. They kept it simple, and they didn't report seeing anyone hanging around. We collected the clothes they were all wearing that day along with their footwear. For elimination and in the hope that it would turn up something. We got lucky. Parks' clothes were the only ones that had bloodstains which were a match to Ruth. Both on his shorts and trainers. There was also the skin and blood matched to Jay found on the old railway sleeper where Ruth died.'

'Did Jay explain that?'

'What could he say? He had a scrape and bruise on his shin. He said he had fallen in the mine.'

'Could you be certain that the clothes taken from the others were the same clothes they were wearing that day?' Meadows asked.

'Yes, I had seen Naomi and Amber myself and we also had the photographs taken with Naomi's camera.'

'So you had no doubt that Jay acted alone?' Meadows asked.

'No.' Dylan shook his head. 'During the interviews and the trial he never once suggested that someone else was involved. I mean, he kept saying that someone else must have killed her, but he didn't indicate that he had help or someone witnessed the killing. If he had been in close proximity to her when she was murdered then that would go some way to explaining the blood on his trainers and shorts. That was never used as a defence. Do you think that he had help from one of the others and protected them?'

'I don't know,' Meadows said. 'I can't see that Jay would have protected someone all these years. We will have to look at all the evidence again and retest the clothing. What explanation did Jay give you for the blood on his clothes?'

'He said that Ruth had cut her leg when swimming and he carried her up the bank.'

'It's the same explanation that he gave us. Did you ask the others about that incident?'

'Yes, of course, but they all said it never happened.'

'What did he say about the blood on his trainers?'

'He had no explanation for that. He said he had gone into the mine to look for Ruth and he could have stepped in the blood. The thing is, if that was the case, he would have seen the blood. There was plenty of it where she died.'

Unless it was too dark, Meadows thought.

'We put the right one away, I'm sure of it,' Dylan said.

Meadows nodded. 'Thank you for talking to us.'

'I hope I've been of some help.'

Meadows stood. 'It's been good to get a first-hand account. Reading case notes only gives you the facts, not impressions or gut feelings. I'll let you know if there are any further developments.'

'I'd appreciate that,' Dylan said as he walked them to the door.

'Thanks for the tea and biscuits,' Edris said as they walked down the path. 'Well, we're none the wiser,' he said as he pulled open the car door.

Meadows pulled his seatbelt across his chest, put the key in the ignition and paused before twisting. 'Interesting, don't you think, that Naomi's parents sent her away. What if it was more than the fact she didn't look after her sister that day?'

'What, you think the parents thought that she had some hand in the murder?'

'It wouldn't be the first case of sibling murder. What if the girls didn't get on? What if Naomi snapped that day? We only have Naomi and Amber's word that they left Ruth sunbathing. Other than the torn clothing there was no evidence of sexual assault. It's too early to see Amber. I think we should pay Naomi another visit. See what she has to say about being sent away.'

Chapter Twenty-one

Naomi sat down on the park bench and pulled up her hood. She felt like the wind was penetrating her skin and wrapping itself around her bones. She hadn't felt warm since the detectives had called to see her. The memories of the past kept creeping up on her and bringing back feelings that she had tried to bury. Then Aiden had come to her house. She had hidden behind the curtains and waited until he had given up. Now she was afraid he would appear when she was out. He could be following me, she thought. She glanced around the park. A group of young mothers were heading towards the play area and there were a few people walking dogs. She tried to calm herself, told herself she was being paranoid. She knew what Aiden had told David, but she didn't trust him or Callum.

An elderly couple walked by and said hello. She returned their greeting. David will never get to be old, she thought. A sadness pressed down on her shoulders. She took out her mobile phone to check the time and tried to distract her wandering mind by playing a game. When she looked up again she saw Amber walking towards her. She hadn't changed much over the years. She wore a green parka coat with her long red hair flying behind her like ribbons. Naomi stood up and smiled and was pleased to see Amber smile back.

'Thank you for coming,' Naomi said.

'I was so happy to hear from you. It's really good to see you, chick.' Amber put her arms around Naomi and squeezed tight. 'It's been so long,' she said.

'You all right to sit here for a while?' Naomi asked. 'It's a bit cold.'

'It's fine,' Amber said and sat down next to Naomi. 'We have so much to catch up on. You go first, tell me about your husband and children.'

They talked about family, marriage, and work and the time moved swiftly. Amber didn't mention David, or the past, and Naomi was grateful for that. It meant she could lead the questions without being taken down a path she didn't want to go.'

'I was sorry to hear about David,' Naomi said. 'It's so sad for his wife and kids. It's unimaginable to think what they must be going through.' As soon as the words left her mouth Naomi realised how stupid they sounded. It wasn't unimaginable, she had been there, experienced the grief and trauma.

'Yeah,' Amber agreed. 'I thought about sending a sympathy card, but what do you say? I saw him not so long before he died.'

David hadn't mentioned that fact to Naomi and she didn't know why she felt a sudden pang of jealously. You're being ridiculous, she told herself. 'Yeah, he came to see me too.'

'That must have been difficult for you,' Amber said and gave Naomi's hand a squeeze.

'A little, it brought back a lot of memories I'd rather forget. There are things from back then I've never told anyone, not even my husband.'

'Nor me. I wanted to get in touch,' Amber said. 'At first I didn't know how and then the years seemed to fly by. Facebook made it easier to find people and I admit I did look you up.' She smiled. 'I guess I didn't want to be a reminder of what happened back then.'

'It never really went away,' Naomi said. 'I've just kept it below the surface. You were a good friend, and it wasn't my choice not to see you or keep in contact.'

'I realised that,' Amber said. 'It's just so nice to see you again.'

'Do you see anyone else from school?'

'No, well, I hadn't for years. Then David turned up, then not long after I'd heard about David, Aiden came to my house. He was waiting outside for me. He was acting strange. To be honest, he gave me the creeps.'

'He was always a little creepy,' Naomi said.

Amber laughed. 'Yeah, he was always hanging around. One time in school I caught him watching me and Callum kissing.'

'He probably fancied you.'

Amber pulled a face. 'Ew, I hope not. I don't think he ever had a girlfriend. He's married now. No kids from what I can see on his profile.'

'You didn't send him a friend request, did you?'

'Hell no.'

'What did he want?' Naomi asked.

'I don't know. The police had been to talk to him about David. Apparently David went to see him and was asking questions.'

'The police came to see me too.'

'I'm seeing them later,' Amber said. 'Did David tell you about the emails he got?'

'Yeah, I had the same thing.'

'Oh, that's just sick. What sort of person would send an email like that, to you of all people?'

'I take it you got them,' Naomi said.

'Yeah, I deleted them.'

'So that makes all of us,' Naomi said. 'It has to be Jay sending them, but I don't understand why.'

'He thinks we know something.'

'Like what? He was the one with Ruth's blood on his…' Naomi turned her head away and sucked in the air.

'I know,' Amber said, 'but we all lied about a lot of things that day.'

'But about nothing important. So what did Aiden say?'

'He wanted to know what I was going to tell the police. I told him I was going to tell them the truth and he should do the same.'

'Did he seem worried?' Naomi asked.

'Yeah, I guess so. What would Aiden have to be worried about?'

Naomi wanted to know the answer to that. 'I don't know. You don't think that Aiden had something to do with what happened?'

'Well, he wasn't with us,' Amber said. 'He was the one that said Ruth was alone with Jay.'

'David had his doubts about Jay being guilty. Do you suppose Aiden told him something? Maybe David remembered something about that day.'

'He would have gone to the police. Aiden hinted that Callum had opportunity.'

Naomi could feel her mouth getting dry. 'He was with you, wasn't he?'

'Not the whole time.'

The thought made Naomi shudder. She couldn't be certain where any of them were or what they had seen. She took a bottle of water from her bag and unscrewed the top.

'Are you OK?' Amber touched Naomi's arm.

'Yes, it's just thinking about the past always makes me feel a bit sick.' Naomi forced a smile. 'I'm OK, we need to talk about it. First the emails, then David, and now Aiden is creeping around. I don't feel safe.'

'Me neither. I'm not letting Aiden in my house again. Do you think I should tell the police about him?'

'I don't know. He hasn't done anything but talk to you. Perhaps I'm just being paranoid. Maybe Jay is just messing with our heads. Trying to get us to turn against each other.'

'Someone killed David,' Amber said.

'Yeah, and Jay got out of prison a year ago. As a member of the victim's family I had to be informed.'

'Did David speak to Jay?' Amber asked.

'If he did, he didn't tell me.'

'So, what did you tell the police?'

'Not a lot. Only what I had to. If I was you I'd do the same. The rest is embarrassing.'

'Yeah.' Amber laughed. 'I'm sure they've heard worse. Don't worry, I won't tell them about, well... you know.'

Naomi wasn't prepared for Amber to bring that up. She felt the knot in her stomach tighten. 'Thank you. David didn't know. I never told him so it's just between you and me.'

'And I'll keep it that way,' Amber said.

'I'm going to have to go, my shift will be starting soon. I'll give you a call when I'm free. You know, I have never been back to Dinas Rock. Have you?'

'No.'

'I was afraid to go, I guess I should. Maybe take up some flowers, try and lay the past to rest,' Naomi said.

'I can go with you if you like,' Amber said.

'Would you? That would be great.' Naomi stood. 'I'll call you.' She gave Amber a hug before heading back to her car.

On the drive to work Naomi played over the conversation in her mind. What Amber had told her made her nervous. It was bad enough that Jay was out of prison but at least he had to keep to the terms of his license and not approach her. Aiden was a different matter, he could be dangerous.

Naomi was glad to get into work, change into her uniform and start on the ward. The norovirus was still causing problems and she had to wear a plastic apron and latex gloves. It wasn't comfortable but she didn't mind. Her main concern were her patients. She felt so sorry for them. It was bad enough to be ill or recovering from an operation without getting this horrible sickness on top. All thoughts of the past were pushed to the back of her mind as she carried out observations and did what she could to make those under her care feel more comfortable. She was just dealing with a particularly poorly patient when another nurse beckoned her over.

'There are a couple of detectives here that want to speak to you,' the nurse said.

'Oh.' Naomi felt her stomach flip. She didn't want it brought here. This was her place of safety.

'I'll take over for you until you get back.'

Naomi could see the curiosity in the other woman's eyes, but she offered no explanation. 'I'll be back as soon as I can.'

Outside the ward Naomi peeled off her gloves and apron and scrubbed her hands. She took her time. Part of her was angry. What was so important they had to come to her work? They could have waited. She saw the two men as she approached the reception area. It was the same detectives that had called at her house.

'Sorry to disturb you at work,' Meadows said. 'We did try at your home first.'

'I don't have a lot of time,' Naomi said. 'We're busy here at the moment.'

'We won't keep you long,' Meadows said.

Naomi didn't want to talk to them but if she put them off, they would only come back later. She didn't want that on her mind as she worked.

'We can use the staff room. There shouldn't be anyone in there.' She turned and walked briskly down the corridor. Inside the room, she grabbed a mug, put in a tea bag, and placed it under the urn. She didn't offer tea to the two men as she didn't want them to stay long enough to drink it.

She took her time stirring the tea and once she felt composed, she turned to face them.

'What can I do for you?' Naomi took a seat and crossed her legs.

Meadows took a seat and placed his hand on his knees while Edris pulled out his notebook and sat down opposite.

'We've been talking to a number of witnesses who gave statements at the time that your sister died,' Meadows said.

'Murdered. Died sounds like she just dropped down dead.' Naomi was aware that she sounded rude. 'I'm sorry, it's a period in my life I don't like to talk about. It was a bit of a shock when you turned up at my house and started asking questions about Jay Parks.' She tried to force a smile.

'That's understandable,' Meadows said. 'I'm sorry we have to ask these questions. Would you mind if we went over the statement you made to the police that day?'

'Can I ask why? I thought you were investigating the murder of David Harris.'

'It's a line of enquiry we are following. I can't give you specific details, but I assure you it is necessary.'

Naomi nodded. 'OK, what do you want to know?'

Edris flicked through his notebook drawing Naomi's attention. Up until this point he had remained silently observing.

'Could you tell us what you remember about that day at Dinas Rock? We understand your sister Ruth wasn't meant to go with you that day.'

Naomi wondered where they had got that information. Probably from her parents. The thought made her feel nauseous. She dreaded to think what they would say about her.

'No, it was my mother who insisted that Ruth went out with Amber and me that day.'

'Did Ruth usually go out with you and your friends?' Meadows asked.

'No, that's because I rarely went out. My parents didn't approve. They thought anyone other than themselves was a bad influence on me. I guess they were right in the end. At that age you don't see the dangers. Now I have my own children I worry all the time.'

'Were you annoyed that you had to take Ruth with you that day?' Meadows asked.

Naomi remembered the resentment she had felt that day. It seemed so petty now. 'Not really. It wasn't like there was anything planned that taking Ruth would have spoiled. You know what it's like when you are a teenager. You just want your own space. I probably complained to my parents, but I didn't argue with Ruth. It wasn't her fault.'

'The three of you got a lift with Amber's brother,' Edris said.

'Yes, it would have been a long journey by bus, and it was hot that day. Ruth thought that Amber's brother was just driving past the bus stop and offered us a lift. It wasn't a problem.'

'Do you think Ruth would have told your parents about the car ride?' Edris asked.

'No, she would have been in as much trouble as me.' Naomi allowed herself a smile at the thought. Her parents thought Ruth was their little angel. Even more so after she died.

'Can you talk me through what happened when you got to Dinas Rock?' Edris asked.

'That's all in the statement I gave to the police at the time,' Naomi said.

'If you could just tell us what you remember,' Meadows said. 'It may be that you forgot something at the time. I imagine you would have been traumatised and not thinking clearly.'

Naomi wondered what Callum and Aiden had said. She was sure they would have stuck to the original story. 'When we arrived we took some photos and then went up to the river by the old silica mine. I'd told my parents I had a school project and needed to photograph the area. It was just an excuse to get out for the day. The boys turned up and said they were out walking. They stopped to talk then went on their way. We had a picnic then I went off with Amber to take some more photos. We left Ruth sunbathing by the river. When we got back, she wasn't there. The rest you know.'

'We had a different account from a witness that claims you arranged to meet up with the boys,' Edris said.

Naomi felt the heat creep up her face.

'I understand this is difficult,' Meadows said, 'but it would be better if you are honest with us. I appreciate that you may have not wanted to tell the police everything about that day at the time. You were all young. You won't be in trouble now for leaving out a few details.'

Naomi nodded. 'I don't suppose it matters now but yes, we did arrange to meet the boys. You have to understand how difficult it was for me back then. I didn't want my parents to find out. I was in enough trouble as I hadn't looked after Ruth. I was so afraid.'

'David was your boyfriend,' Meadows said.

'Yes, only for a brief time.'

'So, you arranged to meet David at Dinas Rock with the other boys,' Edris said.

'Yeah, although they did come later. That bit was true. It was only supposed to be David, Callum, and Aiden. I didn't know that Jay was going to turn up. He came later than the others.'

'Whose idea was it to meet by the silica mine?' Meadows asked.

'David's. He had been hiking up there with his family. They liked that sort of thing. He knew the area well and thought it would be quiet as it was off the main track.'

'Did you go into the mine?' Meadows asked.

Naomi took a guess that they already had the answer to that, but she had no idea how much the detectives knew.

Most of it was embarrassing and she cringed at the thought of telling the whole story to these two men.

'Yes, we all went in to explore the mine. I think I took a few photos.'

'Including Jay Parks?' Edris asked.

'Yes.' Naomi watched him scribble in his notebook.

'You all shared a joint,' Meadows said.

Naomi thought that he was probably saving her the embarrassment of bringing up the subject.

'Yes, I only had a few puffs.'

'How did Ruth react?'

'She wasn't happy about it. She went back outside, and I followed her.'

'What happened then?' Meadows asked.

'The boys joined us, and we all had something to eat. The boys went off for a walk and I went with Amber to take some more photos. Ruth was laying on the patch of grass by the mine.'

'Did Ruth jump into the water before you all went off?' Meadows asked.

'She might have gone swimming. I don't remember if she went in the river before or after we came out of the mine.' An image of Ruth stripping off surfaced in Naomi's memory. She could picture them all laughing and clapping. David's hand warm on her waist then moving up and slipping under her bra. Her body tingling with excitement.

'How did you feel after you had all eaten?' Meadows asked.

'What do you mean?'

'Well, you had all smoked cannabis, maybe had some alcohol. At that point, did you feel out of control? A little high, like you had taken something stronger?'

Naomi could feel the heat rising in her body and her stomach twisting. She was almost at her limit. She could only go so far with her memories before she needed to run. The panic would overcome her, and she didn't want anyone to witness that. It made her feel so weak and pathetic. 'Things were a little hazy. I suppose I felt good. Excited and carefree.' She had done things she wouldn't have usually done. The thought made her feel sick, then angry. She had thought the drink and cannabis made her act the way she did that day but what if it wasn't just that?

'Who brought the cannabis?' Meadows asked.

'Jay. Yes, definitely Jay.'

'What did you eat and drink after you came out of the mine?'

'I don't know. We all brought food with us. We pooled it all together. We had cakes and sandwiches. I think someone brought a bottle of cherryade. Do you think Jay drugged us all?'

'We think it's possible that you all took something at that stage. Maybe unknowingly. As for what was spiked and who spiked it we're not sure. As far as we are aware, Jay didn't bring any food or drink with him that day.'

Naomi remembered David handing Jay a drink when he arrived. 'No, I don't think he did. I thought it was just the weed making me feel odd. I had never smoked it before.'

'What was Ruth doing when you left for your walk?'

'Sunbathing or she could have been asleep.'

'Did you leave before the boys or after?' Meadows asked.

'We all sort of left together. Maybe not Jay and Aiden. They were sitting on the concrete slab that overhangs the river.'

'How long were you gone?'

Naomi shrugged. She really had no idea. 'Maybe an hour, I don't think much longer than that.'

'When you got back from your walk, were any of the boys around?'

'No.'

'Who came back first after you and Amber?'

'David and Callum, then Jay. Aiden was last.'

'Which direction did they come from?'

'I don't know. I wasn't really paying attention. I think Jay came across the bridge and Aiden down the path. Yes, he said he had walked the track that leads to Penderyn. He said he hadn't seen Ruth going that way.'

'Then you all split up to search?'

'Not straight away. We thought she had just gone off for a walk and would come back. When she didn't turn up we decided to search.'

'Did any of you search the tunnel?'

'Ruth didn't have a torch so we didn't think she'd have gone in there. I'm sure one of the boys looked anyway. I tried ringing her, I had to go back up top to get a signal. Her phone kept going straight to voicemail.' A coldness crept over Naomi. All the worry and fear from that day gnawed a hole in her stomach. She put her arms tight around her body.

'Are you OK?' Meadows asked.

His concern brought a tightness to her throat, and she felt tears sting her eyes. 'I'm sorry,' Naomi said. 'I don't like to think about that day. It may be sixteen years ago, but it feels like it happened yesterday.'

'I understand,' Meadows said. 'You are doing really well. Who suggested looking in the mine?'

'Jay.'

'Did anyone offer to go in with him?'

'No.'

'Did he have a torch?'

'I don't think so, unless Callum or David gave him theirs. Amber and me went up the opposite bank to look. Aiden and Callum went to the car park and David went to the old gunpowder works.'

'How long was Jay in the mine?'

'I don't know. We all met up again by the bridge. The boys went home, and Amber stayed with me. That's when I called my mother.'

'Did you have any contact with any of the group after your sister was discovered?' Meadows asked.

'No, Amber was with me at the time, and I saw her once, maybe twice after.'

'We understand that you went to live with your auntie.'

'Yes, not long after that.'

'Why was that?' Meadows asked.

'My parents thought it best. They didn't want me around for the trial.' She couldn't tell them the real reason.

'Did your parents blame you for what happened to Ruth?'

'No more than I blamed myself.'

'When David came to see you and you spoke to him on the phone it wasn't about a reunion, was it?'

Naomi didn't want to talk about David. Seeing him had brought up the feeling of first love and the pain that went after. She guessed the police would know about the emails by now. 'He wanted to talk about that day and what I remembered. He told me about the emails he'd received.'

'What did you tell him?'

'I told him to delete them.'

'Is that what you did with the ones sent to you?' Meadows asked.

'Yes.'

'Why didn't you report it?'

Naomi wished she had now. The police could have traced them and put a stop to it. They had been stupid, and David would still be alive if she had handled things differently. She should have persuaded him to leave things alone. 'I suppose I didn't want all the questions. I didn't want the past dragged up.'

'Did David give you any indication that he thought Jay may be innocent?'

'He thought the emails referred to the fact that we had lied about meeting up. He also thought that Jay might have seen something that day.'

'Like what?' Meadows asked.

'I don't know. I told David everything I remembered. There couldn't have been any other explanation for what happened to Ruth. Jay was the only one with Ruth's blood found on his clothes. David said he would need to speak to Aiden and the other two. He said Callum had got the same email. I don't know if Aiden got one. I think David was going to meet Aiden. I can't remember exactly what he said at the time. I was telling you the truth about that phone call. David had been drinking and he wasn't making a lot of sense.'

'OK,' Meadows said. 'I think that's about it for now unless you have anything to add.'

'I can't think of anything now but if I do, I'll let you know. Can I get back to work now?'

'Yes, we're sorry to have kept you.' Meadows stood. 'One more thing. Could you tell us where you were on the morning of Tuesday 8th March?'

Naomi didn't have to think about it. Her life was well ordered. 'I would have been here. Early shift that week so in at six.'

'Thank you.'

Naomi couldn't get out of the room quick enough. She could feel their eyes on her back as she walked down the corridor. She guessed they would stop at reception and check that she was in that Tuesday morning. That would set the tongues wagging. She just hoped that no one would have the balls to ask her outright what the police wanted. Outside the ward she took a moment to gather her thoughts. Please let that be an end to it, she thought as she pushed open the door.

Chapter Twenty-two

Meadows parked the car in front of Amber's house. A mid-terrace in Ystrad. In the passenger seat Edris stretched and yawned loudly.

'Tired, are you?' Meadows asked.

'Yeah, we haven't stopped all day. The same story over and over again and we don't seem to be getting anywhere.'

'It's the same story with variations. It's those inconsistencies I'm interested in. I still think Naomi is holding back on us. It will be interesting to hear Amber's version. Maybe she'll be the one to tell us what the others are hiding. The fact that she asked us to wait so she could be alone gives me some hope.'

'Well, let's get on with it then,' Edris said. 'I still have to study tonight.'

Meadows laughed. 'You poor thing. After we've spoken to Amber, I'll drop you off home.'

'Great, you can stop off at the chippy on the way. I'm bloody starving.'

'You're always hungry.'

The front door opened as soon as they stepped out of the car. Amber looked from one to the other and smiled.

'Thank you for waiting to see me,' she said. 'I thought it best not to have any distractions.'

'No problem,' Meadows said as he followed her inside and into an open-plan living room which was separated from the kitchen by a breakfast bar.

'Would you like a cup of tea or coffee?'

'No, we're good thanks,' Meadows said. 'Did the officer that called to arrange the visit explain why we needed to talk to you?'

'Yes,' Amber said as she tucked her hair behind her ears. 'About David Harris.'

'Yes, and also Ruth Williams. Have you had any recent contact with David?'

Amber shifted a pile of washing and sat on the chair. 'He came to see me before he, erm, died. He wanted to talk about that day with Ruth.'

She's the first one to give a straight answer, Meadows thought as he took a seat next to Edris on the sofa. 'What did he want to know?'

'He wanted to know what I remembered from that day and if I thought it was possible that Jay didn't kill Ruth. He'd had some emails that had upset him.'

'We've seen the emails that were sent to you all. The implication is that you all lied about that day.'

Amber fidgeted in her chair. 'Yes, I suppose we all did.'

'We've read your initial statement,' Edris said. 'We know you all arranged to meet up that day. What else did you lie about and why lie?'

Meadows saw the colour rise in Amber's cheek. It was clear that Edris wanted to move along with her version, and he was short of patience.

'I suppose we all wanted to protect Naomi. Things were difficult for her back then and she was my best friend. With my hair colour, and my parents in their wisdom choosing to call me Amber, you can imagine what school was like. It wasn't much better for Naomi. We all wore the same school uniform but there were differences that made her stand out. She didn't have the latest fashion coat or shoes. No make-up or jewellery. I guess we stuck together at school. After school and at weekends it wasn't easy to meet up. Naomi wasn't allowed out to mix with others. We would make up excuses for her to leave the house. One was a camera club.' Amber smiled. 'She would come over to my house and change. She always had a stash of clothes she kept hidden that her auntie bought for her. They were considered unsuitable by her parents. She said it was the only time she felt normal.

'That day she was in a state when we couldn't find Ruth. She thought Ruth may have got the bus home and told her parents about the boys. She was afraid of how much trouble she was going to get in but knew it would be far worse if she didn't call her parents. I remember the horror on her face when she made that call and her mother said that Ruth wasn't at home. I was standing next to her and could hear her mother shouting. After Ruth was found we all stuck to the story that we just happened to see the boys there. We didn't want to cause any more trouble for Naomi. We didn't lie about anything important.'

'You all claimed that Jay had arrived separately from the other boys, and you saw him go into the mine alone,' Edris said.

'He did arrive after the other boys. I didn't know he was coming, and I did see him go into the mine. Even if we said we had met up with the boys that day it wouldn't have made any difference. Jay was charged and convicted. I don't know why David thought he may be innocent.'

'Why don't you talk us through what you remember about that day,' Meadows suggested. 'We are not here to judge what you got up to as a teenager.'

'I guess it's more embarrassing than anything else,' Amber said. 'We took some photos when we arrived and then sat on the bridge drinking wine. I had a bottle hidden in my bag I'd nicked from my parents. Ruth didn't notice we were drinking. She was paddling in the river. It was hot and the wine made us a bit light-headed. We moved down to the river and messed around there for a while. Callum, Aiden, and David turned up. They made it look like they were out for a walk. They went off for a while then came back to sit on the grass. Jay turned up and jumped in the river. Then we all went into the mine to explore. Callum and David had torches, so we went down one of the tunnels. After, we sat just inside the mine and smoked some dope. Things got a little silly and we played a game of truth or dare. Jay went down to one of the tunnels on his own.' Amber's face creased in concentration. 'Erm, I think it was then that Ruth got a bit stroppy and left the mine. Naomi and me followed her outside.'

'Was she upset about the boys being there?' Meadows asked.

'Yeah, and because we were smoking weed. Ruth didn't smoke it but Naomi did. I think Naomi was worried that it was a step too far for Ruth. Ruth wanted to go home but we persuaded her to stay a little longer. We told her we would have a picnic and then make our way home.'

Naomi didn't volunteer any of this information, Meadows thought. Did she know about the GHB and thought by giving it to Ruth it would buy her more time?

'So, you all ate and drank. More alcohol?' Edris asked.

'Yeah, we had some shots. Ruth didn't, I don't think she did. After that things got a little weird.'

'Did you take something?' Meadows asked.

'No, but I felt more than just drunk. I was kinda removed from myself, but I felt good.'

'What were the others doing?' Meadows asked.

'Naomi and David were lying on the grass together, kissing. Jay was sitting on the concrete slab that overhangs the riverbank. He was just staring at the water. Callum was next to me and Aiden was sitting next to Ruth. Then Ruth stood up and started stripping. We all laughed and started clapping. It seemed so funny at the time. She took off her top and trousers and then went down the bank and into the water.'

'Did Jay go in after her?' Meadows asked.

'Yeah, he did. She tried climbing up next to the waterfall but slipped. She seemed to be struggling and kept going under. I don't know why none of the rest of us went in to help. It's like we lost all sense and just kept laughing.'

'Do you remember if Ruth cut her leg when she fell?' Meadows asked.

Amber bit her bottom lip in concentration. 'Erm, I'm not sure. She was messing around like she couldn't get out of the water and up the bank. Jay put her on his back and was coming up the bank. Then he went back to the water and set her down. She sat in the water for a while, maybe she was cleaning her leg if she did have a cut. Jay then helped her back up the bank. I think she might have complained about her leg. It's strange that Jay was the only one to help her. Thinking about it, she could have drowned if Jay hadn't gone in. To then go and attack her...' Amber shook her head. 'David thought that it was odd. He asked me if I thought Ruth fancied Jay. I think she did flirt a little. Maybe it went too far.'

'What did Jay do after he pulled Ruth from the water? Did he stay near her?'

'No, he asked for a drink as he hadn't brought anything with him. I think David gave him a can of something. He went back to sitting on the slab. Next to Aiden.'

'What about Ruth? Did she ask to go home again?' Meadows asked.

'No, she seemed contented. She lay down on a towel, face down. I think she fell asleep.'

The thought struck Meadows that Ruth could have taken a bad fall. Maybe knocked her head. They could have all panicked. 'Did she give any indication that she wasn't feeling well?'

'None at all. If she was feeling ill, she didn't say anything about it.'

'I'm guessing something happened after that,' Meadows said.

'Yeah.' Colour rose in Amber's cheeks. 'Naomi and David were lying together. His hands were all over her and she didn't seem to mind. I don't think any of us were taking that much notice or were even embarrassed by the display. Callum suggested we go for a walk together alone. I knew what he meant by it. We stood up and I think I said something like "get a room" to Naomi. She whispered something to David, and they got up. As I walked away I saw them going in the opposite direction.'

'Where exactly did they go?' Edris asked. He'd been busy writing up notes and now looked up with his pen poised.

Amber seemed thrown for a moment. 'Erm... I'm not sure. They went towards the bridge so I'm guessing they went up the other side somewhere or in the tunnel.'

'Where did you go?' Edris asked.

'We stayed on that side and walked further down river. There's a large overhanging rock which hides you from view, so we went under there.'

'I think we can probably guess what happened next, so I won't embarrass you by asking for details,' Meadows said. 'The only thing I will ask is if it was consensual.'

'Yes,' Amber said. 'He didn't force me. Looking back I know I was stupid. Drinking and smoking weed, what did I expect? I don't think I would have gone with him if I'd been sober but that wasn't Callum's fault. After we erm... Callum and me sort of had an argument. Well, we were shouting at each other then laughing hysterically. I don't know if I was laughing or crying. It was a mixture of both.'

'What was the argument about?' Meadows asked.

'I think I said something like "Is that it?" and he got pissed.'

Meadows felt his lips twitch. He could imagine how a young Callum would get insulted by a comment like that.

'I take it you weren't there long.'

'No, well, I stayed longer. Callum went off in a huff. I didn't want to go back and join the others. I thought Aiden and Jay would still be there with Ruth and maybe they would be laughing at me. I also felt very tired and couldn't be bothered to move for a while. I'm not sure how long I stayed there.'

'Who was there when you went back up?'

'Naomi was in the pool. There was no one else there. I joined her for a swim. She was just floating on her back. I asked her how it went, and she didn't say much. I guessed her experience had been like mine. We got out, dried off and lay in the sun. I think we must have dozed off for a while. David came back and woke us. Then Callum and Jay, Aiden was last back. It was then that we realised that Ruth was missing and not with the others.'

'How did everyone seem to you? Were they acting out of character?' Meadows asked.

'Everyone was a little subdued. I think we were probably sobering up. Naomi was worried about Ruth going off and that she would get in trouble with her parents.'

'What about Jay?'

'If you're asking if he was acting like he just killed Ruth then no, he was no different than he had been the rest of the day. We split up then to look for Ruth. That's when Jay suggested looking in the mine. The rest of us went off in different directions. We met up again later. Jay was sitting by the river. I thought later that Ruth could have been hiding in the mine all along and Jay found her, that's when he killed her. None of us were around.'

'But you don't think that now?' Meadows asked.

Amber shrugged her shoulders. 'I don't know. I'm sure it was Jay who said he was going to go home first. Then Naomi said the others should go as well before she called her parents. Jay left and Callum, David, and Aiden followed. It was Aiden that later said he had left Jay with Ruth. Aiden was really upset after Ruth was found. I think he was upset that he had left Ruth alone with Jay that day. He didn't speak to me after it happened. Kept to himself. I only saw Naomi once after that then she was sent away to live with her auntie. I went from having a boyfriend, a best friend, and being part of a group to being alone. I was interesting for a couple of weeks after, as I had been there that day, and everyone wanted to know the details. After that no one bothered with me. I was glad to leave school.'

'Did Naomi tell you why she was being sent away?' Meadows asked.

'Erm, no. I think they just wanted her out of the way. Protect her from the trial.'

'But she never came back.'

'No.'

Meadows got the sense that Amber knew more about Naomi's situation than she was telling. 'Did you see any of the others after you left school?'

'No, I ran into David a couple of times in the supermarket. I haven't seen Callum or Aiden, not until a couple of days ago when Aiden turned up outside my house.'

'What did he want?'

'He said you had been to see him and he wanted to know what I was going to say if you came to talk to me. I told him to just tell the truth. I think perhaps he was worried about smoking dope. I suppose it wouldn't look good with him being a solicitor.'

Maybe it's more than that, Meadows thought. 'Did he ask any questions about that day?'

'He asked me where I was that day and if I was with Callum the whole time. He seemed to think that Jay had killed David and that he could be coming after us. He wanted to know if I had spoken to Naomi. To be honest, he was making me uncomfortable, so I asked him to leave.'

'Has he tried to contact you since?'

'No.'

'OK, I think that's about it for now.' Meadows looked at Edris.

'Could you tell us where you were on the morning of the 8th of March from 7 a.m. until around 9.30 a.m., just so we can eliminate you from our enquiries?' Edris asked.

'Oh, erm. I would have been here with the kids getting them ready for school. I usually drop them off just before nine. My husband left for work about 7.30 if that helps.'

'We'll have to confirm with him.'

'OK, I've never spoken to him about that day. It's not that I've made myself out to be perfect. It's just I was embarrassed about my behaviour and lying. To be honest, I can't see how it would've made a difference if we had told the truth at the time.'

'Perhaps not, but there could've been something that was missed.' Meadows stood. 'We appreciate you talking to us and being so frank,' he said. 'If anything comes to mind or you get any more emails or contact from the others involved that makes you feel uncomfortable, let us know.'

Amber saw them to the door and closed it behind them.

'I think we should bring Aiden in for questioning in the morning,' Meadows said.

'Yeah, his name keeps coming up,' Edris said.

'And he has continually lied to us. I want to know why he is so interested in what Amber remembers from that day. The fact that he wanted to know what she was going to tell us is also suspicious. Perhaps it's not only smoking dope that Aiden doesn't want us to know about.'

Chapter Twenty-three

Jay was sitting in his cell staring at the wall. Over the past year he had got used to his own space. His flat hadn't been big but in comparison to the cell it felt like a castle. It was his first home, a place just for him. He had started to get used to the privacy and being able to make his own decisions. It was the little things he missed. His own bathroom, coloured cotton sheets on his bed, playing his guitar in the evening, and turning off the light when he wanted. These are the small things that ordinary people take for granted, he thought. Those on the outside got to choose their own food, the time they ate. In here every aspect of your life was dictated. Jay had appreciated all those things when he had been out. He didn't want to earn lots of money, drive a nice car, or even go out drinking. He just wanted to be free. To own his own life.

It hadn't taken him long to settle back into the routine inside and in the few days he had been back it felt like he had never left. Part of him wished he hadn't been released. Then there would be nothing to miss. My life is destined to be this way, probably until I die, he thought.

Visiting time was called and Jay made his way out of the cell to line up with the other inmates. He tried to shake off the depression, but his thoughts shrouded him in darkness. He felt like turning back and hiding in his cell. Even that wasn't an option. You couldn't hide away and block out the world in this place. The only thing that made him put one foot in front of the other was the thought of Mason in the visiting area. He could imagine his brother's disappointment and worry if he refused to see him. If Mason could make the effort to come, the least he could do was see him.

The visiting room was filled with chatter and the noise made him feel disorientated. Mason waved when he saw him, and he made his way across the room under the watchful gaze of the prison guards. He knew them all well. He treated them with respect and they in return treated him fairly and often passed the time talking to him. They had been surprised to see him back and some had showed sympathy for his situation. Although in their eyes he knew he was seen as just another convicted criminal.

'You OK?' Mason asked as he took his seat.

'Yeah, back where I belong,' Jay said.

'Don't say that,' Mason said. 'I'm trying to get some money together. I'm going to find you a good solicitor and get you out.'

'Don't,' Jay said. 'I don't want you wasting money or your time. The best legal team in the world couldn't get me out of here. I'm seen as a danger to society.'

'Don't give up,' Mason said. 'You didn't kill David, did you.'

Jay wondered if this was more of a question than a statement. 'Did you?'

'What? No.' Mason looked like he'd been slapped. 'Why would you even ask such a thing?'

Jay felt bad for taking his dark mood out on his brother. 'I'm sorry. I thought for a moment that... well, that you think I'm guilty like everyone else.'

Mason leaned forward. 'You know I don't.'

Jay looked around. All the other inmates were engrossed in conversation with their own visitors. No one was listening to what was being said at his table.

'The only chance I have is if the police find David's killer and I get parole again. I can't see that happening. Look how it turned out last time.'

'I told the police I sent those emails without you knowing. I told them you had nothing to do with it.'

'You shouldn't have done that. You'll get into trouble. You don't want to end up in here.'

'They can't do anything to me. It's not like I threatened any of them. Anyway, it's true I did send them, and the police traced them to me.'

'Yeah, but you did it for me.'

'You didn't know that someone would die as a result.'

'No, but it's still my fault. If we hadn't sent the emails, then David would still be alive. The police said he was trying to help me. Got me the job. He was always the nicest one out of them all.'

'It's down to the murdering bastard that killed Ruth and let you take the blame. None of this is your fault. You gotta stop thinking that way. Just hang in there.' Mason lowered his voice. 'The police are looking into Ruth's murder. I reckon they will reopen the case.'

'How do you know?'

'Amber came to see me again last night. She said the police are asking questions about that day at Dinas Rock. They wouldn't be doing that if they thought you were guilty.'

'What else did she say?'

'She's spoken to the others. Aiden is rattled by all accounts.'

'Yeah, he should be.'

'You should tell the police what you told me.'

'What's the point? They won't believe me. They need to find the information for themselves. It's the only way they will get to the truth.'

'Maybe, I should give them all another push.'

'Don't, it will get back to you and the police will be looking at you for David's murder. Stay away from it all.'

'I can ask Amber to help.'

'No, we don't want the police knowing she's been in contact with you. Anyway, we don't know if we can trust her.'

'I don't trust any of them, but Amber was the one to contact me,' Mason said. 'I can't see that she had anything to do with Ruth's murder. The police won't find out I've talked to her. She doesn't phone. Only turns up in person.'

'Why does she want to help? She was in the pool with Naomi when I got back from my walk. What if the two of them... or was David there?' – Jay rubbed his hands over his face – 'I don't know if I can trust my own memory anymore.'

'I can't see Amber and Naomi killing David and why would one of them have killed Ruth?'

'I don't know,' Jay said. 'I'm not sure of anything anymore. I'm tired. Tired of hoping, tired of...' He wanted to say tired of living, but he didn't want to put that on Mason. 'I'm just tired.'

'I know,' Mason said. 'Let me fight for you. I'm sure Aiden had something to do with Ruth's murder. He's been talking to the others, asking them to keep quiet. Why would he do that if he had nothing to hide? David must have guessed and confronted him. Yeah, the more I think about it the more I'm sure it's him. He's going to pay for it.'

'Don't say that. It sounds like you're going to do something stupid.'

'He just needs a gentle push to tell the truth.'

'Just leave it, promise me.'

Time was called and the inmates started to file out of the room.

'I'll see you soon,' Mason said.

'Thanks for coming.'

Jay left his brother and went back to his cell where he lay down on the bed. He turned over the conversation in his mind. Worry gnawed at his stomach. Enough of his life had been wasted. He didn't want the same for his brother. He thought of the detective that had been to see him. He had listened to his side of the story and didn't make him feel like a criminal. Meadows, yeah that was his name, Jay thought. Maybe he should take a chance and talk to him again. Maybe he would be the one to look further. He hoped so as he didn't know how much longer he could bear this life.

Chapter Twenty-four

Meadows gathered the team around for the morning's briefing. He updated them on what had been gained from the interviews the previous day. Everyone's interest had been peaked when Edris relayed Amber's version of events.

'Sounds like they had a hell of a party,' Blackwell said. 'Between the sex and drugs, it's no wonder they all kept their mouths shut.'

'Yeah, you would expect that of teenagers but what reason do they have for keeping quiet now?' Meadows asked. 'Blackwell, Valentine, how did you get on with Naomi's parents?'

'Funny lot,' Blackwell said. 'They didn't give much away. I told them that it was a follow-up call after Jay's release. Asked if they were coping and if they had any concerns. They said no and that was about it.'

'They didn't even invite us in,' Valentine said. 'Made us stand on the doorstep.'

'I did ask them how Naomi was doing and that got a reaction,' Blackwell said. 'The mother looked as if I'd just dropped my trousers. Pure disgust on her face. She said as far as they were concerned they lost two daughters that day. I asked her why and she said–' Blackwell looked at Valentine.

Valentine looked at her notebook. 'Her exact words: "Naomi brought shame on this family, and we could not tolerate the sin or sinner under our roof."'

'What's that supposed to mean?' Edris asked.

Valentine shrugged. 'She must have done something for her parents to never speak to her again. Maybe they found out about the drinking and sex.'

'Yeah, but you'd expect them to punish their daughter, ground her, not banish her,' Paskin said.

'Unless it was something more serious,' Meadows said. 'Suppose they suspected that Naomi had killed Ruth or had some hand in it.'

'I think if that was the case they would have turned her in,' Blackwell said. 'They seem that type.'

'You could be right,' Meadows said. 'On the other hand, they wouldn't want it known. We need to find out why Naomi was thrown out.'

'Well, forget getting the information from the parents,' Valentine said.

'See if you can track down the aunt. She may be willing to shed some light. How did you get on with the rest of your enquiries?'

'We checked out Mason Parks' alibi. He was on the production line the morning David was killed,' Blackwell said. 'There is no chance he could have slipped away. The supervisor gave me a tour. If Mason had left his position it would have brought the line to a standstill. Everyone takes a break at the same time.'

'Naomi was at work, we checked it out,' Edris said. 'No one can confirm that Callum was in early, same for Aiden. We just need to check out Amber's alibi. It narrows it down a bit.'

'We've checked out most of the ex-cons that Jay served with. Just a couple of alibis to check,' Valentine said.

'Yeah, I think you may be right and one of that lot' – Blackwell pointed to the board – 'killed David Harris.'

'And Ruth Williams,' Valentine said.

'And if that's the case it's going to cause a media storm,' Blackwell said. 'Glad I wasn't around at the time.'

'We'll deal with that if that's the case,' Meadows said. 'All we should be concerned with now is getting to the truth. If Jay Parks is innocent then the only ones to blame for his false imprisonment are those who lied to protect themselves. They've hidden behind a wall of silence for sixteen years. I think David wanted to break that silence. Amber has given us more information than any of them. It's only a matter of time before the truth comes out. We need to find out what really happened that day at Dinas Rock before someone else dies. Paskin, what have you got for us?'

'Physical evidence gathered from Dinas Rock at the time of Ruth Williams' murder should be here later this morning. I've requested use of the conference room as I doubt we'll have the space in here. I've also run background checks on the six that were there that day and their families.' She paused and flicked through her notes.

'Callum Vaughan left school after his sixteenth birthday and went to work for his father. As you know he practically runs the business now. Two siblings, both married and moved away. Callum has been married twice. His second wife worked in the office and rumour has it that he likes to play around. No recorded offenses and I found no suggestion of physical or sexual violence. I checked up on the haulage business for any illegal activity. It appears all above board.'

'Just because he kept himself clean over the years doesn't mean he's innocent,' Blackwell said. 'Rich kid, he'd have had the money to buy GHB. Probably had a good few pairs of trainers and similar clothing to give to the police at the time for testing.'

'According to retired Dylan Finch the clothes taken from all the teenagers were checked against photographs taken with Naomi's camera. But we will recheck this. What else have you got, Paskin?'

'Amber Thomas dropped out of school. She later went to college to study childcare and got a job in the local crèche. She married Jordan Richards and had two children. Active in local groups, lobbying the council for better amenities for young children, that sort of thing. She has one brother. He was questioned at the time of Ruth's murder and had an alibi for that day between dropping off the girls and picking up Amber later that day. Nothing to note in her family background. Naomi Williams, now Collins, went to college after leaving school. She retook the final year of school having taken six months off. I guess the leave was due to the trauma of her sister's death. I need to follow up on this, see if she had any counselling. She trained to be a nurse and other than maternity leave she has worked continually since qualifying. Her employment record is exemplary. She married Adam Collins and has two children.'

'That leaves Aiden Edwards,' Meadows said.

'Aiden was the only one out of the group to go to university. He studied law then took a job in Bristol before moving to Swansea. He is married with no children. He is an only child, parents still together and alive. Again, no recorded offences and no history of violence. You all know Jay's background. His father still works as an accountant but his mother is virtually a recluse. Mason has a record, possession. He went away with his parents to stay with relatives after Jay's arrest. They stayed away for a year then sold the house. There nothing in the family background. No relatives that came up on the radar that could be potentially helping Jay and Mason.'

'What I don't understand is this,' Valentine said. 'If Jay didn't kill Ruth, then whoever did would have had some evidence linking them to the murder. There's no way they wouldn't have got some blood on them. Look at the original photos. There was a pool of blood, and she was moved. What are the chances that Jay got blood on his clothes from an earlier accident then he just happens to step in her blood? I can't see it.'

'Yes, but Jay wasn't covered in blood and like you say there would have been a considerable amount. Why wasn't there any on his T-shirt?'

'It looks from the evidence that she was dragged to the water by her arms leaving a trail behind,' Blackwell said. 'The footprints show that Jay's trainers picked up the blood and left a trail coming out of the mine. So maybe he wasn't so careful on the way out.'

'He didn't have a torch,' Meadows said. 'It's possible that when he went to look for Ruth he didn't see the blood.'

'He could have washed himself off in the water,' Paskin said. 'Cleaned his hands, maybe he didn't have his T-shirt on at the time. They had all been swimming so he could have just been wearing shorts.'

'That goes for any of them,' Meadows said. 'I think we can be certain that Jay didn't kill David Harris which leaves one of the others. Their motive must be to keep him quiet about what he found out about Ruth's murder. Anything on social media?'

'Nothing that stands out,' Paskin said. 'Amber and Naomi are now friends on Facebook. There's a page set up for David. I'm monitoring it. So far anyone that's posted has expressed sympathy and said what a good guy he was.'

'Then I think it's time to put the pressure on the others. Starting with Aiden Edwards,' Meadows said.

* * *

When they arrived at Aiden's office, they found two people waiting in reception and the secretary on the phone. She looked flustered and Meadows could hear her rearranging appointments. He quickly became aware that there was a problem.

'We need to speak to Aiden,' Meadows said as soon as his secretary had put down the phone.

'He's not here. He didn't come in this morning.'

'Have you tried calling him?' Edris asked.

She bristled at the question. 'Of course. I've called his mobile, his landline, and even his wife. No one is answering.'

The tension in her voice put Meadows on edge. For her to be this worried it must really be out of character, he thought.

'Has this ever happened before?' Meadows asked.

'No, he always calls if he's going to be late or is sick.'

'OK, thank you.'

Meadows hurried to the car with Edris keeping step.

'Do you think he's done a runner?' Edris asked.

'Either that or he's in trouble,' Meadows said as he started the engine. 'It's worrying that his wife is out of contact.' He put on the lights and siren and picked up speed as he left the office car park.

The traffic cleared a path for them and they arrived at Aiden's address in minutes. Meadows jumped out of the car. The first thing he noticed was the two cars parked in the driveway and the closed curtains.

'Better call it in,' Meadows said. 'We may need to break down the door.' He hammered on the front door and peered through the letter box. All was quiet and still. 'Let's try round the back.'

Meadows took the side gate with a feeling of foreboding. Round the back of the house was a conservatory. The door was locked so he pressed his face against the glass. He could see a woman lying on the floor fully clothed. Meadows angled himself to see further in. He could see Aiden's legs; the rest of his body was obscured from view.

'Call an ambulance,' Meadows called to Edris. 'I can't see if they are breathing.'

While they waited for help they tried all the windows, but they were locked. They couldn't find a ladder to try the top windows. Meadows looked around for something to break a window with but there was nothing that would have enough force to break through the double glazing. He could feel his frustration mounting. If they are still alive inside precious seconds are being wasted, he thought. It was a great relief to see the police car pull up followed by the ambulance. It only took two swings of the battering ram, and they were inside.

Meadows led the way followed by a paramedic. Aiden was lying in the doorway between the kitchen and the sitting room, his wife near the kitchen table. Meadows stepped past Aiden leaving the paramedic to attend to him and knelt by Aiden's wife. She was cold and pale, but he managed to find a pulse.

'She's still breathing,' he said.

'Same here,' the paramedic said.

Meadows moved her hair and looked at her neck for any sign of a puncture wound.

A second paramedic entered the kitchen and Meadows moved away. As oxygen masks were put on Aiden and his wife, Meadows snapped on a pair of gloves and looked around.

'I'll check upstairs,' Edris said.

Meadows found a set of keys dangling in the locked conservatory door. He walked to the broken front door and found the same.

'All secure up there,' Edris said.

'Not a break-in then,' Meadows said. 'I didn't see any marks on Aiden's wife's neck to indicate she'd been injected.'

'Maybe they did it through the clothes, or if it was someone they knew they could have eaten or drank something,' Edris said.

'It's risky. They could have called for help. There's also the fact that they would have let that person leave and locked up after them,' Meadows said. 'But not impossible, especially if they didn't realise they had been drugged. Call in SOCO.'

Meadows went back into the kitchen and looked around. On the table was a bottle of red wine and two glasses. He picked up the bottle and saw there was only a thin layer of liquid covering the bottom. He sniffed the contents but could only smell alcohol.

'I'm sure I saw a bottle of wine on the secretary's desk in Aiden's office yesterday,' Meadows said.

'It's an expensive bottle,' Edris said.

'I wouldn't know, I never drink the stuff. Most people have a preference though, don't they?'

Edris shrugged. 'Don't ask me, I'll drink anything especially if it's free. Do you think it's been spiked?'

'It would be one way of doing it. I'm guessing that the bottle was meant for Aiden and the only reason he's still breathing is that he shared it with his wife.'

Meadows watched the paramedics loading Aiden and his wife onto stretchers.

'How are they doing?'

'Oxygen levels are low,' the paramedic said.

'Better get them checked out for GHB or a similar substance at the hospital.'

'OK,' the paramedic said as he lifted the stretcher.

'Well, that puts Aiden out of the picture,' Edris said.

Meadows nodded. 'And I can't see Jay sending an expensive bottle of wine from prison. Let's go and see Aiden's secretary again. See if she took a delivery yesterday.'

Aiden's secretary was tearful when they told her the news.

'Did Aiden have anything delivered here yesterday?' Meadows asked.

'Yes, some documents and a thank you gift,' she said.

'A bottle of wine?'

'Yes, why? Oh, do you think that it was poisoned?' Her voice quivered.

'It's possible. How did it arrive?'

'It came with the post. Usual postman.'

'Did you open it?' Meadows asked.

'Yes, that's my job. It was well wrapped inside a box.'

'With a note?'

'Yeah, it said something like "Aiden, all good now. Have a drink on me. C".'

'Do you have the packaging and note?' Edris asked.

'The packaging I threw away and the note I gave to Aiden with the wine. The bins are emptied every evening.'

'OK, we'll send someone over to take your fingerprints as you handled the bottle. Would you also be able to provide the officers with details of the refuse collection?' Meadows said.

'Of course. Will Aiden be OK? I don't know what to do.'

Meadows got the sense that the secretary was about to break down. 'We don't know at this stage, but they survived the night so that's promising. The best thing you can do is keep things here running smoothly until he gets back. I'm sure he'll appreciate that.'

* * *

Meadows' mind was whirring as he drove towards the hospital. 'Give Blackwell a call and tell him to bring in Callum Vaughan.'

'You think that the wine was from Callum?'

'It's possible although he would be stupid to put his initial on the note. He doesn't have an alibi for the morning David was murdered and he hasn't been honest with us.'

'Yeah, and he had opportunity to kill Ruth,' Edris said as he placed the call.

At the hospital, Dr Hill led them to a side room for privacy.

'How are they doing?' Meadows asked.

'Still unconscious. We've got them both on ventilators to assist their breathing. Their oxygen levels were extremely low when they were brought in. I've sent off bloods and as soon as we have them back we'll know what we are dealing with. You asked for them to be tested for GHB. It fits with their condition. If that is what they've ingested, then it is known to depress the respiratory system. If that's the case, then there isn't a lot we can do for them except assist with their breathing and hope they regain consciousness. There is also the possibility that the lack of oxygen could have caused damage to their vital organs.'

'If it were GHB and was put into the bottle of wine, and if Aiden drank the bottle himself then my guess is it would have been a lethal dose.'

'That's a lot of ifs.' Dr Hill smiled. 'But given the condition of the patients and if that were the case then yes, I think it unlikely that Aiden would have survived.'

'Thank you,' Meadows said. 'We'll have an officer posted outside their room.'

'That leaves three out of the six,' Meadows said as he walked down the corridor. 'One in jail, one fighting for his life, and the other dead. It's clear that Aiden knows something and it's possible he's not the only one. Our killer is either Naomi, Amber, or Callum. We have to work out which before someone else dies.'

Chapter Twenty-five

Blackwell was already in the interview room with Callum when Meadows arrived back at the station. He sent Edris off to grab some lunch and knocked on the door before entering.

Blackwell announced Meadows' arrival as he took a seat. Callum was sitting next to his solicitor and this time he didn't look so sure of himself.

'Callum was just talking us through his movements yesterday,' Blackwell said.

'And I asked you to explain why you have brought me in here,' Callum said.

'To help with our enquiries into the murder of David Harris. I recall I explained that to you,' Blackwell said.

'Yes, but now you're asking me about yesterday.'

Blackwell nodded at Meadows.

'Aiden Edwards and his wife were found unconscious in their home this morning. For the benefit of the tape and your solicitor, Aiden, together with yourself, David Harris, Amber Richards, and Naomi Williams gave witness statements in the Ruth Williams case in 2005.'

Callum paled. 'Are they going to be OK?'

'We don't know,' Meadows said. 'We will be asking the other witnesses as well as yourself for their movements yesterday.'

'I was in work.'

'And after work?'

'I went home, ate, watched something on the TV, then went to bed.'

'Did you leave the house at all during the evening?'

'No.'

'What did you watch?' Blackwell asked.

'Some documentary on Netflix.'

'Can you be more specific?'

'Ask my wife,' Callum said.

'We will,' Blackwell said.

'When was the last time you saw Aiden Edwards?' Meadows asked.

'He came to see me a couple of days ago at the office.'

'And what was the nature of the visit?'

'He wanted to talk about the plans for David's funeral and if we could organise some fundraising for Tia and the kids.'

'Was that all?' Blackwell asked.

'Yeah.'

'I think there was a lot more to the conversation than that,' Blackwell said.

'I don't know what you're talking about.'

'Did Aiden ask you about the day Ruth Williams was murdered?'

'No.'

'We've spoken to Amber Richards, or Amber Thomas as you knew her then,' Blackwell said. 'She was very helpful and told us everything that happened that day, so I think it's time you came clean.'

The solicitor held up his hand. 'Where are you going with this? It was my understanding that you wanted to talk to my client in relation to the death of David Harris, now you are implying that he knows something about the Ruth

Williams case. A murder sixteen years ago that as far as I am aware the perpetrator served time for.'

'I can assure you the cases are connected. Your client was involved in both.'

'Wait a minute. I had nothing to do with what happened to Ruth, and David was my best friend. Why would you even think that I had anything to do with his death?'

'You've kept back information about your recent talks with David Harris. Added to that you lied during the investigation into Ruth Williams' murder. You can see how it looks from this side of the table,' Meadows said. 'You've left us wondering why you lied. What is it that you've kept to yourself all these years?'

'OK, fine,' Callum said. 'I lied back then; I was fifteen years old. We did arrange to meet up with the girls that day and we hung out. No big deal. Naomi didn't want anyone to know we were meeting up. I kept quiet because David asked me to.'

'It was a little more than hanging out,' Blackwell said. 'The drinking, the drugs, and then you went off with Amber leaving Ruth alone with Jay and Aiden.'

'Yeah, Amber was my girlfriend at the time.'

'You had sex,' Meadows said.

'Yeah.'

'And then you argued.'

'If you can call it an argument. It was just a stupid falling out, a disagreement.'

'You went off on your own. Where did you go?' Meadows asked.

'I went over the bridge and walked up the other side.'

'Did you see Ruth?'

'No.'

'You've consistently lied to us,' Blackwell said. 'You can see how it looks. We know why you argued with Amber. Let's just say your performance was below par. So, you were pissed. You went storming off, came across Ruth alone and thought you would prove yourself. Is that how it was?'

'No, No!' Callum said. 'I didn't see Ruth.'

'Then why lie to us? Why not tell us about the emails you received? Why not come clean about that day? It makes me think that you did something and didn't want to be found out. Did David know your secret?'

'I didn't kill her,' Callum said. 'And I didn't kill David. He was my best friend.'

'Then tell us what you know,' Meadows said. 'It might help catch David's killer. Don't you want justice for your friend?'

'Yes, but…'

'What are you afraid of telling us?'

'I'd like to speak to my solicitor alone,' Callum said.

Meadows nodded at Blackwell who paused the interview tape.

'You have five minutes,' Blackwell said.

'What do you reckon they are talking about in there?' Blackwell asked as the two of them leaned against the wall outside the interview room.

'Whatever it is, it has Callum worried,' Meadows said. 'My guess is he wants to find out how much trouble he'll be in if he tells us the truth.'

'Do you think he would cover for his best friend? Or maybe they killed her together.'

'If that's the case then who killed David? Unless David wanted to come clean,' Meadows said. 'Or Callum killed Ruth, and David found out.'

'Yeah, and he'll try and pin it on David as he's not around to defend himself. He seems like the maggoty type.'

Meadows smiled. 'He's not the only one that's lied to us.'

They were silent for a few moments then Blackwell checked his watch. 'Right, he's had enough time.'

They went back into the interview room and took their seats before Blackwell restarted the tape.

'You've had time to discuss matters with your solicitor, are you now going to tell us what happened that day at Dinas Rock?'

Callum shuffled in his chair and looked at his solicitor.

'My client wants some reassurance first. Given that he was a minor at the time.'

'I can't give you any reassurances,' Meadows said. 'You know perfectly well that if your client was involved in the murder of Ruth Williams then he will be charged accordingly.'

'I had nothing to do with Ruth's murder,' Callum said.

'I have advised my client that it is not in his best interests to disclose matters relating to that day. However, the information may have some bearing on your case, so you see our problem.'

'How about you ask us a hypothetical question?' Meadows suggested.

The solicitor smiled and nodded. 'OK, if my client, hypothetically, while giving you information, admitted to a drug-related incident, would you pursue a charge?'

Meadows wondered where this was going. Jay had already admitted to supplying the cannabis. That just left the GHB.

'That would depend on if the drugs in question led directly to the death of an individual. Then, of course, we would have to pursue a charge.'

'Just spit it out,' Blackwell snapped. 'We know drugs were used that day and it's obvious now that you supplied them.'

Callum looked at his solicitor who nodded.

'I want to help,' Callum said. 'I did a stupid thing back then, but we were just having fun. I didn't know anyone would get hurt. Nothing like that was supposed to happen.'

'Go on,' Meadows said.

'The plan was to meet the girls and take some food and drink. I took a bottle of vodka. We didn't know Ruth was going until the night before. David asked Aiden to keep her entertained. Flirt a little. I guess there was an understanding that me and Amber and Naomi and David would get some alone time. I got hold of some GHB. It was supposed to be an aphrodisiac or that's what we thought at the time.'

'Date rape drug,' Blackwell said.

'No, it wasn't like that. It wasn't my intention or David's to trick the girls. Come on, you know what it's like at that age. The only thing on your mind is getting laid.'

'Yeah, getting laid and spiking someone's drink to get your own way are two different things,' Blackwell said.

'This is what I was afraid of, that you would think I was some sort of perv. I know what GHB is used for but back then I thought it would get the girls in the mood.'

'Who knew about the GHB?' Meadows asked.

'Just David.'

'So just to be clear, Aiden, Jay and the girls knew nothing about the GHB. They didn't know they had taken it.'

'Yes.' Callum reddened. 'I know it looks bad. Jay brought the weed, that's all.'

'Where did you get the GHB?' Blackwell asked.

'Does it matter?' Callum said. 'No point in getting anyone else in trouble.'

'OK, so what happened next?' Meadows asked.

'We all went exploring in the mine, smoked a joint and played some stupid games. When we got out of the mine the girls were sitting by the river. Naomi was talking about going home as Ruth wasn't happy. They had persuaded her to have a picnic first. Amber would have gone with them so that would have been my day ruined. We had some shots of vodka. Ruth didn't drink, just looked on disapprovingly. I poured the GHB into a bottle of cherryade and shared it out. No one noticed.'

'Your intention was to drug Ruth?' Meadows asked.

'No, we all drank it. I think it affected Ruth more than the rest of us because she was the one to strip off and jump in the river.'

'Did you see Jay go into the river to help her when she got into difficulty?' Meadows asked.

'Yeah, I did. None of us helped him get her up the bank. I guess we were all off our faces and not thinking straight.'

'OK, after that you went off with Amber. How long were you alone together?'

'That I honestly couldn't tell you. There was a lot of kissing and stuff before... well, you know. Then we argued and yes I was pissed off, but more with myself. It hadn't gone as I had planned. I went off for a walk. I wasn't angry, I still felt chilled, but I wanted to be on my own for a while.'

'Did you see Ruth?'

'No, there was no sign of Ruth, Jay, or Aiden.'

'What about David and Naomi?' Meadows asked.

'I saw David on the bank.'

'By the river?'

'No, the grassy bank by the mine.'

'Did you talk to him?'

'No, I wasn't in the mood, and I don't think he saw me.'

'What was David doing?'

'Just sitting there, messing around with the camera.'

'Naomi's camera?' Meadows asked.

'Yeah.'

'So where did you go?'

'I walked across the bridge and up the other side of the river. I sat down on the concrete blocks and had a smoke.'

'More cannabis?' Blackwell asked.

'No, just a regular smoke. Then I went for a walk over the stile. I walked for a while then I met up with Jay. We walked back together. Naomi and Amber were there. They asked if I'd seen Ruth. I think David came back then. I'm not sure where he had been, then Aiden turned up. We hung about for a while. Everyone was quiet. I think we had sobered up a little by then. Naomi started to get worried about Ruth, so we all looked for her. Jay did go into the mine. That wasn't a lie. Jay was the one that was left alone with Ruth, and he was the one to suggest looking in the mine and went in alone.'

'How do you know that Jay was left alone with Ruth?' Meadows asked.

'He was with her when I went off with Amber. Aiden said he had gone off for a walk and left the two of them alone together.'

'When did Aiden tell you this? Before or after Ruth was found?'

'Erm... I think after.'

'So, you assumed that Aiden was telling the truth and you blamed Jay for what happened. You also let Jay take the blame for drugging Ruth.'

'It wasn't like that,' Callum said. 'I couldn't say that I had brought the drugs. It was your lot that arrested Jay and charged him with murder. It was Jay that had Ruth's blood on his clothes. What good would it have done to tell the truth? All that would have happened is that I'd have ended up in trouble. Jay still would have gone down for murder.'

'David didn't think that Jay had killed Ruth, did he?' Meadows asked.

'No.'

'What changed his mind?'

'What do you mean? David never thought that Jay killed Ruth. He was as shocked as the rest of us when Jay was charged. David was the one who wanted us to tell the truth, that we had all met up that day and that Jay didn't bring the drugs. Aiden said we should keep quiet, and I agreed. David was convinced that some randomer had come across Ruth and killed her. Then we heard about the blood on Jay's clothes and trainers. We persuaded David that whatever we said it wouldn't make a difference and that Jay was clearly guilty. We were a little worried that the GHB had caused him to kill Ruth. It was out of character. Jay was always nice, he wouldn't even step on a spider. He was the type to help carry old ladies' shopping and open doors for people.'

'So, you all kept quiet,' Meadows said.

'Yeah, we didn't speak of it again until we all got the emails.'

'What did David say about the emails?'

'He was upset by them and wanted to help Jay. He was convinced there had been some mistake. He wanted to know everything I remembered about that day.'

'What did you tell him?'

'Pretty much what I just told you.'

'How did he react?'

'I don't know. He'd been acting weird since he got the emails.'

'What did you think the emails meant?'

'I thought Jay was pissed about us lying. That he wanted us to come clean about the drugs. I didn't think he'd do anything. Now he's killed David and he tried to kill Aiden. You have to make sure he stays in prison or the rest of us won't be safe.'

'Jay didn't kill David,' Meadows said.

Callum shook his head. 'No, it has to be Jay. Who else would want to hurt David?'

'Someone who, like you, doesn't want the truth to come out. Jay has spent half his life in prison because the investigating officers didn't have all the facts at the time. Things could have turned out differently if you hadn't all conspired against Jay. David might still be alive if you had all come clean, and Aiden and his wife wouldn't be lying seriously ill in hospital. I'd like you to think about that and amend your original statement, it may be sixteen years too late but it's time Jay had some answers, don't you think?'

'What about the GHB, do I have to put that in the statement?' Callum asked.

Meadows couldn't believe that Callum had asked the question. He thought about Amber's embarrassment when she talked about her sexual encounter and Naomi's reluctance to come clean about that day even after all this time. It may be that the girls wouldn't have given consent if they hadn't been drugged. The thought sparked an anger in him although he didn't show it outwardly. I should let him sweat, he thought.

'Yes, you need to put that in your statement,' Meadows said. 'It is one thing that Jay Parks can be cleared of. He wasn't the one to drug Ruth that day.'

'What about me?' Callum asked. 'I've told you everything now. You're not going to charge me, are you?' He turned to his solicitor. 'They can't, can they?'

'That will depend on Amber and if she wants to make a complaint against you.' Meadows stood. 'DS Blackwell will take your renewed statement. I would also suggest that you allow him to take your fingerprints. They will be needed for elimination from the bottle of wine sent to Aiden.' He watched Callum for a reaction to his last comment, but he gave no indication that he was worried about the prints.

Callum shrugged his shoulders. 'Fine, I'll give my fingerprints and anything else you want. But I'm only consenting to show you I'm innocent.'

Innocent was a word Meadows wouldn't apply to Callum. He left the interview room and closed the door. Callum's version of events had only made the case more complicated. They were all drugged that day and that made each of them an unreliable witness.

Chapter Twenty-six

The conference room in the station was filled with evidence boxes that Paskin, Edris, and Valentine were checking against the log.

'Looks like we've got everything,' Valentine said. 'It's a lot of stuff.'

'Everything collected from the scene and the surrounding area. Empty bottles and cigarette butts among other things. Then there are the clothes, and footprint casts. The vial which had the GHB wasn't found but I guess whoever had it disposed of it after,' Edris said.

'It was Callum, he just admitted to it,' Meadows said. 'He put it in a bottle of cherryade and drugged them all. I guess he took the evidence home with him and got rid of it.'

Valentine shook her head. 'It gives me the creeps. They all thought they were going for a fun day out and all along he intended to drug the girls for sex.'

'David knew about the GHB. Callum claimed he thought it was just a mood enhancer at the time,' Meadows said. 'Even if that was the case it doesn't make it right. It's still rape. Those girls didn't give consent.'

'Do you think Callum killed Ruth?' Paskin asked.

'I don't know,' Meadows said. 'He claims he has told us everything but given that he kept silent about the drugs I wouldn't trust anything he says. OK, let's start looking at the evidence and see which pieces are worth retesting given the new information we have.'

The first box Meadows looked in had Naomi's camera and a set of printed photographs. He picked out the camera and examined it through the plastic evidence bag.

'This has a dent in the corner and looks like it might have had a strap.' He pointed to the left side of the camera.

'The dent could have happened at any time before and there's no strap listed in the evidence log,' Paskin said.

'Was the camera sent to forensics?'

'No, it was only taken for the photographs to be uploaded and printed. Naomi had the camera in her possession. She never reclaimed it after the trial.'

'Looks expensive,' Valentine commented. 'I wonder why she never asked for it back.'

'Naomi was sent away before the trial and perhaps her parents didn't want the camera and photos. It would be a reminder of that day. I imagine it would be difficult to look at photos taken hours before their daughter was murdered.' Meadows took the photographs out of the box and laid them out in order along the table.

The first photo showed Naomi and Amber standing close together and posing in front of Dinas Rock. Climbers could be seen behind them scaling the cliff face. Amber wore a high-cut pair of denim shorts, and a light blue cropped top which showed her midriff. Her red hair was fanned out over her shoulders and a rucksack sat at her feet. Naomi's clothes were a sharp contrast to what her friend wore. She wore loose-fitting pink trousers that grazed her ankles and a cream crew-neck T-shirt. Her hair, like Amber's, was loose and hanging over her shoulders.

The next photo was of Naomi and Ruth taken with the same background. Ruth was dressed in the same pink trousers as her sister but wore a short-sleeved white blouse that was buttoned up to the neck. Her hair was tied back and she had a shy smile.

The photographs catalogued their journey up the side of the rock, on to the clearing, to the signpost that showed the paths branching off to Sgwd Yr Eira and Penderyn, and finally the mine and river. Each girl took a turn in front of the camera, sometimes paired together, others just lone shots. Only one photo showed all three, Naomi was in the middle holding the camera at arm's length. It took several shots to get in all their features.

'The days before mobile cameras and selfie sticks,' Edris said.

'If the technology had been as it was now we would have been looking at a lot more photos and possibly a different story would've been captured,' Meadows said.

There were a lot of photographs of the waterfall and pool then random shots of feet dipping into the water, Amber skimming stones, and Naomi and Amber sitting on the bridge with their legs dangling over the edge. There were a couple of the entrance to the mine, taken from both inside and outside. The next three photographs were of the boys walking over the bridge.

'I'm guessing David, Aiden, and Callum,' Meadows said pointing to each of the boys' faces.

'I'm surprised she took photos of the boys given that she wasn't supposed to be meeting them,' Valentine said.

'The previous shots were of Amber and Naomi so I think we can conclude that it was Ruth taking the photographs. Which means that Naomi didn't have the camera the whole time they were there,' Meadows said.

There were no more photographs of the girls and Meadows thought this was probably because the boys had joined them and taken their attention. There was another picture of the mine entrance then a couple of dark shots before the flash lit up what looked like a pillar in the mine. The next one was of Jay and Aiden sitting on the concrete slab that overlooked the river. Jay's head was turned towards the camera, and he had a look of surprise as if he'd been called and wasn't expecting the camera. The last two photographs were too dark to make out any detail. Meadows peered closely then looked back at the previous two photographs.

'These were the last photos taken,' Meadows said. 'Looking at the order it looks as if they were taken after they all came out of the mine. So where and when were they taken?'

'They could have gone back in the mine,' Edris said. 'Naomi could have deleted the others as she didn't want her parents to see the boys.'

'But she left the one of Jay and Aiden,' Meadows said.

'Then maybe Ruth had the camera when she went into the mine and tried to take a photo of her attacker, but the flash didn't work,' Edris said.

'If that was the case the camera would have been found with Ruth. Naomi had the camera,' Valentine said.

Blackwell walked into the room and peered at the photographs. 'Anything interesting?'

'Maybe,' Meadows said. There was something that bothered him about the photos, but he couldn't grasp it. 'I think we should send the camera off for testing. I want to know if the damage happened that day. There may be some minute fragments in the scratch and dent that can be matched to the surface of the mine.'

'Do you want me to move the incident board in here?' Edris asked.

'Yes, it's probably a good idea.' Meadows looked again at the photographs. The young faces full of life and future promise filled him with sadness. Two dead, one in a critical condition, and one whose life had been spent locked away from the world.

'I'll give you a hand,' Valentine said, and followed Edris.

'Can you pin up some of these photos, Paskin?' Meadows asked. He wanted those faces to be the first thing they saw when they came into the room. He wanted them all to stay focused. These people and their families deserved answers. It has been too long, he thought.

'OK, let's get the clothes unpacked and match them to the photographs. I'm sure they will all match as they would have been checked in the first investigation, but it could be that one of them had a similar outfit or pair of shoes to the ones they were wearing that day. Look closely at the details. Every button and mark. Once that's done then they can be sent off for testing.'

'All of them?' Blackwell asked.

'Yes, it's been sixteen years and forensics have evolved. I still don't trust any of their stories.'

'But David was murdered because he knew who the real killer was and an attempt was made on Aiden's life so I think we can rule them out,' Paskin said.

'Aiden was the one to say that Jay was left alone with Ruth. He pointed the finger at Jay, why? What if he was the one left with her?' Meadows said. 'What if he felt so guilty about what he did or was frightened that he was about to be found out and tried to kill himself. He could have drugged the wine.'

'What about his wife?' Paskin asked. 'That would mean that he tried to kill her.'

'It would be one way of ensuring she never found out what he did all those years ago. He could have made a mistake with the dosage. Or he could have known what he was doing and was trying to throw suspicion on someone else,' Blackwell said.

'I suppose it's possible,' Paskin said. 'But we have nothing on him, and he would have known that.'

'It's just a theory,' Meadows said. 'I don't want to rule him out just yet. Then there is David. According to Callum he had Naomi's camera. Was he trying to delete the last photographs? If he was involved in Ruth's murder, he may have wanted to come clean.'

'That's if Callum is to be believed,' Blackwell said.

'It's an odd detail to add if he is lying,' Meadows said. 'What was David doing sitting outside the mine? It's possible that Ruth could already have been dead inside at that stage.'

'But he was with Naomi,' Paskin said. 'That's what Amber said. She saw the two of them go off together.'

'Yes, Amber has been helpful. The only one who has told us the full story voluntarily. Maybe a bit too helpful. If David and Callum had gone off for a walk after they had been alone with the girls, and Aiden and Jay were nowhere to be seen, then that leaves Naomi and Amber. They were the only ones left by the river and claimed that Ruth was missing. What if Ruth had threatened to tell what the girls had been up to. They would want to keep her quiet.'

'I thought it was a sexually motivated attack?' Paskin said.

'That was the conclusion drawn by the prosecution. There was no sign that Ruth had been sexually assaulted. Buttons from her blouse were found on the grassy bank outside the mine. They could have come off in a struggle. Whatever happened started there.'

'OK, so we test all the clothes again. What if we get the same results?' Blackwell asked. 'The only evidence found the first time around was on Jay's clothes and shoes and his own blood and skin on the old bit of track where Ruth died. That's not going away.'

'No but Jay explained the evidence against him. I need to speak with him again and talk through the scrape on his leg. Once the blood was found on Jay's clothes and he was arrested it was just a matter of building a case against him. Why look at any of the others? Take the bloodstains out of the equation and what are you left with?'

'A mess,' Blackwell said.

'It could have been any one of them,' Edris said as he positioned the incident board.

Meadows walked over to the board. 'Which one of these had motive and opportunity to kill Ruth?' He pointed to the pictures. 'Or maybe more than one of them.'

'If Jay was left alone with Ruth and sexed up on GHB that would give him motive and opportunity,' Blackwell said. 'David and Callum had made it clear what they were getting up to with the girls, so Jay took his chance with Ruth. She gets scared and runs into the mine.'

'The same applies to Aiden. Equal motive and opportunity if he was the one left alone with Ruth. Then there's Callum, he was alone and angry with his performance. We only have his word that David was sitting on the bank, it could have been Ruth. He had time to kill her then go off for a walk. He also had opportunity to kill David,' Meadows said.

'If David was alone on the bank as Callum said, he could have killed Ruth,' Valentine said.

'Then who killed David and why?' Edris said. 'I think we can rule him out.'

'Unless someone else helped him,' Meadows said. 'Maybe David felt guilty and wanted to confess so the other party killed him. Then there's Amber. She came back to that spot after Callum left. She could have got into an argument with Ruth. She has an alibi for the morning David was killed but it's her husband that confirmed the time she left for work. He would likely cover for her. The timing would be tight to kill David and get back to take the children to school but it's not impossible. The same applies to Naomi. She had the opportunity to kill her sister and the motive. She had a lot to lose if her parents found out she'd been seeing David. She does have a firm alibi for the morning David was murdered. If we were looking at this case sixteen years ago who would be the most likely suspect?'

'One of the boys,' Blackwell said.

'I think one of the girls,' Valentine said. 'Amber said she lied back then to protect her friend. Maybe she killed Ruth to protect Naomi or Naomi killed Ruth and Amber covered for her. David found out somehow so Amber makes sure he keeps quiet. Naomi was sent away and we still don't know why.'

'OK, Edris can you set up a visit to the prison? The last time we talked to Jay he implied that Aiden knew something.'

'What about Callum?' Blackwell asked. 'He's in the frame and he could go after Amber or Naomi.'

'It could be the other way around and Callum could be in danger,' Meadows said.

'I think we should search his house for any sign of GHB. Look at possible matches to his clothes for the fibres found on David.'

'And see if we can match his shoes to the prints found in the tunnel,' Valentine said.

Meadows looked at the team who all seemed to be nodding in agreement. 'If that's your gut feeling then you should go with it,' he said. 'Apply for a warrant.'

'In the meantime we'll keep Callum under watch,' Blackwell said. He turned to Valentine. 'We can take turns.'

'What!' Valentine frowned. 'You expect me to stay up all night.'

'Nah, I'll watch him tonight, see what he gets up to. We don't want to give him a chance to get rid of anything. You can watch him at work and follow him home, then we'll swap. At the very least we can keep the two women safe if he is guilty. If not then we will also be protecting him from any attacks.'

'Guess it makes sense,' Valentine said. 'I'll go now and make sure he is in work. I can make some excuse to check he's in his office.'

'OK. Blackwell, go home and get a couple of hours' sleep. Paskin, can I leave you to check the clothes and send them off for testing?' Meadows asked.

'I'm on it,' Paskin said.

Meadows turned to Edris. 'You and me can go through the rest of this evidence. See what stands out.'

The rest of the day was spent looking through the evidence and the forensic results. As well as the clothes and litter found at the site there were casts of the footprints.

'They didn't manage to eliminate all the footprints,' Meadows said as he looked at an unidentified size ten. 'I suppose it was summer and anyone passing by would be tempted to go into the mine to explore. Like the tunnel, it's protected from the elements so the prints could stay undisturbed for a long time. There is also an unidentified size five and size seven.'

'Are you thinking that some random person happened to be passing and saw Ruth?' Edris asked.

'No, I think that highly unlikely. One of them would have seen someone hanging around or heard a scream. There was no evidence of Ruth being dragged into the mine. I think she knew her killer. Let's start isolating the prints taken from the group. We should be able to map out their path. The crime scene photos show the prints and markers. Each one was identified but for the prosecution case they concentrated on Jay's prints. We know they all explored the mine so we look at the prints near or concentrated where Ruth died and the water's edge. I'll draw up a floor plan of the mine then we'll add the prints.'

'What good is that going to do?'

'I want to see if one set stands out.'

'Yeah, Jay's prints did that.'

'Yes but now we are working from a different angle. They were looking for evidence to back up that Jay killed Ruth. They already had bloodstains on his clothes and trainers. I doubt they would look closely at every print in the mine.'

'Do we have enough details in the photographs?' Edris asked.

'They are well documented. We just have to fill in the gaps.'

Meadows worked on the floor plan as Edris worked on isolating the group's prints and checking them against the markers on the crime scene photos. They started with Jay's prints using a green marker. The trail led from the entrance of the mine to the second tunnel on the right, moved to the furthest tunnel then back to the entrance. A second trail led directly from the entrance to the furthest right tunnel. They crossed over the point where Ruth had been attacked. The last trail led from the entrance to the mine and just passed the point where Ruth had died. This time the prints left a blood trail.

'Looking at this it does appear as if Jay went in after Ruth and killed her. Then dragged her body to the water's edge. What DI Dylan Finch didn't know was that Jay had been to the water's edge alone earlier that day,' Meadows said. 'Even if Jay did say this in his interviews it was too late. He had already lied. He didn't have the others to back up that story. Amber has now confirmed it. Without that information the footprint trail tells another story. We know that Jay walked in a third time. They all confirmed that. We also know that Ruth's body was dragged to the water's edge so it's likely that her body would have gone over the killer's footprints, yet Jay's print impressions are well defined.'

Edris peered at the photographs. 'I guess it backs up your theory that Jay didn't kill Ruth but it could be argued he went in a third time to check that he didn't leave anything behind. It was then that he stepped in the blood.'

'I think he would have been careful to avoid the blood if he knew it was there.'

'Yeah, I suppose. OK, next we have Aiden's prints.'

Meadows picked up a blue marker. 'His prints were picked up at the entrance to the mine, the tunnel second from the right and going across into the flooded tunnel. There were also prints near where Ruth died but they all walked back that way.'

'Doesn't look like he went back in alone,' Edris said. 'There's Callum and Amber's prints close to his. But not David's or Naomi's.'

'Interesting,' Meadows said. 'We'll grab a cuppa then look at all the prints at the entrance of the mine. It could be that Naomi and David didn't go further into the mine to explore.'

'Hang on,' Edris said. 'He checked down the log and looked at the photos. 'I can't see David's prints in the mine at all.'

'Naomi said that Ruth wanted to go home. Maybe she went out of the mine and Naomi followed her. Perhaps David never went into the mine. We need to go back over the statements and check all the footprints again to see if David's were missed.'

'We'll be here all night. Do you know how many prints were found? Loads of people came forward to say they had been in the mine. Then there was the mountain rescue team and divers that use the mine.'

Meadows looked at his watch. 'Oh, I didn't realise it was that late. Why didn't you say something?'

'You were on a roll,' Edris said. 'I was waiting for that moment when you say, "I've got it by damn."'

Meadows laughed. 'When have you ever heard me say something like that?'

'Never, but it's how it goes in my head.'

'Sometimes I worry about you,' Meadows said with a smile. 'Come on I'll drop you home. We'll finish this tomorrow.'

* * *

Meadows didn't feel like going home after dropping off Edris. He hadn't heard from Daisy for a couple of days and was worried that she'd clocked his smoking habit and was pulling away. He drove the short distance to his mother's flat and took his keys from his pocket.

'Only me,' he called out as he stepped through the door.

Fern Meadows stepped out of the sitting room. As usual she was barefoot with her long grey hair braided down her back.

'Winny love, if I had known you were coming I would have made some food.'

'I ate at work.' Meadows leaned down and hugged his mother. 'Not too late, is it?'

'Nah, I was just watching some crap on the TV. I'll put the kettle on and you can tell me about your case. I've been following it on the news.'

As Fern made the tea Meadows filled her in on the investigation. Over the years his mother had been his sounding board and always kept his confidence.

'So you think this boy is innocent?'

Meadows smiled. Everyone younger than Fern was a child. 'Yeah, I do. If David Harris hadn't been murdered then no one would have given it a second thought. I got the impression Jay was telling the truth when I met him. I would've expected him to be angry, but he seemed almost resigned to the fact that he will always be thought of as guilty. He was out on parole, so he had nothing to gain by going after the witnesses.'

'You've always been a good judge of character so go with your instincts. You'll get there. You have a way of getting the truth out of people.'

'I don't know about that. Most of the time I think I believe people too easily.'

'Nothing wrong with seeing the best in people. Life would be miserable if we thought we couldn't trust anyone.'

'Yeah, you're right. I just have to figure out which one of them is telling the truth. Then there's the evidence I looked through today. There was something about it that didn't seem right.'

'Sleep on it and it will come to you. Right, that's enough about work. What's the real reason you came to talk to me?'

'I just thought I'd call in. I don't have to have a reason, do I?'

'Of course not. But I know you too well. Why are you not with Daisy tonight?'

'We don't see each other every night. I expect she's busy and she knows I'm working a case.'

Fern raised her eyebrows.

'Daisy called around a few nights ago. It was a surprise visit and I'd had a smoke.'

'And?'

'Well, I could lose my job. I haven't heard from her since.'

'Did she say anything to you about it?'

'No, but I think she knows.'

'You worry too much. So you have a smoke to help you relax and sleep. It could be worse, you could be taking medication. I imagine some of the officers you work with take something. Antidepressants or alcohol. What do you expect with the things you all see.' Fern shook her head. 'You're not a druggy, no more than I am.'

'You use it to help with your arthritis. Anyway, it's still illegal.'

'You need to talk to Daisy. You've always been honest and if you're going to have a chance with her then it's no good keeping secrets. Even if she decides to call it a day it's better than living a lie. You have to be yourself. Now get yourself home and get some rest. You look tired.'

'OK.' Meadows gave his mother a hug and left the house. As he was getting into his car his phone rang.

'Hello, Inspector, it's Dr Hill. Sorry to call you so late. It's been a busy day.'

'No problem,' Meadows said.

'I've had the results back from the test on Aiden Edwards and his wife. You were right. It was GHB.'

'How are they both doing?'

'Much the same. We'll have to see how they do overnight. If they don't come round soon, the chances are they will remain in a coma. Any change and I'll call you.'

'Thank you.' Meadows ended the call. The talk with Daisy will have to wait, he thought, I need to work this out before anyone else gets hurt.

Chapter Twenty-seven

Jay pushed the cart of books towards the library. It used to be one of the tasks that he enjoyed. He had read most of the books and would recommend them to the other inmates. Before he was released on parole he'd even managed to start a book club. Now there was no pleasure in the books. Depression had taken hold of him, and he could see no way out. He had no future, and no control over his life. He would end it if he could, but he was being watched. I don't even have the choice when to die, he thought as he entered the library and started to replace the books.

One of the prison guards entered the room. 'Police to see you, Jay. Are you happy to talk to them?'

'What police?'

'DI Meadows and DC Edris. You don't have to see them.'

'It's fine. I'll talk to them.'

Jay followed the prison guard who took him to a room where Meadows and Edris were seated.

'Thank you for seeing us,' Meadows said as Jay took a seat.

'It makes a change to the day,' Jay said.

'I'm sorry you are back in here,' Meadows said. 'It wasn't my intention when we questioned you. I did make it clear to probation that you were not a suspect.'

Jay thought that Meadows sounded genuine. 'It's fine. The rules of probation are strict. If it hadn't been that it would've been something else. It always felt too good to last when I was out.'

Meadows leaned forward. 'The last time we spoke you told us to speak to Aiden Edwards. Aiden and his wife are both critically ill in hospital. They're both suffering from an overdose of GHB.'

Jay felt his stomach twist. This wasn't supposed to happen. He never intended anyone to get hurt. Did they think that he somehow arranged for Aiden and his wife to be attacked?

'If it's an alibi you want I have got a good one this time,' Jay said. 'I'm sorry for Aiden and his wife but I didn't have anything to do with it.'

'Why don't you tell us about the emails?' Meadows said.

'I...' What does it matter now, Jay thought. 'Mason sent them for me. I told him where to take the photos and what to say. I wrote to David and Callum when I was first convicted. I don't know if they got the letters. Everything was checked and I suppose they may have been destroyed. In any case, I didn't get a reply.' Jay could feel the helplessness he'd felt back then wash over him. No one had listened and his family had abandoned him.

'I never understood why they all lied about that day. Over the years I started to realise that they were just kids and like me they were scared. I thought, now time has passed, one of them would be willing to tell the truth. The emails were a prompt. A reminder of the part they played. I just wanted the case looked at again. Have a chance to clear my name. All it would take was for one of them to admit to bringing the GHB.' Jay sighed. 'Even one of them to back up the fact that Ruth cut her leg in the pool, and I got blood on my shorts helping her. They all saw it. I never thought they would turn on each other.'

'Who do you think killed Ruth?' Meadows asked.

The question took Jay by surprise. It wasn't that his opinion was being asked. It was the question itself that implied that the detective might have doubts over his guilt.

'You believe me?' Jay said.

'Certain things have come to light. We now know who supplied the GHB,' Meadows said. 'Given the new information we've received, we will be re-examining the original case.'

Jay felt his throat constrict. He opened his mouth to speak but no words would come. Instead he could feel the emotion of the last sixteen years building in his chest. Every tear that he had kept hidden gathered behind his eyes. He tried to gulp them back. Stuffed his fist in his mouth and bit down but he couldn't stop it. The dam burst.

Jay let himself cry. He didn't care that the two detectives or the prison guard watched his loss of control. He heard a chair scape back then felt a hand on his shoulder.

'It's OK, Jay,' Meadows said.

The hand on his shoulder, just that small gesture of kindness helped Jay regain control. Meadows asked the guard for some tea and a box of tissues was placed on the table.

'Thank you.' Jay picked up a tissue and blew his nose. 'I'm sorry.'

'You don't have to apologise,' Meadows said. 'Take your time.'

When the tea arrived Jay picked up the cup and took a sip. It was hot and too sweet, but it helped him to feel calmer. 'I'm OK. It's just I waited so long and had given up hope of the case being reopened.'

'We know now that GHB was put into a bottle of cherryade and shared out between you all. You said you felt different after you had eaten with the others. That's the reason why.'

'I remember sitting on the concrete slab looking at the water. Everything looked beautiful and I felt so calm.'

'You were sitting with Aiden?'

'Yes.'

'There is a photo of the two of you sitting together. Do you remember who took the photo?'

'Ruth, she had Naomi's camera. She called me and when I turned she snapped a photo. I don't know if she took any more. I think Naomi told her to put the camera away.'

'What happened after that?'

'David and Naomi were lying on the grass, kissing. Amber and Callum were doing the same. Ruth had spread out her towel and was lying on that. Then Callum and Amber stood up and said they were going for a walk. It wasn't hard to guess what they were planning. Amber said something to Naomi and then she got up and took David's hand. They went over the bridge and Amber and Callum walked down river. Aiden suggested that I take a walk. He looked over at Ruth. I wasn't interested in Ruth in that way so I left.'

'What was Ruth doing when you left?' Edris asked.

'Lying down on the grassy patch. I think she was sleeping.'

Edris wrote in his notebook. 'Where did you go?'

'I went over the bridge. David and Naomi were just inside the entrance to the tunnel. They were kissing and getting erm... physical. Naomi saw me and they both moved further inside. I walked past and up the path on the other side. There are large concrete blocks up there. Part of the old pulley system. I sat down. I had a couple of cigarettes left in the packet that Mason had given me, so I smoked one. I was looking around at the view from the top. Across the river I saw Amber and Callum. They were by the overhanging rock. Amber had taken her top off. I thought if they saw me they would think that I was watching them so I moved away. I sort of hung around a bit then I walked back down the path. It's steep and narrow in places with a drop over the side. I stopped by a tree and looked down at the river. When I looked back up I saw Ruth running up the bank to the mine.'

'Are you sure it was Ruth?' Meadows asked.

'Yeah, well it looked like Ruth. She was wearing pink trousers and her hair was in a ponytail. Naomi's hair was loose that day and Amber's hair is red so it must have been Ruth. She had Naomi's camera.'

'In her hand.'

'No, around her neck. I remember thinking it was funny at the time. She was running and the camera was bouncing off her chest. I thought it would hit her in the face.'

'So Naomi's camera had a strap?'

'Yeah, it was a big camera. With a protruding lens.' Jay cupped his hands. 'You know the type.'

'Did you see anyone following Ruth?' Meadows asked.

'No, I only saw her for a moment then I turned around. I wish now that I hadn't. Maybe if I'd carried on walking down and across the bridge I would have seen who went after her, or at least who came out of the mine. I decided not to go down. I thought Aiden and Ruth were messing around and I didn't want to be in the way. Callum and Amber were also over that side so I walked back up. There's a stile up the top. I jumped over and carried on walking.'

'How long were you gone?' Edris asked.

'I don't know. A while. I started to feel tired, and I was thirsty. I sat down for a moment then headed back. I met up with Callum. He said no one was around so he'd decided to go for a walk. We walked back together. I asked him where Amber was, and he said he'd left her down by the overhanging rock.'

'Did you talk about anything else?' Meadows asked.

'Nothing much. He was on about his holiday. He'd been away scuba diving. Then he said something about his phone. He said he was giving it to Aiden as he'd promised it to him if he kept Ruth occupied. He said it hadn't been worth the phone, but he'd give it anyway. We laughed because I said Aiden must have wanted the phone badly as he'd sent me away. I said it looked like Aiden had been playing tag or hide-and-seek with Ruth. For some reason that was hilarious to both of us. I guess we must have been still out of it.'

'What happened when you got back to the other side of the bridge?' Meadows asked.

'Amber and Naomi were in the pool near the waterfall. We saw them from the bridge. They got out and dried off just before David came back. I don't know where he'd been. Naomi asked if we had seen Ruth. I said she was probably with Aiden. We all sat around for a while then Aiden came back alone. Naomi got worried then. She thought Ruth might have gone off home. We tried to reassure her that it would take too long on the bus and Ruth had left her bag so she would come back. I think it was about five o'clock when we decided to look for her. Naomi was supposed to be home at six.'

'Is that when you went into the mine?' Meadows asked.

'Yeah, I said I'd seen her running up the bank. Naomi said Ruth wouldn't have gone in there alone. I offered to look anyway.'

'What reaction did you get from the others when you said you were going into the mine?' Meadows asked.

'No one offered to come with me or give me a torch. They all said they would split up and look for Ruth. When I came out of the mine they were all gone. I checked down by the overhanging rock then sat on the bank until the others came back. Naomi said she would have to call her parents and that we should go. Only Amber stayed.'

'When did you hear about Ruth being found?'

'The next morning, Callum came round. He said we should keep quiet about hanging out with the girls. He said Naomi would be in trouble and she had enough to deal with. I went along with the lie.'

'When you cycled home that day how were the other boys?' Meadows asked. 'Did you get the impression that something was wrong?'

'Not really. We were all quiet. Aiden more so, he didn't say a word on the way back. I had a headache. I guess from the alcohol and being in the sun all day. I just thought the others felt the same.'

'What went through your mind when you heard about Ruth's body being discovered in the mine? Did you think that one of the group had killed her?'

'No, honestly it never crossed my mind. I thought maybe someone had been lurking around that we hadn't seen, just waiting for an opportunity to catch one of us alone. It sounds stupid now, but you watch so many horror films as a teenager. The police came to ask questions and they took the clothes that I had been wearing that day. They said it was procedure and that they had collected clothes from the others. They said it was just to eliminate me. I didn't think much of it. I gave them my clothes and trainers. I couldn't believe what was happening when they arrested and charged me. The truth didn't seem to matter to them. I had already lied so I suppose they had no reason to believe me. That and the blood on my shorts and trainers.'

'We have statements now that you helped Ruth out of the water and that's how you got blood on your shorts. There was also other evidence,' Edris said. 'Your DNA was matched to skin cells and blood found on part of an old railway track in the mine.'

'When we all went into the mine earlier that day they dared me to go to the water alone. I fell on the way and scraped my shin. The torch wasn't very good. It must have been from then.'

'And the blood on your trainers?' Edris asked.

'I didn't have a torch when I went in to look for Ruth.' The thought of stepping in Ruth's blood sent a shiver through his body. 'I walked in as far as I could go. I kept to the right side as that had been the route we had taken earlier. I called out a few times. I couldn't see much so I gave up. It's so dark in there when you get further in. I said this at the time but…' Jay shrugged.

'You've had a long time to think about that day. I would imagine you've gone over it many times. When I asked you who you thought killed Ruth you didn't answer.'

'I don't want to point a finger at someone else. I know what that's like.'

'I understand,' Meadows said. 'You must have some suspicions.'

'The only thought I had was that I left Ruth with Aiden. Callum was with Amber, and David was with Naomi. I saw them leave before me. Then again I didn't see any of them until I came back from my walk. Just because I saw Ruth run up the bank it doesn't mean that she went into the mine at that time. It could have been later. They all say they saw me go into the mine alone and that was the truth. I honestly went in to look for her. I guess the assumption was I found her inside hiding and killed her. Although she had been missing for quite some time. Maybe they thought I killed her earlier and didn't want anyone going in and finding her. In any case I learnt the hard way what assumptions can lead to. Things are never what they appear. I really don't know who killed Ruth. I thought if I sent the emails one of them would be honest about that day and the truth would come out.'

'I can't promise that we'll find out exactly what happened that day,' Meadows said. 'We are getting closer to finding David's killer and that person or persons are also responsible for what happened to Ruth.'

'I hope you catch them this time,' Jay said.

'Just hang in there a bit longer,' Meadows said as he stood.

'Thank you for listening to me,' Jay said before he was led out of the room.

Jay felt lighter as he followed the guard back to the library. A small light of hope flickered now. It wasn't enough to dispel the darkness completely, but it was a start.

Chapter Twenty-eight

Edris looked back at the prison building. 'I feel sorry for him. Imagine spending half your life in that place for something you didn't do.'

'Sadly he's not the first to be in that situation. Even if we manage to find Ruth's killer and he is freed, his life will still be tainted. People will always have doubts. It's human nature. We need a confession, that way he'll have a chance.'

'I can't see that happening. The killer has stayed quiet this long. I thought perhaps Jay would have had an idea of who killed Ruth. We're still in the dark.'

Meadows stopped next to the car. 'What he said about the camera was interesting. Ruth had it when she was running towards the mine.'

'Yeah, but David had it when Callum saw him.'

'David had it in his hands. What we have to ask is, what happened to the strap? I suppose it could have broken at one end when Ruth was running and it fell to the ground. In that case the strap would still be attached by one end. And how did Naomi get the camera?'

'Well, I guess David gave it to her,' Edris asked.

'Why did David have the camera? The only way to find out is to ask Naomi,' Meadows said.

'She's not going to be happy about speaking to us again,' Edris said with a smile.

'There are a lot of things she is not telling us. I think it's time to push a little harder.'

* * *

Naomi answered the door in her dressing gown. Meadows noticed the dark circles beneath her eyes and the paleness of her skin.

'Sorry to disturb you. We need to ask you a few more questions.'

'I was sleeping. I've been on nights. Can you come back another time?'

Meadows thought that she looked too alert to have just woken up. 'I'm sorry, it can't wait.'

'Fine.' Naomi sighed and stood back to let them pass.

In the sitting room Naomi sat in an armchair with her arms folded. Meadows and Edris took a seat on the sofa. Meadows waited for Edris to open his notebook before speaking.

'We need to ask you a few more questions about the day your sister was murdered.' Meadows noticed Naomi shrink back into the chair. 'We've spoken to Callum and Amber and they told us what happened that day. I don't wish to embarrass you and I understand why you didn't tell us. We now know that you were all drugged with GHB and that would have made you lose any inhibitions.'

'I guess you are talking about me having sex with David. Jay may have drugged us all, but I'm still ashamed of my behaviour that day,' Naomi said.

'It wasn't Jay. That's all I can tell you.' Meadows sat forward. 'Naomi, you have nothing to be ashamed about. It's important that you talk us through what happened that day. I promise you we're not going to judge your actions. You went into the tunnel with David?'

'Yes, I went with him willingly. He didn't force me into anything.'

'How long were you in there together?'

'I don't know. Not that long. After we did the deed we just sat there for a while.'

'Who left first?' Meadows asked.

'David.'

'Did you follow him straight away?'

'No, for a while I couldn't be bothered to move. Then I felt cold, so I got dressed and went out.'

'Did you see David when you got outside?'

'No, I walked across the bridge. There was no one around so I went in the pool to erm... to wash. I stayed in the pool then Amber came in for a swim.'

'When you went into the tunnel with David, did you take your rucksack with you?'

'No, I don't think so. I'm sure I left it on the bank.'

'What about your camera?'

'My camera?' Naomi looked confused.

'Was your camera in your bag? You said in your original statement that you went off with Amber to take photographs. We now know that is not the case. So what did you do with the camera?' Meadows asked.

'I don't know. I guess it must have been in my rucksack because I gave it to the police. You probably still have it unless my parents collected it.'

'Did your camera have a strap?'

'Yes, a neck strap.'

'Was the strap with the camera when you gave it to the police?'

'Yeah, I think so. Everything at that time was a bit of a blur. I felt like I was in a nightmare. I'm sorry I can't be certain.'

'That's OK. Can you remember anyone else using your camera that day?'

'Ruth took some shots, and Amber used it to take photos of me and Ruth.'

'Any of the boys use the camera?'

'No.'

'After Amber came to join you in the pool, who came back next?'

'I don't know. You can't see from down there. When we got out to dry off, Callum, Jay, and David were there. Aiden came back last.'

'How did they seem to you? Were any of them acting out of character?'

'No, they were quieter than they had been earlier. We all sort of chilled out on the grass. I asked them if they had seen Ruth. They said no. I thought she must have gone off for a walk.'

'It must have been a terrible shock for you and your parents,' Meadows said.

Naomi nodded.

'You were sent off to live with your aunt before the trial and you stayed with her.'

'Yes, until I got a place of my own.'

'Why was that?'

'I'm sure I told you last time we spoke. My parents thought it best at the time.'

'I think there was a bit more to it than that,' Meadows said.

'No, if you met my parents you would understand.'

'We've spoken to your parents.'

'You've no right to do that,' Naomi said.

Meadows could see the fear in her eyes. 'We are looking into the original investigation. New evidence has come to light that casts doubt on Jay Parks' conviction.'

'What new evidence?'

Meadows ignored the question but was interested in her reaction. Her arms were folded, and her hands gripped her upper arms so tight you could see the tendons in the back of her hands. 'We are looking at all the evidence and retesting the clothes taken from each of you. We had to talk to your parents to inform them.'

'What did they say?'

'Perhaps it would be better to hear your version of events.'

'No.' Tears filled Naomi's eyes. 'I don't want to talk about it.'

'I appreciate it's difficult, but you must see how it looks. Your sister is murdered and a few months later you are sent away and don't return. Did they blame you for her murder?'

'Yes, I was her older sister and was supposed to take care of her.'

'It was more than that, wasn't it?' Meadows said.

Naomi nodded and let the tears come. She took a tissue from her dressing gown pocket and dabbed her eyes.

'They couldn't forgive you, could they?'

'No.'

'What was it they said, Edris?'

'A sin they couldn't forgive,' Edris said.

Naomi covered her face with her hands and sobbed.

'They knew what you did to Ruth,' Meadows said.

Naomi's hands flew away. 'What! No, I didn't do anything to Ruth. They meant...'

'What did they mean?'

'I was pregnant.'

The words stunned Meadows for a moment. A silence filled the room. It wasn't what he was expecting. He thought Naomi was about to confess.

'You were pregnant by David?' Meadows asked.

'Yes, there was no one else. That day at Dinas Rock was my first time. Just my luck that I would get myself into trouble. What are the chances?' Naomi shook her head. 'With everything going on I didn't notice I was late. My mother was the one to bring it up. I think she had her suspicions that I had meet up with the boys that day. She dragged me off to the doctors. It was so humiliating. Abortion wasn't an option with them, and they couldn't bear the shame of having me around. They sent me to stay with my auntie. She wasn't like them. She arranged for a termination. My parents never forgave her, or me. I took some time off school then went back to redo the year. A different school where no one knew me was the best thing that happened.'

'Did David know about the pregnancy or the termination?'

'No, I never saw him after that day. The only person that knew was Amber, and she kept my secret. I never told my husband.'

'It doesn't have to go any further,' Meadows said.

'Thank you.'

'One more thing. When you arrived at Dinas Rock you went into the mine with Ruth and Amber, is that correct?'

'Just inside the entrance to have a look.'

'Then you all went in as a group?'

'Yeah.'

'Did you go into any of the tunnels?'

Naomi bit her lip in concentration. 'No, I don't think so. No, Ruth wanted to go out. She hadn't really wanted to go in and explore with the others. She was fine just looking in the entrance but that was it. She left so I went with her.'

'What about David? Did he go with the others to explore?'

'I don't know, he might have. He came out not long after me.'

'But he did go in?'

'Yes.'

'OK.' Meadows stood. 'We'll leave you to get back to bed. Thank you for talking to us. I understand it's not easy to have the past dragged up.'

'Well, now you know everything. I suppose you can never keep a secret. It catches up with you. Perhaps it would have been better out in the open. I should have shamed my parents, but I was never brave enough. If they hadn't been so strict on us things could have turned out differently. They have never seen their grandchildren. Not once tried to contact me. I think even if Ruth hadn't died that day, I would have still been banished. I think the last thing my mother said to me was that I was a whore.'

Meadows' phone trilled and he excused himself.

'Hello, Inspector, it's Dr Hill. I thought you'd like to know that Aiden Edwards has woken up.'

'We're on our way,' Meadows said.

Chapter Twenty-nine

Aiden was sitting up in bed with his head propped up on a pillow when Meadows and Edris arrived. He had a drip in one arm and an oxygen tube clipped to his nose.

'Hello, Aiden,' Meadows said as he pulled up a chair. 'How are you feeling?'

Aiden shook his head. 'My wife still hasn't woken up and they won't let me get up to see her.'

'You need to rest for now,' Meadows said. 'I'm sure they will tell you as soon as there is any news. Do you remember what happened?'

'No, well, I remember getting home from work. Chrissy came in just after me. I opened a bottle of wine and poured us both a glass. We sat talking for a while. I felt good. We didn't even bother to make a start on dinner. I remember pouring another glass then nothing. I woke up here.'

'We believe the wine you drank was laced with GHB.'

'What? Why would anyone do that to me and Chrissy?'

'I don't think the wine was meant for your wife. Was it the bottle that was delivered to your office?'

'Yes, it was a gift.'

'From who?'

'I thought Callum had sent it.'

'Why?'

'There was a note signed with the initial C. Callum always liked to show off with money.'

'You hadn't been in contact with Callum for years. Didn't you find it odd that he would send you a gift?'

Aiden shrugged.

'Did you think it was a gift for keeping quiet?'

'I don't know what you mean.'

'I think you do,' Meadows said. 'Come on, Aiden, don't you think it's time you told us the truth? Isn't it enough that your wife is seriously ill? You both nearly died. We've spoke to the others. They've all come clean about that day at Dinas Rock. We know about the drinking and the cannabis. They all went off and left you alone with Ruth.'

'Oh God.' Aiden put his hand to his mouth and run his fingers over his chin. 'I didn't kill her.'

'Then tell us what happened.'

'When we were cycling to Dinas Rock that day David and Callum asked me to keep Ruth occupied. They wanted time alone with Amber and Naomi. I knew what they meant. I didn't want to go. It was supposed to be a day out with the boys. I turned round to go home. I wish I had but they persuaded me to go with them.'

'Callum offered you his phone in return for keeping Ruth busy,' Edris said.

'Yeah, it sounds pathetic now. Callum had the best of everything. He was getting a new phone for his birthday. The one he was going to give to me was only six months old. It was too tempting at the time, especially to a teenage boy whose parents struggled to pay the bills. I thought it would be easy, talk to her, maybe flirt a little. That's all.'

'You all went into the mine together. We know at this point Ruth wanted to go home. Did something happen in there that made her uncomfortable? Did you take the flirting a bit too far?' Meadows asked.

'No, she was unhappy about us smoking weed. We all knew what Naomi's parents were like. Ruth was younger than us and I suppose you would call her innocent. We didn't see it like that. She was spoiling our fun. After we all sat on the bank and had something to eat and drink she was OK. Really chilled out. Then she stripped off and jumped in the pool. We all clapped and cheered. We watched her try to climb up the rocks by the waterfall. She fell and was struggling. That's when Jay went in to help her. I was jealous. I was the one that was supposed to be keeping her occupied and she was all over Jay. She called him her hero. Looking back I think he was. If he hadn't gone in to help her, she probably would have drowned. The rest of us just looked on and laughed.'

'The others went off then and left you alone with Ruth,' Meadows prompted.

'Yes.' Aiden picked a glass of water from the bedside table and took a sip. 'I think I had too many shots of vodka and the weed on top. I... I didn't kill her. I'm tired. Can we do this another time?'

They were so close now that Meadows didn't want to stop the interview. It was clear that Aiden was ashamed of what happened next. Did he take it too far and accidentally kill Ruth? Meadows wondered. If I let him think that he had some justification for his actions maybe he'll tell us.

'It wasn't just the cannabis and alcohol,' Meadows said. 'You all took GHB.'

'No,' Aiden said. 'I didn't take any other drugs.'

'You all shared the food and drink?'

'Yes.'

'The cherryade you drank was laced with GHB.'

Aiden shook his head. 'I honestly didn't know. That's why I didn't feel myself.'

'You would have felt relaxed and aroused,' Meadows said. 'It's understandable that you would act out of character. Is that what happened? You were left alone with Ruth, and you were tempted?'

'Yes.' It was almost a whisper. 'I'm so ashamed. Ruth was lying there and I... well, David and Callum had gone off with the girls. I knew what they were getting up to. I had just seen Ruth in her underwear and I... I wanted sex.'

'Did you attack her?' Meadows asked.

'No, it wasn't like that. She was lying on her stomach. I went up to her and touched her. She was half asleep and she didn't seem to mind. She turned over and I kissed her. I came on a bit strong, and she got upset.'

'What do you mean by a bit strong?' Edris asked.

Colour rose in Aiden's face. 'I felt her up. Tried to get my hand up her blouse. She started to struggle and her blouse tore. I'm not a pervert. I've never forced myself on a woman. It was just that one time. I lost control for a moment, but I stopped. She got up and put on her rucksack and grabbed Naomi's camera. She was crying. She said she was going to tell Naomi and was going home to tell her parents. I tried to stop her. I grabbed hold of her rucksack, but she wriggled out of the straps. I dropped the bag on the floor and chased her over the bridge. She went into the tunnel and I let her go. I didn't follow her in.'

'What did you do?' Meadows asked.

'I went back over the bridge and up the other side to the main path. I took the path to Penderyn. I found another mine. I went inside and hid out there. I dozed off for a while. I was cold and stiff when I woke. I was going to go home but I'd left my rucksack down by the waterfall. I was hoping that they all would have left but they were just sitting on the bank. They asked me if I'd seen Ruth. I didn't tell them what had happened. I wanted to go home and get away from them all. I figured I wouldn't have to see any of them until it was time to go back to school. By then I hoped they would forget about it. If it came up, I would deny it and say Ruth tried to kiss me and I wasn't interested. That was my plan. Then Ruth was found, and I was scared. I told David and Callum I had left Ruth with Jay.'

'Jay was accused of attacking Ruth,' Meadows said. 'You could have explained how her blouse got torn.'

Aiden looked horrified. 'I would have got the blame for killing her. It would have been me in prison.'

'So, you let Jay take the blame,' Meadows said.

'There was evidence against Jay. It's not like my silence put him in prison. All these years I've been ashamed of what I did. I could never forget that day.'

'Did you tell all this to David when he came to see you?'

'Not all of it. I told him Ruth was with me and then she went into the tunnel. I didn't tell him why.'

'What did he say?'

'He asked if I'd seen anything else. I told him no and that Jay knew I was alone with Ruth and that's why he sent the emails. He said not to worry as he knew I didn't kill Ruth.'

'Did he say who he thought had?'

'No, just that it wasn't Jay. He said I should tell the police the truth when they came to talk to me.'

'Did David say he was going to talk to the police?'

'Not exactly but that's the impression I got. I tried to persuade him to leave things as they were. Jay was out of prison, so it didn't matter.'

'One more thing,' Meadows said. 'When you all went in to explore the mine, are you sure that David was with you?'

'Yes.'

'And he went down to the water's edge in the flooded tunnel?'

'Yes.'

'What about Naomi?'

'No, she only went in one of the tunnels. She didn't go to the water. She went back with Ruth and Amber.'

'OK. I'm going to send someone to take your statement.'

'What will happen now. Will I be charged?'

'That will depend. You withheld vital information in a murder enquiry. You also had motive and opportunity to kill both Ruth and David.'

'I didn't kill them. I've told you everything now.'

'You lied to us on more than one occasion.'

'But I was drugged. Someone tried to kill me and my wife.'

'Which you could have done yourself. While the investigation is ongoing you are still a person of interest.' Meadows stood up. 'We'll be applying for a warrant to search your house.'

'Fine, look all you want. You won't find anything.'

'We'll leave you to get some rest now,' Meadows said.

'You were a bit hard on him,' Edris said as they walked back to the car.

'He forced himself on Ruth. Then put the blame on Jay. It serves him right. It's his turn to know what it feels like to be a suspect, and no one believes you.'

'Do you think he killed Ruth and David?'

'I don't know. We have all the witness statements, the physical evidence, but no crime scene in Ruth's case. It makes things more difficult. I want to go up to Dinas Rock. It will give us some perspective on the positions of them all and the view they had.'

'In the morning?' Edris asked.

'No, I think we should go now.'

Chapter Thirty

Meadows stood on the concrete platform that overhung the bank of the river. The recent rainfall had swollen the river and the waterfall thundered into the pool. He let his eyes trail the water. It cascaded over a ledge to a second pool then bubbled over rocks re-joining the river. It was mesmerizing.

'It's going to get dark soon,' Edris said.

'We've got about an hour. Besides, we've got torches.' He turned to face Edris. 'Unless you're sitting or standing here, or standing on the bridge, you can't see down into the pool.'

'Your point?' Edris asked.

'I don't know. If Callum came from that direction,' – he pointed down river – 'he wouldn't see if Aiden, or one of the others, were in the pool washing off. Trying to get rid of any evidence.'

'You can't completely wash away bloodstains,' Edris said.

'No but they could have tried. They could certainly clean the soles of their shoes.' Meadows moved to the right. 'This part slopes down. Amber and Callum wouldn't have seen anything until they got to this level.'

Edris walked over to the grass patch at the foot of the bank that led up to the mine. 'This is where Ruth was lying. They found the buttons from her blouse here.'

'If Aiden is to be believed, she struggled with him and ran across the bridge.'

Meadows tried to visualise Ruth's path as she ran from Aiden. He walked over the bridge. The entrance to the tunnel was still cordoned off with tape and flowers were laid at the side. He looked back. 'If Aiden left Ruth here and made his way back to the main path, he wouldn't have seen Ruth cross back over and run to the mine. If she ran into the tunnel as Aiden said she would have come across David and Naomi in a compromising position. It wouldn't have been long after they entered the tunnel.'

'It depends how far in they were, and if David took his torch,' Edris said.

'If she did see them then she would have had a shock,' Meadows said.

'Where are you going now?' Edris asked as Meadows followed the path around the side of the tunnel.

'Jay came this way.' Meadows climbed up the bank and stopped at a large oak tree. 'He had a clear view of the mine entrance from here,' he called down. 'It was summer so the tree foliage would have been thicker. Once he moved he wouldn't have seen anyone following Ruth.'

'Aiden could have been waiting over the other side for her,' Edris said as Meadows climbed back down.

Meadows nodded in agreement. 'The next one on the scene was Callum. He claims he saw David sitting on the bank by the mine entrance and had Naomi's camera in his hands. What if Ruth tried to take a photo of David and Naomi in the tunnel? There were photos that were too dark to see any detail. Naomi and David wouldn't want anyone seeing those photos. Maybe David was checking to see if she managed to capture any and was deleting them.'

'So David chases Ruth out of the tunnel?' Edris asked.

'Maybe. He would have been in a state of undress. He'd be a minute or so behind her which is why Jay wouldn't have seen him. Come on.'

They walked back across the bridge and Meadows made his way up the bank. He stepped over the broken fence and to the mine entrance.

'Whoa, we're not going in there, are we?' Edris stopped at the fence.

'Yep. Sixteen years ago we would've been going in to look at the crime scene. I want to get a feel of the place.'

'Feel? Dark and spooky. What more do you need to know?'

Meadows laughed. 'Come on.'

An icy draft ruffled Meadows' hair as he stepped through the entrance of the mine.

'It's bloody freezing in here,' Edris said pulling up his hood.

'Plenty of light here,' Meadows commented. 'You can see quite far in without a torch.'

'OK, you've seen now,' Edris said.

'Anyone would think you were scared.'

'Did you read the sign? Danger, does that mean anything to you?'

'It's been here over a hundred years. I don't think we are in any immediate danger. We'll stick to the left-hand side. It's the path they took and leads to the tunnel where Ruth was found.'

As they walked the light faded and they switched on the torches. Meadows shone his torch around. The beam picked up overturned trams, years of rust leaving them laced with holes. The ceiling was held up by interspaced pillars. Thick trunks of layered sandstone.

'Beautiful colours,' Meadows said running his fingers over a line of quartz. He trailed the beam outwards, and the tunnels could be seen branching off and disappearing into darkness. 'It's like the Mines of Moria in here.'

'Yeah, and look what happened there,' Edris said.

'Goblins,' Meadows said putting the torch under his chin and grinning.

As they moved further in the light from the entrance faded, and darkness closed around them. Meadows could hear Edris breathing close behind.

'Stop creeping behind me,' Meadows said.

'I'm not creeping. I'm staying close. It's always the one at the back that gets it.'

'Then go in front of me?'

'I'm not going first.'

A few steps further and Meadows stopped. 'It was about here that they found a pool of blood and the trail leading into the tunnel.'

'Poor kid,' Edris said.

Meadows tried not to think of the scene that happened in this spot. The fear Ruth must have felt. 'Turn off your torch for a moment.' He pushed the switch on his own.

They were thrown into almost complete darkness. It took a few moments for their eyes to adjust and even then visibility was poor.

'Jay wouldn't have been able to see much. Unlikely he would have seen the blood. He didn't go much further in than this when he was looking for Ruth.'

'That also means the killer wouldn't have been able to see,' Edris said switching on his torch.

'If David ran from the tunnel or Callum or Aiden chased her in, I can't see they would have had a torch. Maybe Ruth stopped here because she couldn't see her way any further.'

'Unless they saw her go in and they grabbed a torch to look for her. They knew she wouldn't be able to get out without being seen,' Edris said.

An idea came to Meadows. 'If both Callum and David killed Ruth then maybe David was going to confess and that's why he was killed.'

'Then why was David going around asking questions?'

'Good point. In any case whoever killed Ruth would have needed a torch to move her to the water. Let's see how far in they had to go.'

They moved along with neither speaking until the ground sloped and they entered the tunnel on the far left. They came to a smooth surface of water which was only disturbed by the odd drop of water. It made a plink plunk sound which echoed in the silent mine.

Near the edge of the water the beam from the torch picked up the ground below before it disappeared into inky blackness.

'Looks deep,' Meadows said. 'Probably slippery. Ruth's body was pushed someway in. There is no current which means they would've got into the water and pushed or pulled her as they swam. The water would've been freezing and I imagine it was not easy to get out, especially if they were fully clothed.'

'Perhaps they stripped off to move the body and that's how they managed to avoid getting blood on their clothes.'

'It's possible, and given that the wound was at the back of the head, blood would have hit the ground and not spattered her attacker,' Meadows said.

A clink clunk sound coming from the next tunnel made them both jump.

'What was that?' Edris asked.

'Sounded like a stone falling.'

'Let's go,' Edris said. 'This place gives me the willies.'

* * *

After dropping Edris at his flat Meadows drove home. His mind was whirring. Now he could picture the group at Dinas Rock. The laughter, the sun, then everything turning sour. The problem came with the fact that none of the witnesses were reliable. If he could trust Aiden and it was the case that Ruth ran into the tunnel, then the most logical explanation was that either David or Naomi chased after Ruth. If it was David then it was likely he had help from Callum. Maybe David didn't chase Ruth and Callum met up with her on the other side. Then again Aiden could have been waiting. All these thoughts went through his mind as he turned down the track that led to his cottage. He was tired and hungry and knew that he would spend best part of the night trying to figure out the case.

The first thing he noticed was Daisy's car parked outside. The curtains were drawn with light glowing behind. Meadows opened his front door and was met by the smell of frying onions.

'This is a nice surprise,' Meadows said as he walked into the kitchen.

'Good, I hope you don't mind.' Daisy turned down the heat before turning to Meadows and kissing him.

'Coming home to dinner being cooked. What's there to mind?'

'It's just stir fry. You've got just enough time to get changed.'

Meadows took a quick shower then joined Daisy at the table. She poured herself a glass of wine as he filled his glass with elderflower water.

Meadows loaded his fork and took a bite. 'It's good.'

Daisy smiled. 'I know you've been busy with the case, so I thought I'd treat you.'

'I thought you were avoiding me,' Meadows said.

'Why would you think that? I know what you're like when you are working a case. I'm not one of those clinging women. We both need our space.'

Meadows was tempted to leave it at that and not spoil the evening. Mum's right, he thought. It's no good keeping secrets. He'd seen the damage it can cause.

'The last time you came around I–'

Daisy held up her hand. 'You're in the middle of an investigation. Probably stressed. Do you really want to get into a discussion about your box of weed?'

'Erm… right. So you saw it?'

'Saw it? I smelled it.' Daisy laughed.

Meadows was relieved that she didn't seem angry. 'I was going to tell you.'

'I knew you would eventually. It's not the sort of thing you bring up on a first date. Don't worry about it.'

'I thought you'd be shocked.'

'Why? Given your background and the fact you spend your holidays in Peace Valley, I would be naive to think you've never smoked. No one is perfect.'

'I'm far from perfect and I know I could lose my job.'

'You've never gone to work stoned, have you?'

'No. I only have a smoke in the evenings. It helps me sleep.'

'Well there you go. I've never seen you touch a drop of alcohol, and you don't say anything about me drinking a glass or two of wine.'

'That's different. Cannabis is illegal and alcohol isn't.'

'But is it any better than smoking a joint? I've known plenty of people with a drink problem. I've seen the results of alcohol on the body. Injuries from a drunken fight. Wives beaten to death by a drunken husband. Can't say I've seen the same result from a joint. Have you ever dealt with a case where the perpetrator was stoned?'

'Erm, just stoned? Herbal cannabis? No, I can't think of any. When you put alcohol in the mix or skunk then it's a different case.'

'There you go. I imagine that you stick to the home-grown variety. No added chemicals. I'm not saying what you're doing is right but it's not my place to judge. You have so many good qualities I'd be an idiot to walk away over this. All I'd say is that you need to build a shed in the garden.'

'A shed?'

'Yeah, to smoke. What I don't see I don't know,' Daisy said with a smile. 'Also, can you imagine Edris turning up unexpected and catching a whiff of cannabis?'

Meadows laughed. 'He'd have a fit.'

'He looks up to you. You don't want to shatter that image.'

'No, a shed it is then.'

'It can be your thinking room. Now that's out the way I think we should take a break. Have a weekend away.'

'I'm up for that. I'll book some time when I've finished with this case.'

'Are you getting any closer to finding out who killed David Harris?'

'I have a fairly good idea. The same person that killed Ruth Williams. I need to check out a few things in the morning. I keep coming back to one person, but it doesn't make sense. For a start I can't see how they could kill Ruth and move her body without a single speck of blood getting on their clothing.'

'Well, it could be that it wasn't picked up in forensics first time around. Techniques have come a long way in sixteen years. Could the killer have changed clothes?'

Meadows thought of the photographs lined up in the conference room. There was something that troubled him about them, but he hadn't been able to figure it out. How could I have missed it? he thought.

'I'm going to have to go. I need to check something.'

'Go, I'll be here when you get back,' Daisy said.

Meadows got into his car and drove towards the station. If I'm right, the case is about to be turned upside down, he thought.

Chapter Thirty-one

Meadows yawned and took a sip of his coffee. He rarely fuelled himself with caffeine but having spent the best part of the night going over the evidence he needed a boost. The time had dragged for the past hour, and he felt a sense of excitement and urgency to share his discovery with the team.

Blackwell was first in followed by Edris, then Paskin and Valentine arrived together.

'Grab yourselves a tea or coffee and meet me in the conference room,' Meadows said.

When the team with cups in hands gathered around the incident board Meadows sorted his notes. He then briefed them on the interview with Jay, Naomi, and Aiden before turning to Blackwell. 'How did you get on with the search of Callum's house?'

'Nothing much. He wears a size-ten boot which is the same size as the prints found near David Harris' body. I've sent them in for comparison. Some woollen gloves, both male and female. Wrong colour but worth a try to match the fibres. I guess it was a bit too much to hope for a stash of GHB.'

'He could have got rid of the gloves,' Valentine said. 'Most people have more than one pair of boots so he could have ditched a pair.'

'We have nothing to link him to either David's murder or the murder of Ruth Williams. The same applies to the others,' Meadows said. 'What we do have is a different version of events for the day Ruth was murdered to the one they all gave originally. Except for David.'

'Still doesn't mean they are telling the truth,' Paskin said. 'One of them is still lying.'

'Yes,' Meadows agreed. 'I looked again at all the statements and listed the common elements. They all went into the mine that day. They all explored further in according to Amber, Callum, and Aiden. Naomi says she didn't go any further than the entrance. She claims she followed Ruth out. Yet Ruth's prints led down to the second tunnel on the right. SOCO concentrated mainly on Ruth's prints and then on Jay's. Then there are David's footprints. Edris, do you want to talk over what you found yesterday?'

'I didn't find anything,' Edris said.

'Exactly,' Meadows said. 'No prints matched to David's footwear.'

'So David didn't go into the mine,' Valentine said.

'According to the others he did. It's the only thing they agree on. Why would they lie about it? They were all together at that point.'

'Wouldn't that have been picked up in the original investigation?' Valentine asked.

'No, they were looking at what was there. Not what wasn't there. At that time not one of them admitted to exploring the mine together. All they were interested in was eliminating the prints that were in the mine. It may have been a different case if David was a suspect. Once they had a bloody footprint matched to Jay's they concentrated on that. I think David gave a different pair of trainers to the police.' Meadows pointed to a photo on the board. 'This one was taken with Naomi's camera. I enlarged the image. It was taken from a distance but if you look closely, you can see they look in good condition. If you look at the ones taken for evidence, you can see a tear on the side. They're on the table.'

Blackwell picked up the trainers and looked at them. He passed them to Valentine before looking closely at the photograph on the board.

'OK, same make, older pair,' Blackwell said.

'People often have a pair of comfy shoes that have worn out, so they buy the same ones again. The question is why would David give a different pair to the police?'

'Maybe he gave the wrong one by accident,' Paskin said.

'That's a possibility,' Meadows said.

'There is also the fact that he had no blood or other evidence on his clothes,' Blackwell said.

'I think we can agree that we don't always send all the clothes from a suspect for testing. It's mainly the outer clothes. Not underwear and socks.'

The team nodded.

'If you look at this photograph of the boys on the bridge.' Meadows tapped the board. 'Look at what they are wearing. David is wearing cropped cargo trousers and a T-shirt. Callum and Aiden are dressed in a similar fashion. Then you have this photo of Aiden and Jay. Jay is wearing shorts and Aiden looks like he is wearing swimming trunks. The boys knew they would be swimming that day. David is likely to have taken something to swim in.'

'OK, if he did kill Ruth then do you think it's because she saw him having it away with Naomi?' Blackwell said.

'I think he would've wanted to protect Naomi. He may have been trying to get the camera from Ruth and didn't mean to kill her. He wouldn't have had time to get dressed fully. It's also possible that when he went into the tunnel with Naomi he was only wearing swimming trunks. I've checked the clothes taken from David. There is no shorts or swimming trunks. Just his T-shirt, cargo trousers and trainers,' Meadows said.

'It doesn't make sense though,' Valentine said. 'If David killed Ruth, then why was he murdered? What's the motive?'

'He didn't act alone,' Edris said.

'Callum,' Blackwell said.

'I don't think so,' Meadows said. 'I think Naomi either helped him cover it up or she was the one to kill Ruth.'

'You're grasping at straws now,' Blackwell said. 'No physical evidence and she has a tight alibi for the morning David was murdered.'

'That's the only sticking point,' Meadows said. 'Just hear me out. When I first saw the pictures taken with Naomi's camera I thought something was off. It's just taken me a while to figure out what. I came back in last night to look at the photographs again and read through all the statements. Look at this photograph of Amber and Naomi and tell me what you see.' Meadows took the photo from the board and placed it on the conference table. He put one of Ruth taken the same day alongside it.

'What am I looking at?' Blackwell asked.

'Valentine? Paskin? Anything strike you as odd?' Meadows asked.

'Well, Naomi is dressed near enough the same as her sister. More like a thirteen-year-old than a fifteen-year-old,' Paskin said. 'Shapeless clothes.'

'I'm thinking she would have made more of an effort if she was meeting her boyfriend. Next to Amber she looks, I don't know, plain, dowdy,' Valentine said. 'You wouldn't have caught me dead in sandals like that at her age. A tighter fitting T-shirt and roll up the trousers would have made a bit of a difference I suppose.'

'But if her parents were strict then she wouldn't have had a choice,' Paskin said.

'When we interviewed Amber she said that Naomi's aunt bought her clothes and she kept them hidden. She said on occasions Naomi would get changed at her house before they met up with the boys. I think Naomi had a change of clothes and shoes in her rucksack. That's why her footprints are only at the entrance to the mine. They go in to take a couple of photos when they arrive. She gets changed in time for the boys to join them. She then changes again before the police arrive. The clothes go back in her rucksack, and no one knows about them. She then just has to get rid of them when she gets home. I've checked. There was an unidentified size-five print found near where Ruth was attacked and by the water's edge. The sole shape is consistent with a wedged sandal.'

'Do you think that David wanted to confess, and Naomi killed him?' Paskin asked.

'Yes, although I'm not sure why he wanted to talk to the others first. Maybe he was planning to take the blame and not involve Naomi.'

'OK, but she still can't be in two places at once,' Blackwell said.

'It's busy at the hospital. Would she be missed if she sneaked out for a couple of hours?' Meadows asked. 'Why don't you and Valentine check it out? Use your charm. See if you can find out who was on shift with her that day and if there is a chance that she could've left unnoticed. That just leaves Amber. She is the only one who would know if Naomi changed clothes that day.'

Blackwell and Valentine left for the hospital and Meadows tried Amber's number. It went straight to voicemail. He waited ten minutes before trying again but had the same result. He tried her landline and an uneasy feeling crept over him when he heard the answering machine.

'Paskin, can you find a number for Amber's husband please?'

'On it.'

'Edris, call Naomi and find out where she is.'

While he waited Meadows placed a call to Callum who confirmed that David was in his swimming trunks when he saw him sitting on the bank of the mine with the camera.

'Amber's husband's number,' Paskin said handing Meadows a piece of paper. 'Jordan Richards.'

'Thanks,' Meadows said as he punched in the number. He was relieved to hear a voice answer. He introduced himself and chose his words carefully.

'I'm trying to get hold of your wife. We need to check out a few details on a witness statement she gave us.'

'Witness?' Jordan said. 'Are you sure it's Amber you want to speak to?'

Meadows could hear children playing in the background. It sounded like Jordan was in a playground. 'Yes, it's an old case. Her phone is going straight to voicemail. It's important we talk to her today. Do you know where we can reach her?'

'Erm… I'm not sure. She's out somewhere. She did say something about where she was going. I wasn't paying much attention.'

Meadows tapped his fingers on the desk. 'Anything you remember will be useful.'

'Oh yeah, she had flowers. Said something about meeting an old friend. Paying her respects. Something like that. She was talking about that guy that got murdered, David Harris.'

'OK, that's great. Thanks for your help.' Meadows ended the call. 'I think she's gone to Dinas Rock.'

'Naomi isn't answering her phone and she not in work. Finished her shift at eight this morning,' Edris said.

Meadows grabbed his coat. 'Come on, we better get up there. Let's hope Amber has gone alone.'

Meadows drove his car with a sense of urgency. Dinas Rock was a forty-five-minute drive from the station. Even with the lights on and going as fast as was safe, he felt it was taking too long to get there. He was aware that it could already be too late for Amber. With luck on their side she wouldn't be too far in front of them.

'Do you really think that Naomi would kill Amber?' Edris asked as the car veered around a corner.

'We have no evidence to arrest Naomi and Amber is the only witness if she did change clothes. We told Naomi yesterday that we had sent off the clothes for testing. It would only need a slip from Amber.'

'But if that was the case why didn't Amber tell us about the clothes?'

'She had no reason to. Naomi wasn't a suspect.'

Meadows' phone rang. He hit accept and Blackwell's voice filled the car.

'Bit of luck at the hospital. The first person we spoke to was on shift with Naomi the morning David was murdered. She said Naomi got a migraine that morning and used the rest room. She covered for her. She doesn't remember seeing Naomi before she left.'

'Thanks,' Meadows said. 'We're just pulling into Dinas Rock car park. I can see Amber and Naomi's cars.'

'I'm on my way in case you need back-up,' Blackwell said.

Meadows jumped out of the car and set off at a sprint up the path. He didn't have time to change into his boots and as he started up the rocky incline he could feel his feet sliding beneath him. He gripped the handrail and pushed on. By the time he reached the top his thigh muscles were screaming in protest, but he didn't pause. He ran along the path. Took the turning and ran downwards. Near the bottom he lost his footing. He put out his hands to break his fall. He felt the impact in his wrist but scrambled up to run the last few yards to the bridge. Naomi and Amber were halfway across.

'Naomi!' Meadows called as he tried to catch his breath.

Both women turned. As Amber looked towards Meadows Naomi put one hand around her throat. In the other she held a syringe against her neck. 'Don't move,' Naomi said.

Chapter Thirty-two

Meadows put up both hands to indicate to Naomi that he wouldn't move any closer. While he caught his breath, he assessed the situation. It would take seconds for Naomi to inject Amber. He guessed she had GHB in the syringe. Once it was in Amber's bloodstream there would be nothing they could do to help her. Edris came to a stop behind Meadows and bent over panting. Naomi's eyes were wild and her hand shook. The needle scraped against Amber's skin.

'Naomi, please let Amber go,' Meadows said. 'I know you don't want to hurt her. She was your best friend. All these years she has kept quiet. She didn't tell a soul about you getting pregnant.'

Naomi stepped back pulling Amber with her.

'There's nowhere for you to go,' Meadows said. 'Let Amber go with Detective Edris, and you and I can talk. Amber has a family. Two small children. I know you're frightened but Amber doesn't deserve this.'

'No,' Naomi said. 'She has to confess first.'

'What?' Amber struggled and the needle pierced her skin.

'Amber, stay still,' Meadows said.

'There is enough shit in this syringe to kill you before you get off the bridge,' Naomi said. 'Tell them what you did. Tell them you killed Ruth and David.'

'I didn't.' Amber's eyes were wide with terror.

Doubt began to creep into Meadows' mind. Could he have made a mistake? Could Amber and David have killed Ruth? Girls often swapped clothes. Perhaps Amber was wearing Naomi's outfit. No that doesn't make sense, he thought. She would've had to come up with an excuse not to give the clothes back. It's Naomi's footprints that are missing. Naomi is the one that lied about exploring the mine.

'We know what happened,' Meadows said. 'We know you had a change of clothes. Amber was the only one other than Ruth who saw you get changed. You wanted to look your best before David arrived that day. You changed back into your spare clothes before the police arrived, didn't you?'

'You bitch,' Naomi said.

'Amber didn't tell us,' Meadows said. 'She never betrayed your friendship. I doubt she knew the significance of the information she had. Amber wasn't the only one there that day. Not the only one who knew what you were wearing. Amber wasn't the only one to keep your secrets. David protected you all these years. Even to the end. He was going to take the blame. That's why he was going around asking questions. He wanted to know what everyone had seen. That way when he confessed, his story would be believable.'

Meadows saw the surprise in Naomi's eyes. Then the doubt.

'You don't understand. David killed my sister. He had to pay for what he did, and she helped cover it up.'

'I didn't, I swear to you,' Amber said.

'Amber was with Callum,' Meadows said. 'By the time she came back to the waterfall you were in the pool washing off your sister's blood.'

'Stop it,' Naomi screeched. 'You don't know what you're talking about.'

'Then tell me what happened,' Meadows said. 'Let Amber go. This has to end now. Enough people have been hurt. What are you going to do? Kill everyone that was there that day? It's too late to stop the truth coming out. You silenced David and you tried to silence Aiden. It didn't work. Aiden woke up, he told us what he saw that day. Is that why you tried to kill him? He saw Ruth go into the tunnel. She saw you and David together. You must've been scared of what she would tell your parents. You were young, you'd been given drugs. I understand you weren't yourself that day. You've worked so hard to make up for what you did. You dedicate yourself to your work looking after others.'

Edris took a small step forward. 'Let Amber come with me. I promise we'll leave. Let me take her home to her children.'

Naomi looked from Meadows to Edris. 'I'm sorry,' she said. She moved the needle from Amber's neck and gave her a shove.

Amber flew across the bridge to Edris.

Meadows turned his head for a moment to watch Edris lead Amber away. Valentine was standing out of Naomi's view.

'Where's Blackwell?' Meadows mouthed.

Valentine pointed down river. Meadows understood. Blackwell was going to try and cross the river and come at Naomi from behind. When he turned his attention back to Naomi she had the needle against the side of her neck and tears poured down her face.

'Don't do this, Naomi,' Meadows said. 'Think of your children. You don't want them growing up without a mother.'

'I'm going to lose them. I'm going to lose everything.'

'You don't know that.' Meadows eyes flicked to the bank on the opposite side. There was no sign of Blackwell.

He would have to keep Naomi talking and distracted if Blackwell were to have a chance to sneak up behind her. The water rushing into the pool should give Blackwell some cover, he thought.

'David came to see you after you all received the emails,' Meadows said. 'I think he couldn't live with the guilt.'

'He told me what he did,' Naomi said. 'He killed Ruth.'

'What's the point of lying now?' Meadows said. 'I think you owe David the truth. He tried to help you. He made sure that the others didn't know anything. He was going to confess and take all the blame. Don't let that happen. Don't let his wife and children's memory of him be tainted. Did he ask you to meet him here, and tell you what he planned to do?'

'No, that was my suggestion.'

'You brought GHB with you.'

'Yes, because he had given it to Ruth.'

'It was Callum that spiked the drinks,' Meadows said. 'David knew that. I'm sure he would have told you.'

Naomi dragged the needle across her skin. Meadows could see the track mark it made on her neck. 'So, you met David here. How did you persuade him to go into the tunnel?'

'I said I wanted to look. That it had been the place where it all started. He followed me in. I didn't have a torch. We used our phones. David was in a state. He was drinking most of the time. He said he wanted to go to the police. I didn't want to see him go to prison. I knew he wanted to die.'

'Did he tell you that?'

'He said he couldn't live with himself. I had the syringe in my pocket. I pretended to trip. When he helped me up I put one arm around his neck and injected him with my other hand. He didn't fight me. He just lay down quietly. I stayed with him until he went. I saw how peaceful he was. Then I changed into my husband's boots that I had hidden in my rucksack. I walked around a bit. I thought it would cause confusion. I didn't want David to die but it was the only way.'

'He had a family,' Meadows said.

'So do I and that's why I can't face going to prison. I don't want to be around when they find out.' Naomi pushed the needle.

'You owe them an explanation,' Meadows said. 'They need to know why. Only you and David knew what really happened that day. I can take a guess but I'd rather you tell me. I'm sure you didn't intend to kill Ruth. I understand the life you had. The restrictions imposed by your parents. You arrange a day out to be with your boyfriend and they make you take your sister. You must have been upset that day. Ruth giving you disapproving looks, threatening to tell your parents that you met up with a group of boys.'

'No, it wasn't like that. Ruth wasn't like that. She wasn't allowed to do anything. Not allowed to have friends. She wouldn't have told our parents about the boys.'

'She was upset after you explored the mine.'

'Yes, she wanted to go home. It's because we were smoking. She didn't like it. I told her I would take her home after we had eaten. I just wanted a bit more time with David. I would've taken her. She was the one who started messing around. She stripped off. I didn't care. I was happy. She seemed to be having a good time and it meant that we could stay. Then I went into the tunnel with David. We weren't in there that long. I thought I heard Ruth call my name, but we were too busy to take any notice. Then a flash went off. I was naked with David on top of me. It took me a moment to realise what was happening. The flash kept going off. Ruth said something about me setting her up. She screamed that she didn't want sex with him. I didn't know what she was talking about. I pushed David off and got up. She ran off when I was putting my clothes on. By the time I was crossing the bridge she was scrambling up the bank and disappeared into the mine.' Naomi trembled and the needle scratched her neck.

Meadows could see Blackwell pulling himself up on the opposite bank.

'David followed you?'

'Yes. We went into the mine. Ruth wasn't far in. She was crying. She said she was going to show Mum and Dad what I had done. I told her to give me the camera, but she wouldn't. She turned and ran further into the mine. It was dark. I caught up with her and grabbed the camera. She was pulling away. I yanked on the strap. The strap broke and she fell backwards. The camera landed on the floor. I thought Ruth was messing around when she didn't move. I knelt beside her and shook her. David was standing there just staring. I told him to go and get a torch. When he came back I saw the blood. I was kneeling in it. It was all over my hands. I wiped them on my top.'

'Why didn't you call for help?' Meadows asked.

'I thought she was dead. It didn't look like she was breathing. I didn't know what to do. David kept saying we've killed her. He said we needed to hide her. It was his idea to take her to the water. We dragged her. David went into the water and pulled her along. I didn't know she was still alive. David killed her by putting her in the water. That water was so cold. David was shivering when he got out. We left her there to die alone.' A tear slid down Naomi's cheek.

Blackwell had reached the bridge. 'Then you went to the river,' Meadows said.

'Yes, we were careful getting out of the mine. We walked into the second tunnel first, then retraced our steps from earlier that day. David peeked outside of the entrance. There was no one around so I ran down to the water. I took off my clothes and tried to scrub them. David came down after me. It was then that I remembered the camera. David went back in to get it. When he came back he told me he had deleted the photos and put the camera in my bag. Then he left.'

Blackwell was close now, Meadows just needed to give him a few seconds to reach her.

'What about the strap?'

'David said there was blood on it so he would get rid of it. Amber came and—'

Naomi's words were cut off as Blackwell grabbed her wrist.

'No!' Naomi struggled as Blackwell squeezed her wrist until she dropped the syringe.

Meadows let out a breath of relief as he crossed the bridge.

'It was an accident,' Naomi cried. 'I didn't mean to hurt her.'

Meadows thought of the marks he'd seen on Ruth's back. The post-mortem evidence showed she struggled with her attacker. He wanted to believe Naomi, but her life had been crafted in lies. Her upbringing had taught her to be deceitful. It was her only way to be a normal teenager. Those lies had stayed with her all her life and he guessed that she recreated that day and convinced herself. He looked over to the mine. He doubted they would ever know what really happened that day.

Chapter Thirty-three

One month later

Meadows slung his jacket over his shoulder as he walked out of the station. It was Friday evening and the promise of a free weekend spent with Daisy gave a lightness to his step. He had spoken with the team about the move to Ystrad Amman. They had all agree to go with him, even Blackwell.

'Detective Meadows.'

Meadows turned and saw Jay walking across the car park.

'I was hoping to catch you,' Jay said as he got nearer.

Up close Meadows could see that Jay's face was fuller. His eyes a little brighter.

'Hello, Jay. It's good to see you. How are you doing?'

'I'm good. I've been meaning to come and see you. I wanted to thank you for everything you have done for me. Words seem inadequate.'

'I was just doing my job,' Meadows said.

'You were the first one who listened to me. You believed me when no one else would.'

'I think you should give yourself and your brother some credit. If you hadn't been brave enough to send those emails then the truth may never have come out.'

'I don't know about brave. Stupid more like. I still feel so bad for what happened to David. It sounds like he was going to tell the truth.'

'I think so,' Meadows said. 'Don't blame yourself. It was Naomi that took his life.'

'I kinda feel sorry for her. I went to see her. I guess I wanted answers and some closure.'

'Did you get your answers?'

'Not really.' Jay smiled. 'In the end it was just bad luck. If I hadn't gone into the water to help Ruth. If I hadn't gone back into the mine to look for her. Ifs won't change the past. I've just got to move forward now.'

'Do you have any plans?'

'Callum gave me a job. It's OK. It will tide me over until I get my compensation. Aiden is helping me with that. Free of charge. Once things are settled I think I'll move away. A fresh start. There is nothing here for me now but bad memories. I thought my father would contact me once the news broke. I suppose too much has passed between us.'

'Well, don't shut the door completely. He may still come around.'

'Maybe, anyway, I'll let you go. I just wanted to let you know that I am grateful.'

'I'm so happy for you. I wish you all the best,' Meadows said.

'You too.'

Meadows watched Jay walk away. He was glad Jay was moving on. Too many times people held on to the past. They harboured anger and regret which only caused damage to themselves.

'Have a good weekend,' Blackwell said as he walked past.

'I will.' Meadows walked to his car eager now to leave. It was time to forget work and enjoy life. Even if it was just for the weekend.

List of characters

Police:

Detective Inspector Winter Meadows
DC Tristan Edris
DS Rowena Paskin
DS Stefan Blackwell
DC Reena Valentine
DCI Lester
DI Dylan Finch (Retired)

Others:

Daisy Moor – pathologist
Mike Fielding –SOCO
Chris Harley – technical forensics
Oliver Wilson – probation officer
Fern Meadows – Winter's mother
Seren Hardy – work colleague of David Harris
Dr Hill
Mason Parks – Jay Parks' brother
Ruth Williams – victim
David Harris – victim

Witnesses:

Naomi Collins
Jay Parks
Callum Vaughan
Aidan Edwards
Amber Richards

If you enjoyed this book, please let others know by leaving a quick review on Amazon. Also, if you spot anything untoward in the paperback, get in touch. We strive for the best quality and appreciate reader feedback.

editor@thebookfolks.com

www.thebookfolks.com

Also available:

Following a fall and a bang to the head, a woman's memories come flooding back about an incident that occurred twenty years ago in which her friend was murdered. As she pieces together the events and tells the police, she begins to fear repercussions. DI Winter Meadows must work out the identity of the killer before they strike again.

When the boss of a care home for mentally challenged adults is murdered, the residents are not the most reliable of witnesses. DI Winter Meadows draws on his soft nature to gain the trust of an individual he believes saw the crime. But without unravelling the mystery and finding the evidence, the case will freeze over.

When a toddler goes missing from the family home, the police and community come out in force to find her. However, with few traces found after an extensive search, DI Winter Meadows fears the child has been abducted. But someone knows something, and when a man is found dead, the race is on to solve the puzzle.

When local teenage troublemaker and ne'er-do-well Stacey Evans is found dead, locals in a small Welsh village couldn't give a monkey's. That gives nice guy cop DI Winter Meadows a headache. Can he win over their trust and catch a killer in their midst?

All available FREE with Kindle Unlimited and in paperback.

Made in the USA
Monee, IL
05 October 2021